MW00380750

"ALFREDO'S LUCK"

Michael Ludden

Cover by Winter Park, Florida artist Larry Moore

ISBN: 1494484242
ISBN 13: 9781494484248
Library of Congress Control Number: 2013923014
CreateSpace Independent Publishing Platform
North Charleston, South Carolina

CHARACTERS

Metro-Dade PD
Tate Drawdy – detective
The chief
Hugh Brice-Whittaker – Tate's partner
Robert Einburg – deputy chief
Booker Hollingsworth – detective

The cons
Herbert Dodds
Otis Chandler
Paul Albert Rutledge
Jackie Boy Barnett

The prison
Johnny Cordele – tower guard
Grady Osmund – superintendent
Grady's wife – Nell
Grady's brothers – Buddy Lee & Fred
Adam Pinckney – prosecutor

Miami
Sharon – Tate's girlfriend
Ricky – Sharon 's son
Lex Dean – FBI
Tommy Becker – FBI
Christine DeSilva – U.S. attorney
Alfredo Gonzales – wealthy broker
Isabel Marquez Gonzales – Alfredo's wife
Robert Simons – Alfredo's business partner
Juan – Alfredo 's driver

The Keys
William Conover – fishing captain
Andrew Driskell – police chief

The Cubans
Col. Manuel Ortiz
The mechanic

Venezuela
Major Emilio Duran
Capt. Milos Saab

PROLOGUE

TATE DRAWDY popped in a CD and headed for the interstate, keeping it good and loud during the vocals, cranking it up hard for the breaks.

It was sunny and cool, the sky the sort of blue southerners like to claim as their own. He'd thrown on a baseball cap, a flannel shirt, jeans, pair of old running shoes. It had been days since he'd bothered to shave.

He pulled alongside an old couple in a big Beemer. The light went red. Tate tilted his head back, cigarette dangling, adopted a pose suggesting imminent death and played air guitar until the light changed. They stared, shaking, helpless. He could see their crooked little fingers scrambling for the windows.

In the back, his hands cuffed, Herbert Dodds, the human refrigerator, stared out the window, flinching every time Tate reached for that knob.

Tate had volunteered to take him north. He owed a guy a favor. He'd gotten one of the department's unmarked cars, wedged a big boom box into the front seat, headed up the road. Traffic was heavy. He caught Herb's eye in the rear-view mirror.

"Johnny Winter."

Tate, shouting.

Herb was beginning to understand the consequences of crime, the meaning of remorse. Tate turned off the music.

"Where you from?"

"My name's Herb. I'm from Okeechobee. I stole a car."

"And you got stopped."

"Yessir."

"Cop needed surgery, am I right? You crushed his hand?"

"Didn't mean to. I just reached out, took hold of it, squeezed too hard. I got scared is all."

"What were you scared of?"

"Thought he was gonna arrest me."

"What about that thing in the jail? Heard you pulled a TV off the wall."

"Yessir."

"And threw it out the window."

"Yessir. I wished I hadn't done that either. They was playing this game, where somebody asks these people a question and while they're thinking about it, this music plays. It got to driving me a little nutsy."

Tate nodded. He hit the button on the CD.

Herb was gonna keep his mouth shut. But he was miserable.

"Wonder if I might ask, this being a long drive and all. Maybe every so often we could take a breather from that music. Just for a minute. Just a minute. Then you could play it some more. I'm just asking… real respectful."

"That's good thinking Herbert."

Herb was looking more pound puppy than dangerous cargo. Then Tate saw the Chevy, a big Suburban pushing through the traffic, coming up fast. He'd seen it once already this morning, sitting in front of his office.

Another right behind it. Both were black, with heavy tint on the windows.

Broad daylight in the middle of town. Tate didn't think it would make much difference. They were about 10 cars back. Herb was saying he liked a cool breeze.

"Herb… shut up."

He fished a key out of his shirt pocket, held it behind his head.

"Get the cuffs off."

He was looking for a side street. Herb was working on the cuffs, not asking. Tate pulled the shotgun out of the rack on the dashboard, held it back to him.

"Two Suburbans... half a block back."

Herb turned to see. The Chevys were banging fenders now, forcing people out of the way. There wasn't much doubt. Couple of folks seemed to think blowing their horn might help.

"I popped a couple of dopers yesterday. Somebody wants to object."

Herb was twisted around, looking, neck spilling out over his shirt collar, his fingers wrapped like tree roots around the gun barrel. The air was still now.

The big man shook his head. "Geez."

"We don't have a lotta choice here compadre."

Herb turned back to look at him. Sweat began to trickle down the sides of his face.

"I never done nothing like this."

"Just don't shoot any women and children."

The Chevys were two cars back now. One of the drivers was leaning out, shouting something. He was waving a gun. There was a crunching sound. The car behind them suddenly lurched up onto the sidewalk.

"Do we wait for em?"

Tate slammed it into park.

"Come out low and fast. Straight at em."

Later, he would remember it. Spinning from the car, the pavement glistening in the sun, digging hard against it, stunned the big man was keeping pace, a scream, horns, a burning deep in his throat and behind his eyes, the recoil as he pulled the trigger, the sudden explosion of glass and metal, shards floating past him like ornamental birds.

It was a surprise, them coming out of the car like that. Tate got the shooter. The driver opened the door and ran. Herb let out a scream, put a shot in the air, got both his guys to put their hands up. And then the place was crawling with cops. As soon as things were under control, Tate got Herb back into the car. Herb snatched up the cuffs, wrapped them around his wrists and held them against his stomach.

"Forget the cuffs. Hey, I bet you scared the Starbucks crowd real good, coming out shooting in that orange jumpsuit."

"I hope there's not a lot of trouble about it. Mebbe I could just say I sat here while you took care of it."

"Don't think that'll work. We had about two dozen witnesses. And what was that Johnny Weissmuller thing?"

"Huh?"

Sure enough, The chief thought giving a con a shotgun was the worst thing he'd ever heard.

"Let's call it improvisation," Tate said.

Tate's perfectly coiffed boss spit hard enough to crack the concrete.

"You got to be kidding me."

"I don't blame you for being pissed off. You can roast me. Or maybe you get real upbeat about how no citizens got hurt and you don't condone it, but this is the kind of war we're fighting."

The chief worked his jaw real hard.

"Get outa here. Take the man to FSP. Do not say squat to anybody. Then I want you in my office. And find a frickin razor before you come to see me."

Tate hopped in the car, threw on the blue light and got through to the interstate. It was a Crown Vic, so people tended to get out of the way when they saw it in the mirror. Tate liked to run up behind somebody real fast and wave em inside with a snap of the finger. Hey, enjoy the perks of the job.

"What's gonna happen? We're in for it, right?"

"Dunno. Good chance. Let's stop for a bite, what do you say?"

"That would be real good. You know, I don't have any money on me right now."

"I can cover you."

Herb thought about it for a minute. He looked at his hands.

"I tend to want to eat a good bit. You just say when it gets to be too much."

And so began the friendship between Tate Drawdy, tough guy detective, and Herbert Dodds, a young man who'd spent much of his life carrying things other people couldn't manage, picking them up in one house, setting them down in another. It was a life without complication, until now.

Herb was headed for Florida State Prison, the place they call the End of the Line.

1

SUNDAY

OTIS CHANDLER began to chant as he struck out along the fence. It was remarkable, really. Sun warming the ground, Otis gliding along like some incredible thoroughbred.

And now he was calling out this weird sermon-like thing, parsing the words in time with the soft crunch of his Nikes on the sand, the sound echoing over the grounds.

Birds stopped their pecking. The iron boys turned to watch. For a moment, the whole yard got quiet. Otis finished his first lap, still boldly proselytizing as if there were no need to breathe.

Thirty feet above, Johnny Cordele checked his watch, then leaned over the railing to scan the northern fence line. He studied the yard quickly, then, squinting, a moment out east, then south, then dropped down onto his chest for the next set – extra slow.

In the distance, the last of a faint haze clinging to the ground, hiding the bottoms of the trees. Otis, doing his own counting, watching the ground for Cordele's shadow to reappear. Three minutes went by. Three minutes and three seconds. Then Johnny C. was up again, sticking his sissy jaw out over the tower ledge, resting the M-16 inside his elbow, daring somebody to try something.

It was hot early. Everybody was outside. In the shade of the old west wing, long-timers stirred dirt around tomatoes coiled through battered wire baskets, bending to pluck caterpillars off the squash. A couple of the big shepherds jounced and barked, testing their pipes.

In a moment, Johnny would be back on the floor starting his crunches. But Otis had his own regimen to think about. He'd have just two hours, then they'd call him in.

Tall, lean, bushy brown hair hanging wherever it fell, he had spent the last five of his 29 years here and all he ever did was run – always the same route, as far and as long as they'd let him.

Not a cloud in the sky. A peaceful morning, a great stage for the whiz kid. Otis, a prodigy, a dazzling child born of ordinary parents who didn't understand.

He loved Shakespeare. And Satchmo. Some of the guys in school thought he was funny. The girls, a little creepy. He never raised his hand, but always knew the answers, just slouching there, his long legs sticking into the aisle. When the teachers did call on him, the way he trotted out the information made them squirm.

He'd curl one lip up under that beaked nose, cross his arms. Half the time he'd have to explain his answer and then everybody was picking out colleges and Otis didn't want any part of it. As if dutifully finishing a disappointing book, he gradually succumbed to crime.

Otis was helping himself to a rather nice stereo that day, got into an inconvenient pissing match with an indignant homeowner, shoved him so hard he split his skull. A good man gone.

In an absurd way, Otis thought he was getting what was coming to him. He'd mounted no defense, hadn't even wanted the lawyer.

The shrinks said he was a sure bet to kill again. Otis had smirked at that.

Wipe that smile off your face, mister.

And then young Otis had something to say.

"Rather lofty sense of authority, your honor, seeking to control what I think. It smacks of arrogance, as does the visitation by your so-called experts. I feel I have to offer my sympathy to anyone who comes into your courtroom."

That pissed the judge off. Otis got 20 years. His lawyer said it was an easy appeal. Otis told him to let it go.

Today, his mantra would be a Randall Jarrell piece, a nice rhythmic selection he'd read the night before.

As he came around to the West Tower, he shifted into a sideways gait, first one leg stretching out behind the other, then in front, alternating. Another 40 yards and he'd shifted again, now running backward, still stretching, still keeping pace. It was strange and elegant, Otis dancing in mid-air, calling out the words, everyone staring.

And in the midst of it all, Jackie Boy snipped quickly through a dozen links on the first fence, right down against the ground where no one would see.

This was one big-ass prison, nothing but single cells. The destination of last resort. No lightweights here, except for the grunts. You couldn't have psychopaths slicing the carrots, so the help had to come from elsewhere – junkies, car thieves, molesters – the punks of the system, folks who could become trustees. They could run the mail, do paperwork, clean up.

Everybody else was a player. Murderers, rapists, bad guys who'd escaped, been caught, escaped again. When all the other avenues were worn out, they sent them here. That's why the single cells. No roommates.

There was Death Row, and Q wing – that was for the wackos, the guys who rubbed shit all over themselves or threw it on everybody else. The guys who needed to jerk off in front of the guards. The guys who'd done stuff that pissed off the other cons so bad they'd get hurt if they were left in population.

All the incorrigibles in one place, spit and polish, not a speck of dust. Everything freshly painted all the time, fences gleaming in the sun, razor wire floating on top like some kind of Christmas extravagance.

It was not the kind of place where you let folks wander off whenever they felt like it.

2

MONDAY

YOU WOULD have thought that somebody would have seen 10 guys crawling under the wire. Ten guys. How could you not see that?

Well, somebody did see, but not until they were all the way out to the woods, and that was half a mile away. They'd gotten under the first fence, cut through the second, run two dozen yards to a drainage ditch and used it for cover for a couple hundred yards. One of the other guards spotted them as they got to the trees.

They'd cut through near Johnny Cordele's tower. Johnny, it turns out, was working on his abs at the time. Johnny was let go.

The guards mobilized in Jeeps and on horseback. There was still some light and six were caught within a couple of hours. But though there were cops out there and troopers and deputies and even some very snotty city guys in suits, four slipped through.

There was Paul Albert Rutledge, who'd murdered his first and second wives with a shotgun as they sat talking in a diner. They was comparing notes, he said.

There was Otis. Hell, he could have started running and just kept on going. He was probably in another state by now.

There was Dodds. Nobody was real sure they wanted to find Herbert, not by themselves, anyway. Herb might toss you over a house.

And there was Jackson Boyd Barnett, a former Ranger who'd gone bad.

Jackie had been handed a life sentence for the murders of a French telecom executive and his wife in a Jacksonville hotel.

After he'd shot each of them through the head, Jackie had folded his victims' hands together. It turns out that a former colleague of

Jackie's recognized the trademark. It turns out that Jackie had done some killing before he left the employ of the federal government.

• • •

THE YOUNG woman made the turn off U.S. 301 onto State Road 20 and started the back-roads portion of the trip home, her favorite part. It was a winding two-lane past farms, cottages with tidy gardens, front porches and plants hanging under tin roofs.

Somewhere along the way, she would peel off to find a back road where the street names changed from states and flowers to somebody's last name. She had spent the morning in meetings in Tallahassee and didn't expect to get home until dark.

Sunset was approaching. She turned off the highway and passed a road grader chained to a flatbed truck parked along the side of the road. The pavement turned to gravel. Someone had pulled an SUV up into the trees, an old Wagoneer.

It was getting dark. She lowered the front windows, eased her foot off the gas. At an intersection with a dirt lane, two men walked into the middle of the road. One of them had his arms around the other, holding him up.

She stopped 30 feet back and stuck her head out the window.

"What's wrong?"

"My buddy's been hurt. Can you help?"

She didn't like it. Something about their clothes. He seemed confident and she didn't like that.

"I passed a store about a mile back. I'll send somebody back out to you."

He didn't reply.

She cut the wheel, backed up and turned to go the other way. But she couldn't move. Two men, standing in front of the car. One of them looked like a circus strongman, bursting out of a sweater and pants two sizes too small. His buddy had a gun.

The guy with the gun got in the front seat. The other three squeezed into the back. The first two got in without much trouble. The car tipped hard to the side when the big guy folded himself in against the window. But nobody hesitated. Nobody thought about putting him up front. No democracy here. Guy with the gun's the boss.

She slid her seat up as far as she could.

"What do you want with me. You can have the car."

What was the point? They knew she was scared shitless. Why hadn't she just run?

"You're going to drive us a considerable ways south and then we will find something else. Do not make any effort to fuck with us in any way."

He was intelligent, disdainful. He put the gun on the floor in front of him. He saw no need to threaten her, no need to point the gun. She would do as she was told. His knees were crammed against the console. He looked at her. She fumbled for the release, found it and realized there wasn't any room. She shrugged and put the car into gear.

He didn't speak, simply pointing when he saw a sign leading to the interstate. Nobody spoke, in fact. She couldn't figure it out. They were bank robbers, maybe, or escaped cons. Why weren't they talking about what to do next, where to go?

And where did they get those street clothes? Had they already killed somebody?

She looked in the mirror. Bluto just stared out the window, seeming to enjoy the view. The smarmy guy on the right stared back, which was a comforting thing. He'd like to pull over to the side, rape me and get a burger. The guy in the middle had his head back, his eyes shut. Boss man was reading a well-worn novel. He was tall, fit and not at all good looking, with a nose like a hawk. Even without a gun, he would not have seemed approachable.

She drove with her elbows clenched against her sides, swallowed for the thousandth time. She thought she might puke, but she needed to maintain the pretense of control.

"What are you reading?"

"Never mind."

He didn't even look up. So far, she thought, this is going really well.

3

THERE'D BEEN escape attempts before, even a few times when somebody got loose for a little while. Fights, strikes, fires, rapes, killings. Hell, it was a prison. But nobody had ever put together a mass breakout.

Somehow, they'd found a way to work together. That was pretty sinister. These guys were lone wolves.

Otis believed he was a superior being. He had zero desire to muck with the general population. Rutledge, very much your typical son of a bitch. No boundaries.

The scariest was Jackie Boy. Baddest guy in the place. Diabolical. How he'd managed to fool the armed services into thinking he was elite soldier material was a rather unpleasant facet of his charm.

And there was Herbert, not so much a criminal type as a guy who just didn't fit. Herb could put phone poles in the ground, pluck washing machines, any job that let him roam. But at some point, there would be trouble. Somebody or something would aggravate him to the point that he reacted. Herb was not a thinker.

Grady Osmund, superintendent of the prison, headed for his office, loosened his shirt, tossed his jacket and tie onto the back of a chair. It was a renovated space at the back of what had been an old house on the grounds. Nothing fancy, but the furniture was nice and there were plenty of chairs, big windows on one wall. In the bookcase behind the desk, a close-up of Grady's wife, Nell, sitting on the back porch reading. On the walls, early maps of Florida and a panoramic shot of The Swamp, stuffed to the top decks with 93,000 Gator fans.

He called in the supervisors for S wing, the area that included Otis' and Jackie Boy's cells, and the T and D wings, where Herbert and Paul Rutledge lived.

They spread around a conference table.

"This isn't just embarrassing, gentlemen. These guys' faces are going to be on the front page of every newspaper in the country tomorrow. And the headlines are going to say they're the worst specimens anybody's ever seen. And they'll be right.

"I don't need to tell you what kind of mayhem these men might inflict, three of em anyway. So let's get right to it. Jason, we'll start with you."

"Not sure I can think of much that will help, Grady. I don't remember seeing these guys together. And Jackie Boy's never been social. Come to think of it, he's been working out pretty hard though."

"Doing what?"

"Lotta weird situps. He does a lot of that oriental crap in his cell and he knocks off a ton of those upside-down pushups."

"Huh?"

"He does a handstand, then he does pushups like that. I've seen him doing it all hours. And he jumps around. He puts things on the floor and hops over them on one foot. I've tried it. It's hard as shit. Course he was always in pretty unbelievable shape."

"So he's been getting ready. What's he been reading?"

"Books – same stuff he's always read... politics, old newspapers, magazines."

"Any visitors?"

"Have to go back and look. I don't remember anything."

"Stick around for this meeting. Then get it done."

There was a knock on the door. A slight, gray-headed woman stuck her head in.

"Your brothers are on their way."

"Thanks, Kate. How are we coming with food and coffee for the media?"

"Everything's just like you asked."

"Thank you. And one other thing, please... See if you can find that Miami detective, the guy who brought Dodds up here. They had some rapport."

She smiled.

"I've got a call in to him now."

A moment later, Grady's brothers, Buddy Lee and Fred, came in. Like Grady, they were big, lanky, hard around the edges. Of the three, Grady had put on more weight, then he was the oldest.

"Hey. We're just getting started. Jason briefed on Jackie Boy. Says he's been working out pretty hard, sticking to himself."

"I'm not so sure about that," said Buddy Lee. "I saw him in the exercise yard two weeks ago. Walked out the door, straight across the grassy patch behind the admin building and right up to Rutledge. They chatted real close for awhile. Struck me as pretty odd. Never saw the two of them together before."

Kate knocked and stuck her head in again. "Phone's for you, Grady. You'll want to take this one."

He picked up, listened for a few minutes.

"This place is wall to wall as it is. A couple more strangers won't catch anybody's eye. Just see the first gateman."

He hung up, put his elbows on the desk, hands pressed together, his chin resting on his thumbs.

"The feds want to talk about Jackie. Interesting. Guy's been gone an hour and they're already in the car."

• • •

THEY WERE cruising down the Turnpike now, south of Orlando, south of the tourist corridor. She had been driving for three hours, keeping her speed just over the limit. She badly needed to pee.

There were some trees near the highway, but mostly it was pale green scrub, flat to the horizon. The moon was up. On either side of the road, power lines, scattered clusters of cattle. Lowlands and forests. Skeeters.

Traffic was light. She thought about crashing the car.

I could swerve into a ditch and then sprint for it. They might let me go. Another driver might pull over. At some point, they'll need gas, or food, or a bathroom. Things are really going to suck when we have to stop.

"Is there anything to read here?" It was the guy with the gun. He'd already burned through the paperback he'd brought. She offered up a binder on first-quarter client assessments.

"Stop at the next exit. You'll stay in the car. I will go inside and pick up something ridiculous at the counter."

Then the guy in the backseat, in the middle, spoke up: "Not here. Further down."

Who's the boss here? She wiped her hands on her skirt, rubbed her eyes. Was there no way to leave some kind of message? She spotted a huge osprey's nest atop a distant power pole. At another time, it might have been peaceful.

At least we don't have any kids yet.

• • •

TATE HAD just gotten home when the call came. He poured a Grande of the good stuff and headed for the car, put the windows up, cranked the a.c., tossed the soccer ball into the back seat and laid some rubber out of the driveway. Tonight he was in a hurry. He stuck a blue light on the roof and put the pedal down, left the boom box home.

The ball was Ricky's. A fair amount of the time, he and Sharon stayed over at Tate's house. Tate wasn't too comfortable with that – not the right thing to do, not with Ricky. Still, he wasn't exactly fighting it.

He had 15 years on her, actually it was closer to 20. Did he really want her to make the move permanently, or was kidding himself? The one time he'd brought it up, she'd balked, big time, said she'd had a bad experience the first time around.

"You can take me this way or not at all, cowboy," she'd said. So Tate wrestled with it. He made Sharon his beneficiary. He wore his seat belt.

So he was older. So what? He was still in better shape than most of the young studs in the office. That was experience, maturity he saw in the mirror. What did she see? Maybe she was being smart.

Maybe what he needed to do… find another line of work. Maybe the cop thing was what turned her off. That was a squirrelly side road. Tate wasn't sure he wanted to do anything else. Hell, he wasn't sure he was fit for anything else.

Born in Atlanta, the youngest son of a family brimming with Coke money. Private schools, good grades, a jock. A lush life before him. He'd wanted to study pre-med and had started out at Emory. Then he wrangled a summer job driving an ambulance for Candler Hospital in Savannah. Great place to learn. Three times as many stabbings and shootings as the other hospitals. Get a real taste of the nightlife.

He ended up spending his off hours with the same crowd, the emergency medical techs, the hospital staffers. And cops. After a time, Tate sort of gravitated toward the cops. Maybe it was the excitement, or the mission. Maybe it was just that he didn't feel much like hanging out with the well-heeled crowd. He'd spent most of his life among their type.

So he stayed, finished his undergrad, drove a meat wagon. A couple of years as a beat cop in Savannah, made detective, took a job with Metro-Dade. Miami paid a lot more. Much cooler town and there was a lot more going on. The gray set in.

He got to Starke late, heading quickly down the hallway toward Grady's office, heels echoing off the hard pine floor. Grady's brothers, a guy from the governor's office. The feds, already there.

The head guy, Lex Dean. Tight mouth, little ears, big future. Doing his best to act as if this was not a disaster, pacing, clearing his throat, talking about how important it was that all the right information got to all the right people and none of the wrong information got to anyone and what an enormous and inappropriate risk it would be to try to take Jackie Barnett into custody. All his buddies were nodding.

Grady thought Dean was putting on an extraordinarily bad performance.

"Lex... seems like you're going to a lot of trouble to avoid getting to the point."

"I'm not sure I understand."

"He's being polite. He's telling you you're full of shit."

This from Tate, who took the opportunity to walk across the room for some coffee, making sure he took a route that brought him chin to forehead with the head fed.

Tate, about 6'3, just under 200 pounds, enough attitude to put off some people. An old girlfriend had told him he was "about as fucking modest as Sean Penn." Then, she had an axe to grind.

Tate poured a cup.

"I'm just guessing here," he said, "but it sorta looks like you have some experience with Mr. Barnett that you're not telling us about. What you'd like to do, it sounds like, is have him killed while fleeing, as quickly as possible. Would you mind telling us why?"

"I'm not sure we need to get into that."

Grady stood. So did his brothers. He nodded toward Dean.

"Kate will show you out."

"Mr. Osmund, I'd like you to stay – please. Look, we were just hoping not to have to get into some of this stuff."

Grady turned toward him.

"Lex, we're wasting time. If you have something, let's hear it. But don't play games. When we take these guys into custody, you won't get near them unless I say so."

Dean opened his hands, palms pointed toward the ceiling. He leaned back, cleared his throat, did his best to reduce the air of superiority that seemed to come naturally to his voice.

"Please," he said, pointing to the chair.

Grady sighed. He sat.

"Let me start with the bottom line. We don't want Jackie Boy leaving the country, if we can help it, and I'm not sure we can. I haven't been told a whole lot. I know Jackie worked for the federal government for five years, mostly in South America, the Mideast. Took on nasty jobs.

"I did talk to a guy I trust. I asked him whether people were afraid that Jackie would spill secrets or something. He said no. He said Jackie is just real bad medicine and a bunch of very senior people had been embarrassed by him, by the fact that they'd hired him, and they didn't want him to go on.

"We understand that you're in charge. We just want to make sure we're there when this goes down. Just to be sure that all the right things are done."

Grady took a gun belt out of the bottom drawer. He turned at the door.

"Lex, I seriously doubt you're this naïve. We will recapture all these people and we will endeavor to take them alive. If you or any of your people interfere, you're going to wish you hadn't."

This time the prison team left without interruption. The governor's man sat, not sure which group he belonged with.

Dean placed a gleaming wing-tip against a chair and propelled it into the desk with a crash.

"Gentlemen, I think we have just had our one and only shot with Mr. Osmund."

4

THEY WERE huddled in front of a mom and pop. A truck-stop next door. Yellow flood lamps 40 feet high illuminated the place like a bad slasher movie. Bacon and diesel fumes, laughter from across the parking lot. Johnny Cash was Walkin' the Line.

She was doing a poor job of hiding her terror. Her head was splitting.

Herbert languished with her in the car. He was eating a peanut butter cup. He nibbled off four sweet bites from each one. Reesee Cups, he called them. Get me some Reesees, he'd told Jackie.

Rutledge was standing in front of the car, twisting a finger into Otis' chest. Short, nasty looking, his oily black hair thinning dramatically up top, dark eyes set wide apart, sloping forehead, childish nose. You could see Rutledge was a piece of work from 50 yards.

He was pushing his grimy little face into Otis' chin, trying to make a point.

"We don't waste her before I play."

Otis put a hand on his shoulder. "I appreciate your frustration, my friend. But it may not be in our best interests to have something to dispose of at this point. Why don't we reassess?"

Rutledge was about to tell Otis where he could stuff it when Jackie Boy strolled back from the office. He took something out of his pocket, dropped it into a bottle of water and walked up to the car window.

"Drink this. All of it."

She took a sip and pulled her head away. Jackie took her wrist and squeezed.

"Now."

She finished it.

He opened the car door, reached in and took her arm, lifting her out. Her knees buckled. Suddenly she was dizzy. Why couldn't she think of anything to say? Her stomach rushed toward her throat.

"You can just leave me here," she gasped.

Jackie held her up and half-carried her into a room. A couple of minutes later, he was back.

"She'll be out for a couple of hours and when she wakes up she'll have a hard time making much sense. I took all her ID. We'll keep the car."

Rutledge was incensed. "You just figure on making all the calls without asking?"

Jackie Boy got into his face.

"You understood what we agreed to."

For a half-second, Rutledge reeled back. Then he thrust out his jaw, snatched the door key from Jackie's hand and burst into the room. Jackie was about to go after him when they heard the crack. Rutledge sauntered back outside and tossed Jackie the key.

"Next time, talk to me."

They got back into the car and headed south. Otis drove. This time, Herbert landed a spot in the front. He got in without speaking.

5

IT WAS past 10. Otis was still driving.

They were winding along a narrow farm road. It had been almost an hour since they'd left the interstate and Rutledge had slept through it all. He sat up and read a small weathered sign for Lake Okeechobee.

"We're getting way out into bumfuck now. Keep on this road, we'll have to start lookin for Injuns."

"Mr. Rutledge, chronicler of the obvious, has made another compelling diary entry."

"Hey, fuck you, Otis. You shit for brains asshole."

Jackie's forearm snapped across the back seat, the heel of his hand driving Rutledge's windpipe against the back of his throat. Rutledge began to choke, desperately flailing his arms, fighting it. Herb flinched so hard he cracked his head on the door molding.

Otis swung the wheel over, sending the car skidding down a dirt lane between rows of orange trees, bottoming hard in a muddy hole before sliding to a stop.

Grasshoppers jack-hammering, still hot as blazes. Somewhere nearby, a sprinkler started a staccato flight. The grove looked like it went on for miles.

Herb twisted around slow like a lighthouse but he couldn't see nobody.

Jackie hopped out, grabbed Rutledge by his shirt collar and the buckle of his belt and shucked him outside, Rutledge was rolling around on the ground, gurgling, waving his silly hands. Jackie dragged him by the heels into the trees and shot him once in the temple, the barrel pressed hard against the side of his face. For half of a second, the body seemed to lift off the ground.

Otis and Herb sat in the car and watched as he bent over the body, doing something with Paul's arms. Herb, shaking his head.

"You understand why that needed to happen, don't you Herbert?"

"Don't know why he couldn't just left him someplace if he didn't like him."

"Paul was going to get us all killed. Paul was resistant to change. He did not understand the need for working together."

"I figured, when he killed that woman, Jackie was going to get him back."

The door opened. Jackie climbed back into the car.

"Tell you something," Herb said, turning in his seat to face them squarely, like a salesman pushing for the get. "I know we got a deal, but I wanna know where we're going to end up. Lotta people getting killed here."

"Let's do that," Jackie said. "Let's talk it through. But first, let's get back to the main road. And let's get a burger."

Herb sighed.

"OK."

• • •

THE SEARCH team was broken into groups – working the phones, coordinating the search. Their first break came from a sheriff's deputy south of Gainesville. Someone had called in about an abandoned SUV on a rural side road.

State troopers and local deputies were knocking on doors.

Tate was thinking out loud. "We might find a theft report. More likely they've commandeered something. Make sure everyone knows to forward any missing-persons calls to us, anything at all that's unexplained. Search the roadsides, make sure they didn't dump the driver."

They'd sent photos across the country, to cop shops, to bus stations, rail stations. Local police were hitting small airports, anyplace the cons might find a boat. Tate figured they were more likely to travel by car.

They would head for a city, someplace where they could disappear for awhile – Orlando, Tampa, Miami – or out in the middle of nowhere. And that is why it was far more likely that some local deputy, a highway patrolman or a citizen would spot them.

Their faces were all over newspapers and tv. The break was huge news. Four bad guys at large – prime time. There'd been a crowd of interviews. Grady was letting one of his captains handle the print people, asking for the public's help, of course, but with care to warn people not to approach the men or even show they'd recognized them.

Grady was doing the television interviews, always outside in the park, surrounded by police cars and choppers. The resources were highly visible.

"We want people to understand several things. We have law enforcement all over the region, and all over the country, looking for these men. We have complete confidence that they will be apprehended very quickly. In the meantime, keep your eyes open and call authorities if you see anything suspicious. Don't assume they are still traveling together. They might be. They might not. If you see anything out of the ordinary, call your local police. These men are armed and dangerous."

There was a tent and coffee. Grady brought Tate a cup.

"I hope we get this over soon. My wife hates this shit."

"Tell me about it," Tate said. "I gotta pretend I hate it too."

"Married?

"No, and this is why."

"Appreciate you coming up. One thing, though."

"What's that."

"The Dolphins cap. You might wanna lose that if you expect to get any cooperation from people. This is Gator country. You look like somebody who's not from around here."

6

TUESDAY

BREAKFAST TIME. The kid was on his way north on I-95. It wasn't the coolest set of wheels he'd ever snatched at a bargain, but it was fine and he'd turn a decent profit. He was sitting on 63 mph. No sense in pushing his luck with a hot car. He'd passed a trooper a few miles back and the guy hadn't even flinched.

He played with the radio. What an effortless score it had been.

Passed a bus, it looked to be carrying a middle school band. A smug little horn player had his face smashed up against the glass, tongue flattened out, one hand holding the trumpet, the other giving him the finger, waving it on a pendulum so he'd be sure not to miss it.

Then all the little band members were giving him the finger. He sped up and got past them.

There must be a wreck up ahead in the southbound lanes, he figured. All of the sudden, nobody was coming the other way. And then he saw a cruiser coming up from behind. Damn. It was more like six cruisers and they were coming like a bat out of hell. The kid eased over to the right-hand lane. He was toast.

The first car stopped a good 40 yards back, then eased up behind him. The rest, stopping all the other traffic. The kid started to get out of his car. He heard a loud squawk.

"Remain in the car. Put your hands on the steering wheel where I can see them."

A chopper settled down in the median. The kid started to bawl.

He'd paid $375 for the car yesterday, he told them. There were three guys, rough looking. He'd sent them to a buddy to hook up with another set of wheels.

Now every cop in the world was pointing a gun at him.

The guy in the chopper, Buddy Lee Osmund, was on the radio.

"Kid says just three. Sounds like Rutledge isn't with them."

The cops unlocked his cuffs and brought the kid over to a car. It would be the two of them, the kid and Osmund, who said he was some kind of prison official, which scared the shit out of the kid.

"You take me to where you met these guys, right now, and don't mess with me and you might just get out of this."

The kid swallowed and sputtered and made it real clear he'd fetch and do laundry.

They crowded around a map spread across the hood of one of the patrol cars. The kid showed them where he'd met the cons and where he'd sent them.

"I want roadblocks on every road out of town," Osmund said. "Stop every car. Put an unmarked a quarter mile short of every roadblock, further if traffic backs up. Start moving teams into the town. You know what to look for, but lay back and do not approach."

Osmund and the kid took the chopper most of the way to Pahokee and set down in a pasture. There were more cops there and one of the guys gave them the keys to an old sedan. It was hot. The bugs owned the neighborhood and the whole place smelled like you'd better not step anywhere.

"I gotta piss real bad," the kid said. "And I'm not feeling so hot."

The cop took three steps and got right into the kid's face. He looked like he'd played for the Packers. Osmund called him off.

"We're in a hurry, son. Piss over there and let's get moving. Anybody have something to eat?"

One of the cops had a burger and fries he hadn't started on yet.

"You eat that and you'll be fine. Now let's get moving."

The kid ate while Osmund drove, one hand on the wheel, the other against the frame of the open window. He looked to be in pretty good shape for an older guy. Maybe not that old. The breeze wouldn't mess up his crewcut. The kid, wondering if they had any openings.

The others followed at a distance. The chopper was in the air. If they ran into the cons, the cops would be all over them.

"Who are these guys and what did they do?"

"They escaped from prison and they killed a woman. That was her car they sold you. They must not have been real interested in you or they would have killed you too."

The kid suddenly felt dry. "Holy shit. I don't know anything about all that stuff. I just bought a car is all. I don't want any trouble with you guys. You just tell me where you wanna go, OK?"

Buddy Lee didn't respond. The kid tried again.

"You think they stuck around?"

"Maybe, maybe not."

He'd finished the burger and fries. They had reached the outskirts of town. Osmund pulled over and the kid got behind the wheel.

"Let's move it."

• • •

THE GARAGE was at the end of an alley and around the bend, behind a shuttered five and dime and a flower shop. It was a brick building with paint hanging like barnacles, maybe 60 years old, with a flat roof, heavy wooden doors and iron bars on the windows. It was locked up tight. The kid went around back and got inside.

He called out: "Perry. Perry, where are you man?" And then he saw the body. Perry was on the ground, between a couple of rebuilt muscle cars, a hole in his head, his hands folded across his waist. The kid could see the scorch marks on the side of his face.

He ran to door and yanked it open.

"Holy shit, man."

Buddy Lee pushed past him. He knelt over the body. Perry hadn't been much, a youngster, wispy growth on his chin, skinny from too much partying. A pair of greasy bluejeans and a t-shirt. He couldn't have held his own in a strong breeze. His eyes were closed, but the pain and the fear had stayed with him. If there'd been an echo, he hadn't heard it.

A couple of the officers huddled with the local cops. The others went out to interview people in the shops along the street. The cons had a good head start.

The kid's hamburger didn't stay down long. He staggered back from the bathroom in the back of the shop and sat on a rusting toolbox, waiting for Buddy Lee to finish instructing the men.

"I can't believe they shot the dude, man. Perry was cool, he wasn't gonna mess with nobody."

"There are half a dozen cars here. Do you know what's missing?"

"No, man. I don't know shit, I think those guys are bullshit, man. Those guys completely suck. Those guys. . . "

Buddy Lee interrupted the kid's monologue, jerking him to his feet.

"I need to know what kind of car they took. Pull yourself together. Look around. What's missing? If you don't know, I need to find somebody who does – right now."

7

A TRIO of gulls splashed down just past the stern. They'd been trolling 20 miles offshore for close to an hour, caps pulled low, shielding their eyes against a glare that penetrated like a dentist's needle.

The Silver Queen rocked slowly from side to side, rising gently as the waves passed underneath. She was a proud 50-footer, not too old, covered in ivory white fiberglass, with a tuna tower that still glistened and four fat swivel chairs bolted to a sun-bleached teak deck.

Then William Conover III, captain of the Queen, gave a shout. He'd hooked into something, looked like a big snapper.

"Hell, boys, you gonna see some big boy fishin' now. Mebbe we'll fry him up cajun, just so you can tell all your buddies you was out for real."

Landing the yellowtail took some time. Conover was letting one of his fares handle the rod. They were paying him money to go fishing and they hadn't had so much to drink that they couldn't follow simple orders.

"What'samatter boy? You outa shape?"

It was his way of letting the customer know that what was happening was routine and that he needed to suck it up in order to walk tall when they put back into shore. These were city boys, but they were good for most of the day, anyhow. And for a healthy bump if they caught something.

Conover was good on the water. He had grown up on his daddy's boat, fishing the waters off Massachusetts, filling out on his mama's big country breakfasts and hard days on deck. He was full grown by the eighth grade and by his twenties he bristled with confidence and had a quick, booming laugh.

He'd joined the Falmouth police out of high school, met a Miami girl on vacation and married her. After five years, she'd had her fill of overcoats and boots. Florida sounded fine. Another five years on a beat with Miami-Dade and he'd saved enough to get a boat.

They headed south for good water, setting up in Sister Creek, just east of Boot Key. It was a great place to be, for a few more years anyhow. Not as tarted up as Key West, but with a few of the amenities that made the tourists feel comfortable. There was a hospital and a little airport. There were restaurants with fishnets and big conch shells and aquariums and watered-down reggae and great big pina coladas.

Mostly there was lots of blue water and plenty of palm trees, fresh air and the smell of the sea.

Pretty nice here, Conover thought. He put up a sign, began calling himself Cap'n Bill and they settled into an easy life that lasted a couple of years until she'd had enough of him, too. Now she lived down the road, He stayed to himself, caught fish, drank a beer, fried up a steak on Saturday nights.

He had watched, grinning, as this foursome drove up in a new Cadillac. Paying customers, babe.

Like everyone, they quickly fell in love with the grinning, sun-scorched Irishman, that New England accent, the blond curly head, top lip buried under a World War I flying ace mustache, his oversized hands, the slap on a stranger's back.

"All right with me if you bring the ladies," he'd confided. "Course we'll get a ways offshore and at times it gets a mite rough. Nothin' to spark you men, but your ladies might not always like it." Sure enough, the women had stayed behind to shop and sun.

That was how the Conover like it. Men could get drunk and leave you a danged good tip, especially if they caught something decent. Hell, tell a good story or two and you could set a few dollars aside. But once the women got on board, it was a whole different thing. What's the fare, they'd ask. Then they'd start to calculate.

The last trip he'd had wives along, he overheard a couple of the wives talking not more than two hours into the trip.

I think a good 10 percent is well within the range of generosity. The range of generosity. Hell if that wasn't a done deal. He could have landed fat old sharks, told them the hairiest jokes they'd ever heard and fed 'em champagne and lobster salad and they still would have given him an exact 10 percent. Best to leave the wives ashore when possible, was Cap'n Bill's motto.

Lots of times, guys weren't so interested in catching anything. Just get em offshore, really. They could say they'd been out so far they couldn't see land anymore. The sea was real big and the sky was real big and they got a bad burn. It all made for a great tale back home.

Then there were some guys who wanted a big catch or they felt cheated. So you had to be able to hook into something.

These guys were pretty easygoing and they'd already caught the snapper, so anything else was gravy. They caught some trash and threw 'em back. An hour later, after they'd wrestled a fat-bellied black grouper on board, they'd had enough.

It had been a good trip. Conover headed in, both turbos running loud and smooth, just the way the slickers liked it, parting the waters, barreling through a shimmery afternoon haze.

8

"THEY'VE CROSSED the line and they'll stay across it."

Grady Osmund was on the phone with his brother. Buddy Lee's frustration was starting to show.

"It's hard to believe they've been at large for this long," said Buddy Lee. "Their pictures are everywhere. We know what part of the state they're in and still there's nothing."

"You know how that works. They'll put on some shades and grow beards and mingle. Let's get them before they get to wherever they're going. I'm coming down. I'll see you in a couple of hours."

Grady threw a couple of files into a soft briefcase, shut down his computer. Then he drove out to the house.

Nell met him at the door. She'd already packed his clothes, his hiking boots, lots of underwear, jeans, shorts, heavy shirts, light shirts, t-shirts, lots of socks, a couple of belts. He always forgot a belt. In a ziploc bag, she'd put headache pills, sore throat pills, stomach pills, hay fever pills. He didn't use any of that stuff. She just figured it was the right preparation for a safari of unknown destination. Somewhere in all that stuff, when he got to rummaging through it, if he ever changed his clothes, he'd find a little note. There was always a note.

"How soon do you have to leave, darlin'?"

"About 20 minutes. They're sending a ride. Fred's going. And Tomas – he knows these guys pretty well. Guy up from Miami who's helping out. Pretty good guy. Don't let me forget – I want to bring him a hat. We've got time to sit out back if you want. Thanks for my stuff."

She grabbed his hand as they walked. It was just turning toward dusk. They sat on a wrought iron bench in the garden, among the lantana, the crepe myrtle and the roses. They watched squirrels run around for awhile.

Grady stuck his head up and sniffed a few times.

"Checking for clues in the breeze?"

"Yup. I think I see 'em now.

Nell kicked off her shoes and put her tiny feet up on an antique wooden bucket they'd turned over for a table. She had on an old pair of baggy string-tie shorts and a retired ban-lon with holes in it. She'd been puttering. She'd washed her face, but her hair was kind of messed up, the way he liked it. Still blond, still sweet looking with those big green eyes.

She'd gotten rounder over the last few years, storing fat for when she got evicted from the tribe. Grady loved her all the more for it. He liked to reach around her when she was cooking and squeeze her tight. She'd hold his hands in one of hers while she kept right on working.

They'd met in high school, in Cross City, about an hour and a half west of Gainesville.

"I was hoping you could teach me to dance," was the first thing he'd ever said to her. "I can see you've got lots of boys hanging 'round you who know already, so I figured you might be getting bored."

She thought he was charming. A bit serious, a bit dangerous, perhaps, but solid, someone who looked like he could do anything he wanted. And he would become the local boy who'd made good.

His Daddy had offered to help, but there were three boys and Grady wanted to carry his own weight. After graduation, he'd joined the Marine Corps, the first to leave home and the first to go to war. One tour in Vietnam and he was home with a battlefield commission and free tuition to the University of Florida, thanks to the GI bill.

He was a walk-on at the university, playing both ways, a linebacker so quick opponents thought he could read minds and a tight end known for vaulting over would-be tacklers. Eventually, like his father, he became superintendent of the toughest prison in the state.

He kept the crewcut.

Grady thought he'd like to take a long walk with his wife, maybe skip dinner. He ran his hands through her hair. He put his arm around her.

"There's nothing to worry about here. I'm chasing some guys who will do anything they can to stay real far away from me. And I'll be with half the cops in the state. Only thing that's gonna happen to me is I'm not gonna sleep so good by myself."

Nell patted his hand. They'd been together a long time. She knew what he was going to say before she heard it.

"I don't have a real good feeling about this, baby. You do what you have to do, but it's not personal. It's not yours. Whatever happens, you just don't plan on doing anything you'd have to explain to me."

He kissed her. "Well, you always worry about me staying up too late. And I promise I'll try not to do that."

She put a hand behind his head and pulled him close.

"Bullshit. Let's get a drink before you go."

In another 10 minutes he was on the chopper headed south. Blue jeans, a short-sleeved shirt, pair of shades and an old .45 in a shoulder holster. It was a lot more comfortable than something on the waist. You could sit down and, if he needed to go someplace in public, he could always put on a jacket.

Besides, they were with a crowd... heavily muscled SWAT guys carrying black nylon zipper bags, so it wasn't a question of being inconspicuous. Inside the bags, submachine guns, Heckler & Koch MP5's. Grady had been offered one and turned it down. He didn't like the show and he didn't like running around in a chopper, but there was too much work to be done to waste time.

Tate had been offered some heavy firepower as well. He laughed it off.

"I'm hiding behind you guys."

It started to rain, muting the churning of the chopper blades. Fred leaned in close.

"OK, bro. Let's try a run-through. You game?"

Grady nodded. Fred needed to talk about things to figure how they sat.

"OK. Let's look at the simple stuff first. They've killed twice, both times for transportation. As far as anyone knows, they haven't stopped to rob anybody, get drunk or get laid. Straight south. Four... well, three, I guess... incredibly bad guys with virtually nothing in common – other than the desire to be free – and they put together a plan, pulled it off and, as far as we know, they're still together.

Grady looked at Tate.

"What do you think?"

"They must have someplace to go, something to do," Tate said. "They might have left with some money. Or they could have had somebody on the outside. Looks like somebody supplied them with a gun."

"They could have stolen one later," said Fred. "But it makes more sense to think they had one all along, or had one planted outside the fence. The breakout was too clean."

Fred, the brother the others wondered about. Must have been the mailman. Probably had those same meet in the middle eyebrows. Fred had farmed awhile, sold real estate, talked about school and, eventually, had come inside to work with his brothers.

He seemed more a city type than his brothers, or the rest of the prison crowd, for that matter. Longish hair, nice clothes and a goatee. Big good-looking guy with a goatee.

"Our team combed outside the fence and haven't found anything," he said. "We've quizzed every snitch inside. Some guys knew a breakout was up, just because of our boys' behavior, but there was no bragging. And there were no requests for help, which is strange, unless you believe they had serious outside help.

"Johnny Cordele, the tower guard, is off the job, but he's still around and he hasn't been spending any unusual amounts of money. If they were smart, they'd pay him off in installments, so he'd stay quiet and stay close. He may still have another paycheck out there.

"We've sweated him pretty hard and he flunks the lie detector across the board. Johnny won't hang tough forever, though. It will scare the shit out of him when Adam charges him as an accessory to the murder of that woman. And now we can add this kid.

"Now let's go to the more sinister stuff. We've heard diddly from the feds. What the fuck is up with that? They're real uncomfortable with something, which means there's something they haven't told us."

"Doesn't smell right," said Grady. "Let's assume the feds are the opposition on this one."

"Yup. And put that against the bad guys heading south. These guys act like they're on some sort of timetable. They're headed for something – another job, a payoff, a meeting."

"You're on the money," said Tate. "If these guys got out on their own, why are they sticking together? And if somebody got them out, who'd want these guys?"

• • •

THE FARMHOUSE hadn't been lived in for a very long time. There were holes in the walls, holes in the doors, holes where windows were supposed to be. But there was some furniture, a few dishes in the kitchen and, once they'd pumped it awhile, the well water still flowed. In the middle of an orange grove, it looked like a good place to sit tight for awhile.

The cons searched the area carefully, grinning at their luck. They were out in the middle of nowhere, not even another farm close by. And the place obviously had not had visitors of any kind for a very long time. They felt confident that no one had seen them start down the overgrown dirt road that wandered back to the house.

And Herbert, always the long-range planner, had chanced to look in the kid's refrigerator before they left the garage.

"Hey. The kid lives here."

Otis and Jackie were already inside the van, ready to go.

"Come on," Jackie shouted.

"Hold on a minute here. This guy's been to the store."

Otis slapped Jackie across the back and they jumped out to see.

Three boxes of Cheerios, four cans of baked beans, two packages of hot dogs, one bag of frozen peas, a jar of spaghetti sauce and a box of linguine, six Snickers bars, two packs of Twinkies, a gallon of milk, a loaf of bread and a case of Old Milwaukee.

They packed it all up, stuffing everything into a styrofoam ice chest the kid had left on top of his fridge.

An hour later, here they were, sitting on a pinewood porch, looking out over acres of water oaks and cypress. Otis, sitting on a box by the railing, Jackie in a rocker, Herbert, sprawled on the porch floor, an array of foodstuffs spread before him.

“It feels good to be gentlemen farmers,” Otis announced. “Life on the outside… the land… the absence of limits…”

“I know what you’re sayin,’ ” Herbert replied, squeezing one eye shut as he carefully folded a Twinkie in two. “You like them candy bars.”

9

WEDNESDAY

CONOVER WOKE at 5. The slickers wanted to go back out and that was good. He'd take it a little easier on Day Two, didn't want to leave them gasping for air. Return business was about as good as it got around here and return guys usually told their friends.

He'd have the boat ready a little after sunrise. He wasn't far from the marina, his place a bad-postured bungalow under some big shade trees with a narrow porch on the front. Linoleum floors, fake wood paneling, an old stove and a refrigerator with a pull-down handle. He liked it.

He rolled out of bed, put on a pot and headed for the bathroom. And then the phone rang. It was Andrew H. Driskell, local chief of police.

"Billy. Get down here right now."

"What's up chief? Lose a puppy?"

"Ain't what I lost, brother, it's what I found. And, unless you parked the Silver Queen someplace else last night, it's what you lost. So haul your ass down here before things get any shittier than they already are."

Conover slammed down the phone. "What the fuck." He was still pulling on his shirt as he ran to his pickup. In two minutes, he was at the marina. Sure enough, the Silver Queen was gone.

He spotted Chief Driskell.

"Andy, what the fuck?"

Andy had on one of those white cop shirts with the shiny buttons and the little stars on the collar, like a bus driver at a theme park.

"Called you as soon as we figured out what was going on, Billy. Now just settle down. I've already called the Coast Guard and everybody else. One of the guys in the cabin over there saw a car pull up. Three guys. Well, from the description, two guys and Sasquatch. He decided it didn't look right. They were trying too hard to be quiet.

"They've been gone for hours. What can I say?"

Conover noticed his right little toe had busted out the side of his sneakers.

He'd never get his boat back. They'd run it aground. They'd dump it and set it on fire. They'd run it too hot and burn up the engines. They were dopers and they'd blow it up. The Coast Guard would chase them. *They'd* blow it up. He'd get arrested. He'd go broke. He'd get some bullshit insurance settlement. He'd be homeless. He'd have to move in with his ex-wife.

His fucking watch was still on board.

• • •

THE DESK was cherry, or a very good imitation. So were the twin bookshelves and the credenza. The photos weren't family shots. Lex Dean was single and his decorative choices reflected his primary interest. There were pictures of Lex with the station chief and some foreign dignitary, Lex at a dais making a speech, Lex getting an award, smiling, hair all slicked up, buttons buttoned. On the walls, his diploma from Vanderbilt, a plaque recognizing his leadership on an FBI management team.

On the desk, a large block of etched glass bearing his name.

The books were all non-fiction, mostly professional management tomes, biographies of American presidents, books on the theory of combat.

He liked to read about the great strategic thinkers ... Genghis Khan, Sun Tzu, the Chairman. He liked to imagine life in a more ordered society, where people were afforded the opportunity to live under enlightened direction.

Life today was just so much chaos, democracy a form of quicksand. He believed in it, of course. But the vast majority of the population was unfit to make decisions, even about their own lives.

The presidential primaries had been going on for months. He held up a newspaper account breaking down the latest skirmishing and shook it as if it were evidence of a conspiracy.

"Look at this. People who never voted in their life are out on the street, writing checks like there was no tomorrow. These assholes are racking up millions a week. We are about to see a Democrat in the White House and they will pull the plug in Iraq… maybe even Afghanistan. Holy shit. Finally, we take some action and we're going to erase it all because of a couple of memorable sound bites. Why do they think the Islamists attack us? Because we've gone soft. The liberals in this country have no stomach for the realities of life, but, oh, we wouldn't dream of doing anything to curtail their right to screw things up for the rest of us.

"Even the Russians are going soft."

Tommy Becker just nodded. Soon enough, Lex would climb down from the soapbox, quit wagging his head and they could get on with it. When he saw an opening, he interrupted.

"You still don't want to say anything?"

"No, Tommy, I don't. I'm not sure what good it would do anyhow."

"Well, what if he gets killed?"

"Then he'll be dead."

The Mafioso pin-stripe was not the typical fare in the Tampa office, but it suited Lex. He left the jacket carefully draped on a wooden hangar behind the door. He was round-faced, had very short black hair that stood straight up because of something he put in it. He'd probably been chunky since the day he was born.

And his ears were too small. People noticed it right away. Then, if they knew him, they figured his ears were about right, considering how much he used them.

The phone rang. It sounded like the cons had made it all the way to the keys, and taken a boat. Grady Osmund was headed south to join the search.

It was time to move. Lex and Tommy Becker and a couple of agents took a quick hop to Miami. Since their meeting in Grady's office, there had been virtually no direct communication between them. Grady's people were cooperative, but the frost appeared to be permanent.

Lex read case reports in the back seat. Tommy was at the wheel.

"What if they put up a fight?" Tommy asked. "Do we intervene?"

"Best-case, they're cornered and they turn in. Worst-case, they're cornered and somebody starts to shoot. Or the other worst-case is a hostage, in which case we don't have much opportunity."

"I'm just wondering how we keep our guy alive."

Dean was blunt: "No reason to, unless he's got something to tell us."

"But didn't you make a deal?"

"Well, if he's smart, he gets the fuck out of there if it goes downhill. And he gets to us."

"Yeah, Ok. Well, what would you like to see happen?"

"They get caught, give up, and we're able to leverage some time alone with them. We separate 'em and we see what they know. We give 'em back."

"How does that solve the Barnett problem?"

"Time will tell, my friend. Time will tell."

Becker could see this wasn't getting anywhere. Lex had never gotten chummy in the past, even on some tough cases. They'd had a week-long stakeout together two years before and Becker still knew virtually nothing about his boss. Now, even though Becker was privy to the complexities, it wasn't likely Lex was going to break the case down any further. Not unless the shit hit the fan and he had to ask for help.

This time, though, they both wanted to save their skins. And Becker could see that might very well put them at odds.

10

ONE BY one, the men drove through the gates and headed up the drive to the big house on the water. They gathered in the card room, a space virtually guaranteed to take the breath of any first-time visitor. It was round, with a ceiling 25 feet high. A second-floor walkway wrapped around the gallery, with soaring glass panels on the east side that straddled a rugged stone fireplace and a chimney that disappeared through the ceiling.

Their host, Alfredo Gonzales, owner of an elite securities brokerage firm, old enough and long since wealthy enough to be retired, but nowhere near slowing down. Dark hair, graying, brushed straight back, medium moustache and a modest start on a belly, he carried a hard set to his jaw but was quick to smile. He was at work before daylight, with meetings most nights – chamber of commerce committees, local economic development groups.

The executive committee for the Cuban-American group he had helped create met at least once a week. If only Fidel could see this place, a young committee member once told him, he would begin to understand the true benefits of capitalism.

Gonzales had laughed.

"If Fidel ever enters this room, he will never see another sunrise."

He was 63, a director of one of the most influential political organizations in the country, with more than 50,000 members and a leadership group that included the most powerful businessmen in Miami and well-heeled Cuban-Americans from around the country. Their strength, the result of decades of political contributions, millions of dollars over the last 20 years, their relentless focus on one objective – toppling Castro's regime – and the unanimity they carried to the polls.

Half a million Cubans had fled the island between 1962 and 1974. Many had stayed in Miami and, like Gonzales, many had been in the United States nearly all of their adult lives. Still they talked and dreamed about returning home.

Some had spent time in Cuban prisons. Older members could recite the names of family and friends lost to firing squads. Despite the years, there was no softening of their position.

For decades, despite the efforts of the U.S. Chamber of Commerce, the American Farm Bureau and the combined clout of all the wheat states, nothing had changed. Thanks to the foundation and its monolithic authority, the embargo that prohibited the sale of American food and medicine to Cuba remained.

There had been attempts, particularly during the Democratic administrations, to make concessions. Now there was another push to loosen the reins. Would it prevail? Gonzalez didn't care anymore. He had played a significant role in the victories. His was a very public role.

But there was another side and another very private association, whose meetings took place in an old warehouse along the Miami River.

A dozen men, not so old, gathered here. And it was here, in a concrete vault under the floor, that Gonzales kept his most prized possessions, the global positioning units, the night vision equipment, his Swiss SG 550-1s.

Illegal to import since the late '90s, the hand-crafted sniper rifles sold for $10,000 apiece, the price you paid for certainty.

They had tried other alternatives – money to the dissidents on the island, radio programs, literature. Nothing threatened Fidel's control. And then the old man got sick and they began to hope once again. Until Raul.

Raul had taken the reins, installed a handful of meaningless changes. The people would be allowed to spend money in the tourist hotels. They could own cellphones, spend dollars, if they had them, even travel a bit. Token gestures, intended to display a desire for progress, to show that Cuba was a part of the world, that things were happening. It meant nothing. It meant more pain, more anger. Gonzales and his men were fed up. And they were frightened. Fidel was growing old, finally slowing down. He might die on his own before they had a chance to put a bullet in his head.

Just lately, Fidel had been feeling a little more spry He was seen again in public. And now he had agreed to appear at a Southern Hemisphere Economic Summit on Margarita Island off the coast of Venezuela.

His last words would be in a speech at an outdoor plaza.

It would not become a part of Gonzales' considerable legacy – the group had decided their activities would remain secret regardless of the outcome. Those who needed to know would know.

• • •

YOU'D HAVE thought the cons would head for the open sea, the Caribbean. But they'd gone north, up the coast. The hunt was leading to Miami.

Grady and the others found a hotel downtown. Tate went home, pulled into the driveway and found Sharon and Ricky kicking a soccer ball out front. She had a nice dinner waiting. They argued about who missed the other the most.

Tate was glad to be back home, hated being out of his routine. He lived in a nice place, ate decent food, got lots of exercise, paid attention to the news, even had a social life. In short, he was not your typical obsessed dysfunctional crime-fighter. But he had the prerequisite belligerence. And he had real good instincts about bad guys.

He'd gone into the office for awhile, made sure the chief saw him. No word. No surprise. The guy would tolerate him right up until the day he fired him.

He dropped off early and he'd been asleep for an hour when the call came.

And now he was walking into one of the hottest mansions in the city, looking for a dead superstar. Hugh was already there. His best friend, his partner, his drinking buddy, the one guy who rarely bitched when he cranked a CD to pain level.

Hugh started in as soon as he came through the door.

"We're just starting to collect the lab work. It's been a couple hours, at the most. He was killed with a soft round, so we may not get much from it. We know it's a huge deal and the chief is upset and the mayor is upset and he says the fucking president of the United States is gonna be upset. I would have had you here sooner, but I've been too busy answering all those other calls, which is why I finally had to get somebody else to call you, so I'm sure you're going to want to chew me a new one."

"Cut it out," Tate said. "What else do we know?"

"Not a lot. We don't know how he got in, or they got in. There's fulltime security on the property. There's a major-league alarm on the place. It looks like some wires have been fiddled with outside, which the alarm people say can't be done without setting it off.

"We don't have any idea whether that happened tonight or two years ago or he could have had a visitor, somebody he knew, and turned it off, or somebody real smart could have turned it off, but the alarm people say that's not likely, which you would expect them to say, so, just yet, I don't know exactly what we have here."

Hugh's last name was Brice-Whittaker. He took some shit for it. It was an English name. Hugh didn't look English, although he was fairly tall and had reddish hair and bushy eyebrows, which perhaps was a bit Brit-looking.

But he had a back-home accent and he cussed a fair amount when it was inappropriate, which didn't seem very British, and he tended to ramble on more than most people and he was the kind of person who could hold his own in a dark alley with the wrong people.

"So what we have," Tate said, "is a murder by somebody who is really good and who did not likely leave anything behind for us to find, am I right? And the splice job is pretty slick. So let's assume that's how they got in without disturbing the guy, who I assume had some real protection around. Does he have a gun?"

"Yup, real nice handgun, sitting in a desk drawer, where it's sat for years, unfired, and his wife knows about it and it's still sitting there."

"Where was he?"

"Sitting at the desk, the same desk, and it looks like he was shot from about eight feet away."

"Doorway?"

"Nope, from the other side of the room. They were in the room with him."

"Anyplace somebody could have been hiding?"

"Yeah. There's a closet and there's that big armoire over there and with just the desk light on, you could maybe hide a small person there, but that assumes Gonzales was so preoccupied that he walks into the room and over to the desk without glancing over that way – and the closet door squeaks, by the way.

"We're doing fibers everyplace, we're doing prints, but, you know, nothing's really ultra-clean, the way some guys leave it. Everything just looks really normal, like nothing's been disturbed. The guy beamed down to the library from his mother ship, shot the hottest Cuban in Miami, and beamed back aboard, no trace."

Tate took a minute, looking around. There was more money in a single room here – in a corner of the room – than he had in his entire house. A gorgeous painting in a golden frame hanging on thin wires from the crown molding. A small fireplace surrounded in rose-colored marble. In front of it, an antique desk, ornately carved, now stained with blood.

He made a few phone calls, placated a few people, or tried to.

When things slowed down a little, he went home to grab a shower. He scanned the newspaper while he ate. The Herald had put out an Extra and thrown it in everybody's driveway. Pages and pages about Alfredo Gonzales, his impact on the country, speculation about motive, clamoring from the community, long passages from everybody who was anybody, pictures of Gonzales with the president, with the English prime minister, with a bank president, with a crowd of neighborhood kids at a housing project he'd funded.

Then Hugh called again. It was about 7:30. Gonzales hadn't been dead for 10 hours yet.

"Tate. Hey listen, this is kind of weird but the dead guy ain't Gonzales. It's one of his vice presidents. Yeah, we had a pos ID from the wife. She lied. I dunno. The coroner flagged it. This guy's got no scars. Gonzales had a triple bypass a couple years ago. Yeah, I'm on my way back over there. I thought you might want to go along."

11

THURSDAY

HE PULLED up to the house, as close as you could get without permission. Hugh was waiting there by the gate. They were buzzed through. The wife, Isabel was her name, was waiting at the front door. Of course she knew they'd be back.

"It was clearly an assassination attempt on my husband's life. There was nothing we could do to save Robert. So Alfredo made a sound judgment. He allowed people to believe that he had been killed."

She was pretty slick, just the right mix of sincerity and authority. A second generation Miamian, she was 20 years younger than her husband, perhaps more. Shoulder-length charcoal hair, straightened, a small gold necklace, a mid-length black dress, pricey shoes, a casual refinement that showed she was quite comfortable in her surroundings. Stunning. And the perfume was hypnotic. Tate reminded himself not to stare.

She brought them inside.

The real dead man's family was gathered there, surrounded by the smell of rich coffee. There was a silver service on the table and a bunch of tiny cups. As for Gonzales, he was nowhere. And nobody was about to help them find him.

"It is not," his wife said, "in the best interests of the country for Alfredo to be available at present."

• • •

ROBERT SIMONS, the dead guy, was a longtime partner. He and Gonzales went way back. Simons was there every week and had a key. It was strictly ordinary, Isabel said, for him to do work there, answer phones, etc. Simons' family said the same thing. And nobody seemed to have a theory. He'd just gotten killed in Gonzales' home office, presumably by mistake.

These people were way close, which was going to make it even tougher to investigate the crime. Even Simons' wife thought it was a real good idea to let the world believe the hit on Gonzales had been a success.

This was not just a business. There was some kind of big-time philosophical bond. But Simons wasn't Cuban. What kind of connection made the death of a family member less important than the relationship?

Tate decided to skip out on the meeting. The group-think was overpowering. He'd talk to them later, one on one. But first he needed to know more about Gonzales. About why somebody would want to kill him badly enough to hire a professional, and why that would come as such a small surprise to his family and friends that they would circle the wagons. Overnight.

He walked outside. It was a big Mediterranean – lots of sandstone and glass with layered gardens that would need constant care. Out front, there was enough room for a couple of football games. The back yard had room for the county fair. That much land was a rarity on Key Biscayne.

The security was pretty remarkable too, although that wasn't hugely surprising, given Gonzales' money.

Tate swung by the garage. No fancy sports cars here, just a stable full of Mercedes, dark and still. One of them was parked outside. A guy was waxing it.

"Hey," said Tate. "Who are you?"

"I'm Juan," said the guy, "Mr. Gonzales' driver."

There was no accent. Juan turned to face him, smiling. Tate walked around the car, dusting a finger along a fender.

"So you know what happened."

"Yes. I'm afraid so. Mr. Gonzales will be sorely missed."

Even the help had been roped in. Tate was impressed.

"Wasn't Gonzales, which I'm sure you know. In fact, why don't you tell me where Gonzales is, so we can save a little time here?"

"I'm not going to be able to help you. I wasn't here last night. I go up to Boca Raton every Tuesday night for school and I don't come back until the next morning."

No acknowledgement the wrong guy was dead, although it was interesting that the hit came on his night off.

"Anybody be able to verify that for me, anybody who saw you last night, saw you at school, saw you maybe between, say, 10 o'clock and midnight?"

"Yes, I can provide you with my professor's name and phone number. The clerk at the hotel can tell you what time I checked in. After that, I'm afraid I can't help too much. I stayed there alone."

"Which hotel we talking about?"

"The Boca Raton Resort and Club. It's on East Camino, close to the campus.

"That's a bit pricey isn't it? What are you studying?"

"Mr. Gonzales took care of my expenses. I'm in the MBA program at Florida Atlantic."

Still using the past tense, and very much at ease taking a lot of snippy questions. The guy was completely unfazed. An articulate, white-collar, grad-school, slick as shit chauffeur. And this guy was ripped. Not a pumped up, body-builder type. No, this guy was the kind of hard body you see in the military.

Juan wasn't just a driver. Juan was a part of the team, whatever that was.

12

IT HAD been a year now since that night. She'd taken the elevator up to the 55th floor of the Wachovia tower, the City Club, the best view in town.

He'd been standing at the glass looking out. He hadn't been approachable all evening, always a crowd gathered around him, someone waiting to speak to him. Tall, self-assured, a black pin-stripe with broad lapels, a peaked handkerchief in his jacket pocket, an old look, very fashionable. She stood beside him, her back to the crowd, hoping they would be left alone for a moment.

"I love seeing the bay from here."

He answered without turning.

"Yes. It is remarkable, all that steel."

And then he looked at her, pleased to see her smile was open, genuine. She was beautiful.

She pointed to the mouth of the river.

"Did you know the city began right there? And if you dug under some of those high-rises, you'd find the Indian mounds where it all began, the first railroad station and the terminal where they shipped the oranges and the tomatoes."

"You like history?"

"I love history. I love knowing how things came to be. And you?"

"It is all that matters," he said. "Understanding the past is the only way to know who you are, knowing where you came from, what must be done to maintain the legacy."

She extended a hand and squeezed.

"I'm Isabel Marquez."

"Alfredo… Alfredo Gonzales."

He hadn't yet let go. She waited, smiling. He studied her face, then released her, leaning closer, taking her arm.

"Would you like to sit down, some champagne?"

"Yes. I'd love to."

She moved alongside, her shoulder was close to his, and scanned the room.

"But… over there I think."

She pointed to a dark corner, a table away from the crowd.

Gonzales caught the eye of a hostess.

"Would you mind asking someone to bring us a bottle of Moet and a pair of glasses?"

"Of course, Mr. Gonzales."

They walked side by side, not touching. He held her chair. She scooted back from the table and turned slightly to the window so he could look at her without being self-conscious.

A simple black gown, slit up one side, her hair tied back, a hint of makeup, a hint of perfume, a loose string of pearls, the heel of her shoe hanging loosely off her foot. She had a small, straight nose, high, pronounced cheekbones. Her mouth, very round and a good chin.

He looked at her neck, the strength in her shoulders, a remarkable figure, not showing it off.

Not a word about each other. They talked about the early settlers, the freezes that had spared Miami, but had devastated much of the state, the evolution of shipping and turn-of-the-century tourism.

A waiter in a tuxedo brought their champagne and two crystal glasses. Linen napkins, marble. Glass on three sides overlooking the bay, the Port of Miami, the beaches and Brickell Avenue, Coconut Grove and the gables.

Her laugh was unrehearsed. He took off his jacket and tossed it over a chair. Later, he made a little joke. She'd just taken a sip of champagne and she grabbed his hand and squeezed it until she was able to swallow. And then she went right on.

Jet black hair, yet she was fair and her eyes were blue. There was a maturity there and something else he couldn't place. Idealism, perhaps.

When it was time to go he walked her to the elevator. As the door opened, he reached out to take her hand, turning it over carefully to examine the shape of her fingers, her wrist.

He smiled.

"Thank you, Isabel."

"I had a very nice time, Alfredo."

She stood in the doorway, her eyes sparkling. He took one last look. She handed him her card as the doors closed.

She was alone on the elevator.

History, she thought.

Bingo.

13

BILL CONOVER parked his old GMC pickup under a shriveled pine and walked out on the dock. A couple of guys were working in the wheelhouse of a medium-sized pleasure boat. They didn't have shirts, didn't need 'em. They were deep brown and it was obvious they were pacing themselves.

"Name's Bill Conover. I'm looking for anybody who knows about my boat, the Silver Queen. Got hijacked out of Boot Key night before last. Three guys took it. Headed north."

A rail-thin salt and pepper mechanic lifted a cold stub from his mouth and stuck out a callused hand.

"I'm Suds. This is Big Jim. A 50-foot trawler, chrome scaffold?"

Conover nodded.

"Mighta seen it. We all heard about your fracas down there. Heard about somebody taking a boat. Mike and I was out drinking in some deck chairs and a boat like that go by. It was about midnight, so coulda easy been your boat. Course we didn't think nothing of it at the time. You fixing to chase them down?"

"Last time I looked it was my boat. Long as it's gone, I got nothing to do. So I figure I'll track 'em down, get it back. Figure the longer I wait, the less chance of finding it."

"So you're stopping at docks on the way. Smart. You got a picture of the boat?"

Conover went back to the car and grabbed an 8x10, still in the frame.

"I'm thinking this is the boat we saw. What do you think?"

Big Jim took the picture, nodded. "Anything we can do for you?"

"You could lend me a bathroom and maybe some coffee for my thermos."

"Sure thing. Grab your stuff and I'll show you where it is. How about a beer?"

"Nope, thanks. 'Preciate the help though. Good place to stop further up?"

Suds led Conover to a map on the inside wall of the bait shop a few feet away. Suds hadn't seen a dentist in a very long time. Conover stepped back. Suds closed the gap, put an arm around him, drew him close.

"Here's where I'd go next. There's usually guys out at night. There's a bar there. Somebody mighta seen something."

The door to the bathroom had a hole where the knob used to be. Inside, there was a fisherman's shower – the kind with a plywood privacy wall and a hook for your clothes. A collection of squashed cigar stubs adorned a small shelf like a roach still-life.

Ten minutes later, he was back on the highway. He had spent all day Wednesday on the telephone – the Coast Guard, every cop in the state. They'd let him know.

That morning he'd started north. As long as he could keep finding people who'd seen something, he'd feel like he was making progress. At some point, when they got closer to the mainland, somebody was very likely to tell him they'd seen the Silver Queen beached, or worse.

In the glove compartment, a .45 automatic.

• • •

ALFREDO GONZALES' team was mulling the options. They'd spent some time thinking about making a call to Washington, maybe talk to the president. Then again, what good would that do? And wasn't it too late for that?

Would they try again? These were not questions they'd been prepared for. Eventually, Alfredo made the decision. Just let them know they failed. It's just another chapter. They will try again, but it might not be for years. Why should we waste time worrying?

That would not do a lot to make Isabel feel better. But Gonzales was not the type to change his mind. He had come back to town quickly from Washington aboard an associate's private jet and he'd gone directly to the apartment downtown. It was a very nice apartment with a picture window overlooking the river and a plasma TV over the fireplace. The shelves were stacked with books, though no one had yet looked at any of them. It was heavily alarmed and the doors were steel. Behind one of the bookcases was a self-contained security room, with soundproofing and several days worth of food.

It wasn't registered in a name that might be connected to Gonzales or any of his organizations. Until now, he'd never been there. No one in his family had been there, nor would they visit now.

There was no phone. He'd talk by cell. It was as private as they had expected they would ever need.

He'd had a nice breakfast, talked with Isabel. He'd spent a considerable time on the phone with Robert Simons' wife, reassuring her that she and the family would be well cared for, letting her know how devastated they all were, thanking her for her loyalty.

It was time to get wired back in. He called Juan.

"How goes it? What do we know?"

"We don't know how they got in, jefe. Nothing's been disturbed. The wall safe has not been touched. It looks like it was purely an effort to kill you.

"You heard about Boot Key? The newspapers are saying that three men stole a charter boat and headed north. The boat has not been found. It may be escaped convicts.

But what if it's someone from the island?"

Gonzales lit a Cohiba. He had traded his customary suit for a pair of running shoes and a warm-up suit.

"Our people should look for strangers, any unusual activity. Anyone close to us needs protection and the children should not be left alone."

"This has all been done. All activities are cancelled. We have asked people to walk the streets and to drive in groups of two and three. We are the neighborhood watch, you know."

Gonzales told Juan to call the group together. They would meet that night at the marina.

"We cannot fail to act. There will be a response. Our people expect nothing less."

• • •

THE LAB guys were still working. Tate Drawdy was sitting at his desk, feet up, thinking. It was the way he worked. To some, it might have looked pretty casual. The tie, knotted a few inches below his open collar. Spongy soled shoes, a checked shirt, tan pants. And tan socks. Tate matched up his colors as well as the next guy.

Tate figured he put in enough hours. Besides, the way stuff was piled a foot high on top of the desk, on the credenza, in piles on the floor, in the chairs, anybody could see he was working.

No piles on the chief's desk.

He took his left hand in his right and began to work it, the thumb pressing into his palm and the fingers tugging slowly across the back of his hand. It was something he did at times when he was deep in thought. But it also was a thing he did in front of others, a suggestion of energy bristling under the surface. He liked that it distracted people and he'd perfected a narrowing of the eyes to go with it.

"You gonna punch somebody with that," a suspect had asked him once in an interrogation. Since then, he'd used it more liberally, although he was learning not to fall into such habits out of the office. Sharon had brusquely slapped away his gathered hands one evening, telling him to leave his work at the office.

"What?"

"You might torment people and maybe they deserve it, but leave it with your hardware by the front door."

He respected the fact that she didn't put up with any crap. Maybe it wasn't such a good thing to have tough-guy habits. At least it was better than chewing on an old cigar or rearranging your balls every time somebody blinked.

Right now he was waiting for the lab analysis from the crime scene. Given the circumstances, he didn't expect much.

So he sat. He ruminated.

Maybe he'd get Sharon a puppy. That would be a clever stunt. Dog's got to stay somewhere, can't be running back and forth all the time. Dog would be like family. One thing might lead to another.

Then, he could imagine that Sharon might not fall for his Machiavellian bullshit.

"You thought I might fall for this Machiavellian bullshit?" she might ask. The last thing he wanted to do was try to work Ricky. He'd tried that and it had backfired miserably.

He was tugging on an earlobe, trying to figure out where in the hell his life was going when he had another cute nugget dropped into his lap.

Hugh called to say that a body had been found in a cheap hotel, a young guy who'd taken a bunch of pills, looked like, with a note that talked about Gonzales.

Tate jumped in the car, got there as the pictures were being taken. The kid – he looked to be in his early 20s – was lying on his back in a hotel room, hands folded. The note was on the nightstand. It was all about remorse and greed; he'd wanted to rob Gonzales and had to shoot him when he was discovered.

Tate had an abrupt response.

"This is such complete bullshit," he said. "This kid had nothing to do with it. They're playing with us."

"Who?"

Hugh was intently scratching a spot on the rug with his shoe. He didn't put much faith in this Santa Claus perp either. But he had to ask.

"Let me see. Where do we start? Look here. The bed is made. The fucking bed is made. He wrote a note, for another thing. He took pills, for another thing. This kid has been whacked and it's the bad guys' way of tweaking us, 'cause now they know the dead guy wasn't Gonzales."

That was enough to royally piss off the deputy chief, the tight-assed Mr. Robert Einburg, who just happened to have shown up shortly after the call went out.

Einburg was a big shot, the department's finance guy. The chief had suggested he visit a crime scene from time to time, soak up a few things. Tate had spotted him lurking in the corner when he came in the door, making sure to remain expressionless when they made eye contact.

Einburg was standing off to the side, hands on his hips, mouth clenched. It was how he stood most of the time, his goopy hair smashed flat on his head, sticking out behind the horn rims, like always.

"You're coming off just a bit half-cocked on this, aren't you Tate? Would you mind telling me how you can dismiss this without so much as a moment of investigation?"

Tate did nothing to hide his exasperation at having to play the teacher.

"There are so many things wrong here, Robert, obvious things. But since you asked... let's talk about suicides.

"Women kill themselves like this guy did. They put on nice clothes. They do their best not to leave a mess behind. They write a note, explaining. You can see their mother-fucking dismay at having arrived at this sorry point in their lives.

"Guys don't give a shit. They suck a pistol. They floor it off a bridge. They don't leave a note. They leave beer cans all over the place. It's very much a fuck-it sort of departure.

"This kid is a punk. The Gonzales shooting was a professional hit, not a robbery, and this kid has no more clue how to disarm that security system than the fucking dog.

"What this is all about is some sick, sorry-assed poke in the ribs from the bad guys to us. And what it means is that they're still around and they're still making plans to do some bad shit. And the fact that they'd whack a kid just to mess with our heads tells us that they're really not very nice people, in case we needed to know that."

Einburg's eyes were kind of milky and his jaw was pulled in tight. He wasn't thrilled at being taken down in front of the crew. He hesitated a moment and then decided to say so.

"You and I have had our differences, Tate, but . . ."

"Ok then. What's your take?"

"I don't know, Tate, without more information. You seem not to need any, though. You can solve a crime just by observing the housekeeping."

Tate had two inches and 40 pounds on Einburg. He softened his tone.

"Actually, Robert, this kid may be our first real hope at something. Who is he? Where's he been? Where was he when they grabbed him? What kinda bad shit is floating around in his bloodstream? We can assume they didn't spend a whole helluva lotta time at Gonzales' place. At least they were in here for awhile.

"And they had to check in, which means somebody saw something. Actually, I'm kind of excited about this kid. But not too excited, because I'm thinking the guys who did this aren't in the business of making mistakes. And whatever clues they've left, if there are any, won't help us much."

It was time for Hugh to jump in. "Front desk clerk called in sick, Tate. We sent a unit to the house.

"Let's just hope we haven't got another body," Tate said. He pointed to Einburg. "Would you like to go along, since you're playing street cop today?"

Einburg turned and walked out the door.

14

MANUEL ORTIZ was napping. It was a sunny day, a few clouds. The air wasn't moving. The windows of his third floor office were open wide, ceiling fan slowly spinning. He had come in late and would go home early, a typical day. Parked in the street below his window, where it was safe under the watchful eye of an officer, his 1957 Chevrolet Bel Air convertible.

Two-tone, blue vinyl interior, fat tires, the widest whitewalls, a tinted windshield that stood almost straight in the air, the distinctive triple notches in the front fenders.

Auto-powerglide, 283 cubic inch V-8, with 270 horsepower. Power steering and brakes, continental kit, day-night mirror, front bumper guards, dual outside rearview mirrors, spinner hubcabs, backup lights and a push-button radio.

It was the pride of Havana and it ran like shit. Just now he was using his inimitable powers of persuasion to obtain a rebuilt carburetor, a factory built 2X4 carburetor if one could be found. Ortiz had gone to the best mechanic in the city, laid some nice cigars on him and asked how long it would take to find one.

The mechanic shook his head.

"Your grandchildren will be gray."

Ortiz had smiled and murmured his sympathies.

"True… True… Nevertheless, it is something I am in need of."

The next day a number of officers had visited the mechanic's shop, separately and at regular intervals during the afternoon. They strolled, picking things up, setting them down, looking under things, asking questions.

On the second day, they returned. This time, they stayed, standing in front of the door. There were no customers. That afternoon, the mechanic locked his doors and hurried home. He washed and shaved before pedaling to police headquarters, where he had politely asked if he might be permitted to speak with the man himself.

When he was shown into the office, Ortiz stood and graciously stepped around the big desk to take the mechanic in his arms.

"It is good to see you."

"I will not rest," the mechanic said simply, "until I have acquired the very finest 2X4 carburetor for the colonel. I wanted you to know."

"This is very good news," the colonel replied. "Very good news."

That night, when the mechanic returned home, a lovely young woman was waiting at his door. She stayed with him through the night. She made him feel young and, in the morning, she rose early and brought him coffee.

He patted the sheet alongside him.

"Business is slow. I don't have to go to work today."

She set the coffee on the table. As she opened the door, she turned to him.

"That is not what I have heard. I have heard you must be there early."

And then she was gone.

And so he went, realizing that, now, Ortiz would require regular reports, perhaps weekly, perhaps daily. He hoped it would not take too long and he wondered if he would ever be paid.

It was the way Ortiz worked. He found a way, yet his own hands were never soiled. Just now, his secretary was making sure that no one disturbed her colonel during his afternoon refresher. Whatever it was could wait.

And then the American called and she knew she must interrupt.

• • •

AT THE Gonzales home, things had changed. More guards, very visible, and clearly not Pinkertons. Outside the gates, they stood in pairs. Inside, there were more. Tate had offered police protection. The city would scarcely raise an eyebrow at an overtime bill for guarding the Gonzales family. Isabel had politely turned them down.

"We feel comfortable with our own people. We appreciate your support."

Where was her husband?

"I'll call you immediately when I hear from him."

Like shit she would. Tate couldn't figure out what the hell was up and her indifference pissed him off to the point that he put a tail on her, on Simons' wife and on Juan, the driver. He put his best guys on Juan. Ordinarily, the wife would have been his first choice. Not now.

She seemed the traditional lady of the house and there was something very strange going on here. Juan was a lot more likely to be a part of it than Isabel, though Tate had offered to make life miserable for the cop who lost a tail on the wife.

There was little, at this point, to grasp. Simons appeared to have no enemies, no money problems, no strife at home. Church-going, well-liked. No one had a harsh word. He was an accomplished financial adviser, like Gonzales. He had worked in Miami for years, after a decade in New York City with one of the big hotel chains. Tate had a guy backtracking for anything there, and they had asked for the wife's permission to look at financial records, but it appeared that Simons was simply in the wrong place.

And Tate was more interested in Gonzales.

Juan was spending his time driving from one neighborhood to another. Everyplace he went, people came out on the street to meet him. After half a dozen stops, Hugh called Tate.

"This guy is unbelievable and the network is unbelievable. He's on the cell the whole time. When he pulls up to a house, there's already a ton of people waiting for him. They talk. They shake hands. They hug.

"And, I tell you what, it's a damn good thing he's got that big Benz. Everyplace he goes, somebody brings out food – casseroles, salads, big old pots, cakes, pies. I'm thinking he better be headed for the homeless shelters now. There's no way anybody could eat all that stuff."

Tate wasn't surprised, though he would like to have gotten his hands on some of that arroz con pollo himself.

"Anything suspicious? Big boxes? Small boxes? Envelopes?"

"Nah."

"Stay on him. And make sure the night crew is fully briefed. Give them a copy of your log. If he hits the same place twice, we'll look at it."

• • •

TATE KEPT one hand on the wheel while he rummaged in the back seat, rifling through a shoebox full of CDs until he found something with the right raunch to it. It was one of his homemade mixes, nothing but blazing blues guitar.

If it ain't breaking glass, it ain't the blues, Tate liked to say. He was a serious aficionado. Most of the time, Tate could tell you who was playing after hearing a couple of licks. This was a Lucky Peterson cut.

Lucky had his good days and his bad. Sometimes he tried to play songs, set a mood. Tate didn't much care for it. He liked it better when Lucky just ripped it up.

Doubt if Gonzales ever listened to Lucky.

"Tater, you're gonna bust my fucking eardrums, man."

"Can you feel it whompin' in your chest? If you can't, I'll notch it up some more."

"I can feel it, I promise."

Hugh stuck his head out the window. It helped carry some of the sound away.

Tate and Hugh had been a team for a couple of years now. Tate, more likely to see the big picture, more impulsive, more likely just to walk in the front door. See more that way.

Hugh, a slogger, a detail guy, like the time the perp had a pair of shoes in the back of his closet and there was some red clay under the heel. It was a small thing and Hugh had figured it out.

They were headed across Biscayne Bay toward a salon where they would take over the shift tailing Isabel. Tate had scheduled himself with the guys tailing the Gonzales clan, saying he'd get a gut feeling if he hung out long enough. And that would lead him to Gonzales.

They saw her SLK 350 parked in front of one of the more expensive places in town. The guys were half a block down on the other side. Tate drove past them and swung around behind. One of the guys in the front car called him on the cell.

"She's just gotten here, so it may be awhile. You guys have a good one. We're headed for the barn."

They waved. Hugh had already ejected the CD. Tate killed the engine, slid the seat back and lit a smoke.

"Thought you were gonna quit."

"I am. Thought you were gonna quit bringing it up."

"Who was it asked me to remind you?"

"Yeah? How about fuck yourself."

He stared at the cigarette, rolled down the window, took another drag. It was a damn good thing Hugh didn't get pissed at him. Actually it was a damn good thing most of the people who knew him didn't get pissed at him, not counting the chief, Einburg, Sharon's mother, Sharon... some of the time, some of the other guys on the force.

He tossed the butt.

"Good. Now, let's think out loud... Gonzales is still hiding out, which means he thinks whoever tried to kill him is still around, yes? Would that be the only reason?"

"Dunno compadre, but his folks are not availing himself of our services, which makes me think they're afraid we're no good, or we're corrupt and we'll give him up, or maybe there's some other reason, but I can't think what it would be, unless there's something they wants to hide from us, too."

"Yup," said Tate. "You've seen all the armor at his place now. He could be damn safe at home. And he knows we'd bust our asses keeping him out of trouble. So let's just assume that he has some other reason for not wanting us to know where he is. Now what might that be?"

"OK, the simplest solutions first, right? He's into drugs, gambling, whores."

"Don't think so, doesn't make sense," Tate said. "This guy is so clean the politicians will do anything to get into his circle. If he was nasty, it would be the other way around."

"Yeah, but he's slick. Maybe he's fooled everybody."

"I'll buy that much," said Tate. "I'll buy that he's slick and that he's fooled people. But I don't see the guy stooping that low. I could be wrong, but just look at the facts. Somebody tries to whack him and everybody immediately lets us think he's dead, when, in fact, it's a close friend of his. And even the close friend's family lets us think Gonzales is dead.

"You know, in most families, if somebody's life was in danger, they'd be talking to us until we couldn't stand it anymore. We'd know who had an affair, who had a falling out with their third cousin. They'd be treating us like father confessors."

He lit another butt and adjusted his back into the seat.

"These guys are not just keeping their distance, they're acting on their own. That independence didn't just start yesterday. And whatever is going on isn't limited to the immediate family. There's a whole group that's in on it. You know what? This is what I'd expect if somebody had tried to whack a guy in the Mafia."

"Yeah, but so what? We don't have anything, we don't even suspect anything," said Hugh. "We're stuck, big-time."

"Maybe so, but I don't just want to investigate who killed Simons. I want to peel back the cover off Gonzales. Something stinks here."

"I'm starting to smell Lone Ranger again, Dude. We have nothing to justify going full bore on the *victim.* You'd better plan on finding yourself in very big trouble if you barge in and screw up."

"Gracias, my friend. Now what I want from you is to help me figure out how we're going to break the Gonzales family code."

• • •

ALFREDO WAS pleased.

"We have much to discuss. But first, let us congratulate Juan for his foresight in bringing this wonderful supper."

He'd had a good long talk with Isabel. They would try to spend a little time together, but Alfredo thought it was too soon. They would work on a plan.

Just now there was picadillo and arroz con pollo, with fritos and yuca, a terrific salad. They ate off paper plates. The beer was cold and the wine was perfect.

There was a large bay inside the warehouse where they could park, but most of them had walked. The team had gathered after dark, making sure not to be followed. Rafael Martinez was the first to speak.

"Some of the young machos want to set up some sort of trap to find out who we are dealing with. I myself think it is those scumbag espia. Is it a distraction?"

Gonzales thought a moment. He lifted some onions with a fork and draped them over his chicken.

"Let's have them put something together and we'll look at it. Obviously we don't want any exposure. Something clever might be appealing. Manuel?"

Manuel Ramos had been with Gonzales for 20 years. He'd come over early, like Gonzales. As he had aged, he had grown round as a barrel. And he was quite proud of his heavy moustache.

Manuel still liked to tell stories about the old days, about arriving in Miami, about being met with welcome bags stuffed with peanut butter and spam, toothpaste and English-Spanish dictionaries.

"It will have to be beyond clever. If it is Castro's scum, is it your assumption they will simply stay here until their job is done? That may be true. It may not. If we kill them, how do we know we killed them all? If we do not kill them, how do we know whether they are still here?

"The easiest way to deal with these assassins is to kill their leader. We came together to kill Fidel. Now we will finish it. Cut off the head and the body withers. If they work for no one, they have no work."

"Well spoken. Who else has a thought?"

It was the reason Juan loved Gonzales. The man could issue orders and they would all follow without question. And yet he led with soft hands. He listened to everyone.

"I think Manuel is right, but only to a point," Juan said. "He presupposes that we work alone. You treat the police as if they are the enemy, as if they are a part of the problem. What if we simply worked to discover who our antagonists are and where they are? And then we provide that information to Drawdy?

"It certainly does us no harm if the police lock up the killers. The Americans put the screws to La Red Avispa and it has done us no harm."

Manuel didn't like it.

"It was not Metro-Dade police who intercepted the communications that led them to the wasp network. Local police did not analyze the encryptions."

Gonzales jumped in.

"You're both right. But I think Juan raises a strong point. We are too regimented in our thinking. There may be a way to make use of law enforcement without jeopardizing our mission."

Juan was glad that he'd had the opportunity to put forth the idea of working, at least unilaterally, with the cops. They were a weapon the group hadn't considered.

When the feds had moved against the WASP network – a Cuban spy ring that had infiltrated military installations and even some of the exile groups – it had been a cause for celebration in Miami.

The WASP leader had been tried and handed a death sentence for his role in the Cuban air attack – when MIGs had killed four members of Brothers to the Rescue, the organization of flyers who patrolled the waters between Cuba and Florida watching for refugees in need of assistance.

Gonzales nodded to Juan. His ideas would be helpful.

"But I think now we should talk about El Loco. The time is getting closer."

Juan passed the desserts, a nice flan, some pudin de pan and café con leche. There was a chorus of laughter.

15

FRIDAY

"HEY GRADY. They found Paul."

Grady Osmund's chopper had landed in the parking lot of the Palm Beach county sheriff's office. A couple of deputies had been offered up as drivers and they were about to head out to meet Buddy Lee when the call came.

"He's alone? He split from the rest of them?"

"He's dead. Busted windpipe and a bullet through the head. Hands folded together."

Fred held up three fingers.

"The count's climbing."

After combing through some papers they found stuffed in a cardboard box in the garage, the cops thought the cons might be driving an old Ford Econoline van. They'd put cruisers on all the main roads, a single-engine plane over the interstate.

The cons could have left the road to wait for things to cool off. They could have found another ride or they might have made it to someplace big enough to hide. Lauderdale maybe.

The brothers found a seafood place. Grady and Buddy Lee and Fred got a table. The rest of the team sat across the room.

Buddy Lee ordered a round of iced tea.

"You want to see what the feds can tell us?

"We've passed along the info. The file on Barnett makes a reference to the victims' hands. Obviously the feds know a good deal more about that than we do, but I'm not real sure I want to be beholden to them, even if it's just for information. I like keeping Dean at arm's length. If they want to offer something, we can listen."

Fred jumped in.

"My guess is Paul wore out his welcome."

"Yeah, we figured he would," Buddy Lee said, "but it raises the question why they brought him along. I can't figure out the advantage to having a group in the first place, unless there's a job, in which case, maybe three guys can do what four guys would have done. And then, of course, why the hell they brought Herb."

• • •

JUAN PUNCHED the horn on the Mercedes and hopped out to shake some hands. It was his second day touring the city.

It is an important time to show leadership, Gonzales had said. Let people know that things are in order. Let them see that we are out and about. What you say isn't as important as the fact that you show a profile.

The group would meet again this evening. Juan had not seen anyone following him, still he drove like his grandfather, creeping along, often circling the same block several times.

Down the street, Hugh Brice-Whittaker washed down a ham and cheese with some chocolate milk. His grimy Chevy sedan looked like half the cars in the neighborhood. He was on until 7. Then Tate would spell him.

The Mercedes inched through Little Havana side streets stocked with low-slung Detroit battle wagons and rusting compacts, mouse-sized front yards decorated with painted mailboxes, skinny palms and bunched-up plastic pinwheels. Hugh kept the windows down so he could smell the pork and the black beans. He got Tate on the radio.

"I don't think he even knows all these folks. He just stops when he sees somebody and tells them who he is and what's going on."

Tate wasn't sure it was that simple.

"Guy's a politician. He's calming fears, keeping everybody on the same page. They all know about the attempt on Gonzales. What's strange is this thing is bringing the community together. He's working off of that, keeping everybody cool, but he's capitalizing on the tension."

The cops knew all about Juan's assurances. Gonzales was fine. The Cuban community had nothing to fear. Castro would be taught a lesson.

Surrounded by a group on the front porch of a small shotgun cottage, Juan embraced an elderly couple. A cab drove up from the far end of the street. Hugh's car was a ways back, but he could see the Mercedes was blocking the road. Juan waved and jogged out to clasp hands with a man at the curb. Suddenly he jumped in the cab. It backed quickly out into the intersection.

"Son of a bitch."

Hugh stomped on the gas, gambling they'd head north. He grabbed his radio and sent another car south as he skipped through intersections, hoping to cut them off. Glancing down a side street, he saw a cab on a parallel course suddenly turn right, away from him.

He was at the wrong end of a one-way street and his way was blocked. There was just room on the sidewalk. He jumped the curb, cut between a couple of parked cars and punched it all the way to the corner.

The cab was headed toward the river.

• • •

THE OLD Whaler putted along, straight up the waterway. Bill Conover had quit asking spectators if they'd seen anything. They must be headed for the city. He rented a small boat and, sure enough, after a long afternoon communing with the egrets and the pelicans, he spotted the Silver Queen beached under a gang of Australian pines. It looked ok.

He motored slowly around behind, then pulled up close, edging the whaler aground so it wouldn't rock. Then he stood on the bow, reached for the Queen's railing and pulled himself aboard. She cranked right up and he breathed a huge sigh of relief. Tying a tow rope to his rental, he gently slid the Queen back, wondering if a benevolent streak had prompted the thieves to push her up into the sand. On the console, in plain sight, his watch.

He'd been cruising slowly, surveying, and hadn't seen anything civilized in a couple of miles. Nothing but a worn-out bait shack. It was a small cinderblock square with a crushed-shell drive, a tin roof and an old gas pump shaped like a jukebox. A rusted-out refrigerator sat out back, next to a pile of scrap wood and some flattened cardboard boxes. The place looked open, but he couldn't see any signs of life.

Conover nudged the Queen into deeper water and headed south to get his truck. He'd moor at the marina where he'd rented the little whaler.

Gulls screeched at him the whole way back.

Two hours later, he was back at the bait shop. He parked the GMC in front of an Orange Crush sign and went inside. The clerk was an old fart who'd spent too much time in the sun.

"You see that trawler beached up in the trees about a quarter mile south of here?"

"You're shitting me. Somebody wreck the thing?"

"Nope. Stole it. My boat. I'm looking for three guys. Would have been through here a day and a half ago and they woulda been on foot."

"Didn't see three guys. There was one guy I saw. He looked for shit. Couple days worth of beard. I gave him the number for Sonny's Cab, only one around here. You talk to Sonny. He come out and got him."

Conover called Sonny. And Sonny came through big time. For $40, he'd take him into the city, to the place where he'd dropped the three guys.

"Deal. Lemme talk to this guy about leaving my truck here."

He got a small leather bag out of the truck and climbed into the front seat.

"Here's $50. Start at the beginning. What they looked like. What they said. What you said. The whole deal."

It was three guys, one of them huge. They wanted a ride into Miami. Once they'd gotten to town, they had cruised some neighborhoods until one of the guys saw a fleabag he'd liked.

Conover found the desk clerk somewhat reluctant, but a couple of $10s was enough. The three had stayed not quite two days. Third floor. One guy went in and out. The other two hadn't left the room.

The clerk had no clue where they'd gone. There was a punk hanging out with him in the lobby. He didn't know a thing either. He said it before he was asked.

The punk was just leaving the motel when a fist caught him across the back of the head and sent him sprawling into the alley.

"Jesus help me."

Conover twisted the .45 into his left nostril and jammed him up against the wall, feet off the ground.

"Talk to me."

Turns out the punk had run some errands, getting food and such. And, yes, he'd found them another place to stay. It was only a couple of blocks. Conover kept one hand wrapped around the kid's throat the whole way over.

It was another fleabag, still a shitty part of town, with busted out streetlights and houses built for people under five feet.

"You can go now, you little fuck."

The punk rubbed at his neck. He backed a few feet away and was about to tell Conover what he thought of him when he gave a start. The captain looked over and saw two men walking out of the motel. Just behind them, a third, so big he had to duck through the doorway.

"Shit." The kid bolted.

Conover still had his gun out. One guy darted to the side, into the dark. One dropped to his knee and fished for a weapon from behind his back. Conover aimed for him and pulled the trigger.

A foot smashed into the side of his face, lifting him off the ground, and then he was on his back, punching, scrambling, pushing him off. A hand tightening around his throat, the flash of something metallic. The guy was strong, too strong. Conover fought to break free, threw a forearm. The knife skittered toward the curb. An elbow crashed into his chest.

"Jackie!"

Suddenly he was gone. Conover's head was swimming, his heart pounding. He gasped, small choking bursts. Then, slowly, his breath began to return. He rolled over onto his knees, collected himself and staggered to his feet. There was a small crowd across the street, staring. Nobody moved in his direction.

He saw the .45, grabbed it and shuffled down the street.

16

A JUNGLE cacophony of cars jammed into too small a space, sirens, toughs shouting from the corner, a rumbling from the bowels of a nightclub a few doors down, head-banging heat from the asphalt and the steel.

Conover thought there was a good chance he'd missed the guy completely. But he'd come pretty close to getting killed himself.

Lights out, curtains drawn tight, he pulled his arm down over his eyes. Sick to his stomach, his back throbbing from where he hit the ground, sore all over from the beating he'd taken and scared shitless. He took a long plunge off one of the quart bottles of Bud he'd gotten across the street and rolled slowly over onto his side. He reached across a wobbly little desk by the bed, pulled on the light and dialed.

"Switch me to investigations, will ya?

"Yeah. Who's working tonight. No. No. Booker? OK, put Booker on.

"Booker. Bill Conover. Yeah. Remember me? Hey I need to talk with you. I'm in town and I just took a shot at a guy. No I'm not sure I hit anything. Well, 'cause I left. There was a couple other guys there who wanted to kill me. So I left.

"Don't get pissy with me, man, I'm trying to do the right thing here. I feel like complete shit. How about you come over here and lemme explain what's happened, OK?

"I Dunno, some shit hotel down by Manuel's. No, I don't wanna come down there. I just had somebody kick the living shit of me and I'm not exactly eager to run around OK? Look, Booker, I swear I'm not shitting you, I just need you to come this way, all right? Yeah, well, it's a shithole, it's right across from that little liquor store, Manuel's Fine Liquors. You know the place?

"Yeah. Right down the street. All right, you know the place? All right. I'm upstairs. Tell 'em you're looking for Bill. Yeah. Thanks."

Booker Hollingsworth came by himself. There wasn't much point in dragging anybody else along. He found the hotel, one of the city's forgotten treasures, flashed his badge at the desk clerk and took the stairs two at a time, which he always did, which may have contributed to his softball-sized calves.

Booker was heavy and short, but he didn't seem to mind. Perpetually good-natured, Booker was married to his high school sweetheart, the prom queen everybody had tried to nudge away.

His name is not Fireplug, she'd say. It's Booker. I like Booker.

A long-timer, he was the best shot on the force, spoke three languages and liked to cut peaches in half and and soak 'em in rum and brown sugar all day, then grill 'em up for dessert in the summertime. On a typical Saturday, Booker and Amy easily would be mistaken for a traditional suburban white-collar couple, working in the yard, exchanging a stack of mysteries at the library. Booker heading down to the basement in the late afternoon for an hour with his clarinet. Big band stuff.

He banged on the door. Conover let him in. Booker started out with a bunch of questions. When they came a bit too fast, Conover sat up straight and pointed a finger.

"Fuck you."

Booker grinned.

"I know what you're saying. Now, where was I?..."

Conover answered all his questions. Then they got back into Booker's car and drove to the hotel.

SATURDAY

THE NEXT morning, Booker sat with Tate Drawdy and Hugh. They waited.

Booker had told Conover to get drunk, sleep it off and show up at 10. That was an hour ago. Booker was wondering if he had screwed up.

Tate crossed his arms.

"I'm glad I got here early."

"Hey... sorry man. I told the guy 10 o'clock."

"No sweat. It's not your fault the fucking guy decides to blow us off. Let's give him another couple of minutes. If he shows any later than that, we'll kill him."

It was Tate's way of being nice. There was a knock.

Tate went to the door. On the other side, a six-foot, 230-pounder, powerful, but past the days of training camp, one side of his face all swole up.

He turned to Booker: "Is this the captain?"

Conover brushed past him and came on in, looking sorely in need of java.

Booker was pleased.

"Hey man, you shaved."

The captain grunted. After the introductions were made, Booker began by explaining what he'd heard the night before.

"Well, there were a few folks who saw some of it, maybe even some folks who saw the whole thing. In any case, there isn't much disagreement. People saw Bill here walking towards the hotel with another man, a small man, when three guys came out of the hotel. One of the three reached behind his back and dropped down like he was going to shoot and Bill fired his weapon, which he just happened to be holding in his hand at the time.

"Folks say a guy jumped up and did a Jackie Chan thing on Bill until his buddy yelled at him. Bill left on foot. The other fellas shoved a gun in the face of a guy driving by, tossed him out and took his SUV. Gray, no make or model. Right now, no stolen car report that matches.

"So, in a nutshell, the story bears out with the witnesses. The street people say the three guys looked liked serious players.

"And now maybe Mr. Conover would like to repeat the story about his boat and how he came here."

So the Cap'n told his tale.

Hugh and Tate were torn between shrugging it off and throwing his butt in jail.

"You're retired, man. What did you think you were doing, coming up here with a gun after three guys who, as far as you know, stole your boat?" Hugh asked.

"I've been trying to figure that out. Curious, I guess; bit of John Wayne, maybe. I was pissed off. I'm still pissed off.

"But you know, I'm thinking about the way this went. Three guys grab a boat and they're banging up to Miami and they grab a hotel and, when I show up, they're balls to the wall. What's up with these guys?"

Booker had done the hospital calls already, right after he'd left Conover. Nobody had come in with a gunshot, at least nobody who seemed to fit this scenario. Anyhow, the hospitals called them whenever gunshot victims came in.

"Sounds like dopers to me," Hugh offered.

Tate brought over another cup for Conover.

"What do you want to do now?"

"I guess I'd like to head on back south, if you guys have no objection. I think maybe I committed a crime, but I'm not sure. I mean, that guy was gonna kill me. They were all gonna kill me, if they'd stuck around for it."

Tate stood, motioned for Booker and Hugh to follow him outside. A few minutes later, they came back. Conover was free to go. They knew where to find him. And they would keep his gun.

Conover borrowed a phone and made a call to his new friend Sonny.

• • •

SHARON PULLED the Mustang up to the dry cleaner's window and stuck her head out.

"Hey. You guys gonna give me my stuff or not?"

There was a shout from the back. "Mahoney's here. Tell her the clothes aren't ready yet so she'll come inside."

"Dougie, you horny asshole, gimme my clothes or my boyfriend comes in here and shoots up the place."

Dougie appeared at the side door, carrying a couple of bundles, taking his time. Tall, with dazzling blue eyes and a smattering of tomboyish freckles, Miss Sharon was quite the traffic stopper.

"Harmless dry cleaning guy murdered for ogling redhead. That's gonna look great on the resume."

"Yeah, sweetie, well he might just pop you in the leg, or worse, and then you'd have to live through the pain. And then your buddy Roberto would dump you like stale pizza. So, best thing for you is just give me the laundry and put it on my tab and I'll just ease on outta here like this never happened."

Dougie opened the side door and laid the clothes across the back seat.

"What you got on, babe? Clothes? You could pick up your stuff after dark. I could open up late for you. You wouldn't have to go to all that trouble, you know, getting dressed and everything."

She lit a smoke and cranked up the CD. "Cool. I'll be back tonight about midnight. You wait for me right here, OK?"

Dougie stood by the door. "You're all jacked up, honey. Big plans?"

"I'm afraid so, my friend. Got a babysitter. Got a reservation. Got some nice bubbly. The old fart been working mucho hours lately. Ms. Mahoney gonna treat him to a real meal."

"You are way too good for that copper. What do they call them? Dicks?"

She patted him on the arm and roared out of the parking lot.

17

OVERSTREET RANCH was 250 acres of dense woods not far from Lake Okeechobee. There were no real roads anywhere close by, which made it perfect. It was one of those unmarked hunting areas set aside many years before, just a skinny dirt road off a two lane, hardly visible, blocked off with a rusty chain between two trees. If someone got past the first bend, they'd see a sign:

Overstreet Hunting Ranch.

Private Property

No Trespassing

Just to be on the safe side, one of Gonzales' people lived in the main house fulltime, with a no-nonsense dog roaming close by.

The group had bought the ranch 10 years earlier, though no record of the transaction had been made. The owners, an old couple who had left no children, got more money than they wanted and a new place to live in Arizona where they could escape the humidity and the bugs.

You drove for a good 10 minutes to reach the house once you'd unlocked the chain at the end of the dirt road. The grass and weeds grew hip high and, during the hunting season, it was typical to see the trunk of an old pine lying across the lane as if blown down during a storm. There was no reason anyone would venture beyond it.

The main house was an old brick two-story. More than a generation before, it had serviced a large estate, but most of the land had been in sugar cane and it had been undercut by the big farms. Eventually, forest had grown up around the place until it no longer seemed connected with the rest of the world. It had a screened porch on the front and, out back, a barn and a tractor shed. Inside the shed, a generator provided electricity and a deep well offered cool water.

The dirt driveway formed a circle leading up to the house and it surrounded a grassy area where the men liked to throw a baseball or grill steaks at a brick fireplace under a huge live oak that shaded half the yard. There was a pair of bent-twig rockers alongside a flat stump that sometimes held a chessboard at the end of a long day.

Behind the house, an open field of 10 acres or more and then more woods, marsh and the lake. Inside, a huge kitchen with a table that could seat a dozen. There were eight bedrooms and a handful of bathrooms. Still, the men often cleaned up under a pair of showerheads atop a pole in the center of a concrete pad by the side of the house.

When they went to the house, they took their food and supplies with them. Nobody local had ever seen them. They arrived at night by four-wheeler or airboat and their weapons practice was virtually silent. For Juan, it was like summer camp.

Sometimes, the committee visited the farm. But most of them, like Gonzales, were older. Money, ideas and a fire that still burned, but they were not soldiers. That task fell to the younger group, no less committed, but far more capable of the task of putting a bullet through the forehead of a Cuban dictator and escaping without entanglements.

They had spent a year developing their strategy. Early on, they'd made a significant investment in intelligence. A member of the committee had developed a friendship with Major Emilio Duran of the Caracas police force. Duran was head of the patrol division. He would be the one to assign security for the trip from the airport in Caracas across to the island and throughout his stay. After Fidel was dead, Duran would serve an additional two years on the force. He would live in the same house, eat in the same restaurants, wear the same clothes.

After two years had passed, he would vacation in Miami and, during that trip, he would become ill. He would see a doctor, who would advise him to retire and find a less stressful way of life. Duran would move very far away and, at that point, he would have access to his bank account. He was a 57-year-old officer with an unblemished record. He was a good choice.

His second-in-command was Milos Saab, a young captain. Saab also worked for the team, though his major knew nothing of it. Saab's wife had given birth just six months earlier and it had been a complicated delivery.

Just three weeks before she was due, she'd been in a car wreck. She had been badly injured and then she was coughing and seemed confused. Lab tests confirmed it. It was called DIC, disseminated intravascular coagulation. It was a dangerous development. Blood clots were forming throughout her body.

It was triggered by the shock, Saab's doctor said. Her condition could worsen. Her body might use up all its clotting factors, and then she would hemorrhage. With a major trauma, the doctor said, DIC doubled the mortality rate.

The difficulty was knowing how, when and if to treat it.

"If! If! What does that mean?"

Sometimes, the doctor said, the patient improves. But the underlying problem has to be solved. We'll watch her blood counts and hope. Otherwise – inflammation, fever and then bleeding from her nose, mouth, eyes, vagina, rectum.

Saab stayed at her bedside most of the day. Later in the afternoon, he had run by his office for a moment when the phone rang. It was the doctor. Could Saab meet him at the hospital? There was a specialist available who might be persuaded to take the case.

Saab rushed downtown. His doctor sat him down. The involvement of the specialist could mean the difference between life and death for his wife and their unborn son. But the specialist had many cases.

When he heard the fee, Saab dropped his head into his hands. It was more than he made in two years.

I have been asked, his doctor said, to tell you there is a potential benefactor, a man who overheard one of the nurses talking about your wife's case. He has asked me to mention this to you. He is a man of wealth, but he wants no publicity. Perhaps you would like to speak to him?

The specialist took the case. Saab's wife and son came home healthy and happy and, when it was over, he received a bill. It was marked paid in full.

Saab's fee was to stand ready to perform a task. He would be a backup. If the major faltered, or if for some reason he was unable to perform his duties, the captain would take his place.

It would be just a matter of days now before one of them was called to serve.

• • •

ASSISTANT POLICE Chief Robert Einburg was feeling particularly erudite.

"The typical murderer is between 16 and 20 and he prefers a .38 caliber revolver or a 9 mm pistol. That's what's easiest to obtain. You can buy them at flea markets or gun shows or in the newspaper classifieds.

"This kid is in his early 20s. He fits the profile. And Simons was killed with a 9mm. All of which lends credence to the notion that the suicide is a legitimate suspect."

They were sitting in the chief's office – the chief, Einburg and Tate. Einburg had asked for the meeting. On a Saturday. The chief's office, a sterile place. He had the prerequisite cop memorabilia on the walls, a framed clipping from the newspaper story the day he'd been promoted. On the desk, in a deep wooden frame covered with glass, a lineup of antique police badges. Pictures of his wife and kids.

It was a hot day, but the chief still wore long pants. Tate, cutoffs and flip-flops. Einburg looked like he'd gotten lost on the way to the golf course.

"I suggest that we achieve a positive identification on the young man. Then we'll be well along our way to deducing motive."

Tate had a question: "How you planning to get the ID on your so-called Suicide Boy?"

"Dental records, I suspect."

Tate tilted his head deferentially toward his supervisor.

"Chief, how about we park Mr. Einburg in front of the tv for a few more days. By then, he ought to have enough insight to solve the crime outright."

Einburg wasn't backing off.

"You care to explain why this doesn't hold water, Tate?"

"As soon as the lab gets caught up, we're going to find out there's no residue on his hands. This little asshole killed himself? Don't think so. He's not strung out. He's probably some pizza delivery fart. Regardless, I'm not sure I see the logic in the whole remorse bit, seeing as how he supposedly thought he'd whacked one of the wealthiest guys in the country and didn't take a fucking thing.

"But I do like the dental idea. Here's what you do, Robert. You've already got your body. All you need to do now is scour the planet for somebody who hasn't been home for dinner lately. Then you've got your missing person. Then you track down his dentist and get his x-rays. Have them sent here and we'll see if there's a match. I think that's pretty much how they do it.

"Course, as I recall, that's usually for people who've been burnt up in some horrible fire or been buried for 16 years or they got washed up on shore or something. In this case, we have a perfectly fine body so we have his fingerprints. And we could take an actual holy shit photograph of the fucking guy if you want. But I do like the dental thing. That's pretty cool."

Einburg looked over at the chief. He'd been sitting with his chin in his hand for awhile, staring over top of his glasses. But now he was leaning back and he was laughing pretty hard. Einburg snapped the cover on his palm pilot and headed for the door.

Tate held out a hand.

"You've got my cell, Robert. Any more light bulbs, you give me a call, day or night, OK?"

18

THE SUN was just beginning to set. It had been a scorcher and it would stay hot for hours. Tate pulled a pack of smokes from a soppy shirt and lit one without taking the binoculars from his eyes.

It was, supposedly, the cool part of the year. What a crock. There were no seasons here. Just hot and unbearably hot. In Atlanta, there'd been a respite. You could build a fire on a pretty regular basis during the winter. Here, there might be a couple of days when you'd open the windows.

He'd gotten to where he liked the tropical thing, the Mediterranean look, the palms and the pulsing nightlife. But he missed the sense of place he'd felt in Atlanta. In the wealthy Druid Hills neighborhood where his parents lived, the houses sat the ground they'd owned for generations.

Here, everything felt temporary, new. You could go to sleep with an empty field out back and wake up to a shopping center.

Eventually, those changes would reach the inner city. Not yet. Here, along the seedier part of the river, things were very much the same.

It was the center of what the city fathers liked to call the river's "urban potential." Shipyards, scarcely used; abandoned buildings; rusting freighters loaded with old clothes, mattresses and other discards headed for Haiti and the Dominican Republic.

They were not far from the site of the infamous River Cops case, a north-shore boatyard where three bodies had been found floating after a police raid on some guys offloading a cocaine shipment. Eight of Tate's predecessors had decided to grab 400 kilograms of the stuff, figuring on improving their standard of living.

Rum-runners, drug runners, illegal-alien smugglers. In a few years, if the city had its way, it would be fancy loft living. For the time being, it was not a good place to bring the relatives.

The old warehouse was surrounded and they had a cigarette in the river. They hadn't seen anybody go in, but Hugh was sure that this was the building.

It was owned by some Latin import firm. They could have spent some time backtracking to make sure there was an ownership connection with Gonzales, but Tate didn't want to worry with it.

"Why does this not surprise me?" Hugh had said. "Let's just hope we're not screwing up completely here."

"Hey. You followed the fucking guy here, am I right? Let's not piss around."

There were lights on inside. It sounded like a radio was playing on the second floor.

Tate keyed his radio. "Let's go look."

A uniform with a battering ram forced the door and they burst inside, only to meet a deluge. Lights strobed. A siren wailed.

Not a soul around.

Hugh cursed his way down every hallway in the place until he found the control panel and disabled the alarms. It took another five minutes to get the sprinkler system turned off. Then Tate's team began wading through the building.

High ceilings and suspended incandescent lamps. Pallets, truck tires, a couple of real estate signs, a case of roach spray. In an office, some empty filing cabinets and, inside a plastic garbage bag in the corner, a pile of fast-food wrappers. It opened onto a large room with a long table, a nice table, with 10 cushioned chairs. In the corner, a desk with some unused legal pads in the top drawer.

Hugh was thrilled. "Welcome to squatsville. Ain't a fucking thing in here. No people. No stuff."

"Keep looking."

They searched, climbing through the rafters, thumping on the walls, sticking flashlights everyplace. They were about to give up when one of the river patrol team offered a suggestion. "You know, Tate, I've seen a couple of old buildings like this with an underground level, for cool storage and stuff."

They looked again. After an hour, Hugh took him aside. "Tate. Ain't no stairs, nothing. We've been outside. We've been inside."

Tate held up a hand. "OK. We're done, for now. Put a couple guys here overnight and get some equipment in here to make sure there's nothing under the floor. We're dealing with serious people here, with serious money."

He turned to leave, then stopped.

"You know what? Get that stuff now. Let's find it now. This was a nice pair of shoes."

"Yeah, and you had your hair just right."

Tate stopped to talk to a few cops before he walked back outside. Hugh had just gotten off the phone with the tech guys. Tate sloshed over and grabbed an arm.

"Hey man. Let's get a beer before we check out. We can have a great time talking about how we don't have a fucking clue about what's going on here."

They found a place with an outdoor deck, someplace where they could drip. Tate ordered the first round.

"Gimme three Buds and give my buddy three Buds. And an ashtray."

They were on their second round when Hugh's cell rang. The team had found a room under the floor.

One of the tech guys met them outside.

"You ain't gonna believe this, Tate. There's a trap door. It's concrete. And underneath it, there's this perfect room."

"Whaddya mean, a perfect room?"

"Come on. You'll see. We haven't gone down yet. Thought you might want to be the first."

There was a simple pull on the floor, but it was well disguised. One good tug on the big trap door and it swung up nicely on a counterbalance. Concrete stairs led to a basement vault. There was a musty smell, but the place was clean.

Hugh spit into a corner. “We got squat here.”

“Bullshit. This ain’t squat. It’s a disaster. Look at what we’re dealing with here. Some wealthy investment guy who’s the hottest shit in this town turns out to be a target. He’s got a warehouse with some kind of secret room. And the whole fucking place is empty.

“We better figure this out right now. As long as Gonzales is still in hiding, we can’t protect him. There are some bad fuckers in town. And if he gets whacked we’re gonna look like we don’t care, or we’re incompetent. Either scenario, you and I are out of work.”

Tate shoved one of the guys aside and headed up the stairs.

SUNDAY

FACE DOWN, pillow on top of his head, hands bent awkwardly underneath, he made no effort to greet the day. Sharon had managed to get up, get dressed, make coffee and eat breakfast and he hadn’t stirred.

And now she was back from aerobics, bouncing into the house, not dreaming she’d find him there, buried into the mattress, deep ravines etched into his face.

Finally the slumbering beauty uttered a sound. What it was, she did not know.

Methodically, and with great care, she slammed the door to the bathroom.

“Oops,” she said.

One at a time, he pulled his arms out from beneath his chest. He rolled slightly to one side, bent a leg and with that leverage rolled himself over onto his back. She could remember when she’d been thrilled to see her child manage the same move for the first time.

He sat up slowly, Lugosi-like, opened his eyes and grinned at her.

"You're up."

"Yes I am," he said. "Yes... I... am."

A moment later, he was back from the bathroom. He'd brushed his teeth. He kissed her.

"You smell great."

"I am dripping with sweat."

"Yup."

She watched as he pulled open a drawer, took out a pair of nylon shorts and some thin socks. He slid his Nikes out from under the bureau.

"You going out?"

"Taking a run. Quickest way to get human."

"It's 90 out there."

"Perfect. Buy you some breakfast in an hour?"

"Ok."

She stood at the window and saw him disappear down the street. He was not a blur.

• • •

JACKIE BOY Barnett pulled the SUV onto a vacant lot in a shitty part of town, under some trees with the butt-end against the fence. He'd snatched a small toolbox from the kid's garage and he pulled out a Phillips head and took off the license plate and stuffed it inside, behind the spare tire. He was starting to look pretty scruffy – a six-day beard, a Cincinnati Reds baseball cap and a faded sweatshirt over some oil-stained jeans. There was a hop in his step. Freedom wasn't so bad, they were getting close and he loved the work.

He'd left Otis and Herb near a dumpy motel about five miles away, on the outskirts of Little Havana, not far from a bus stop, so they could stroll over as if they had just come in.

Jackie waved down a cab and found Herbert in the room watching an old movie. He was eating popcorn, a big bag, grabbing a few kernels at a time with his thumb and two fingers, delicately pushing more between his lips as he chewed. In his left hand, a wad of paper towels he was using to swipe across his mouth

"Where's Otis?"

Herb wiped each finger. He nodded so Jackie would know he'd get an answer as soon as he finished swallowing. He cleared his throat, pointed at the popcorn, stuck a thumb in the air.

"Went for a fucking run. In this heat. And it's 'sposed to storm. Mother fucker's all I can say. Mother fuckin' heat. Course that's all he ever does, is read shit and run his legs. Smart and skinny, that's Otis. Me, I'm gonna take a fuckin' nap, just thinking about it."

"You do that, my friend. Save your strength."

"Damn right."

Herb hurried a few more bites into his mouth, rolled onto his side. The mattress seemed to curl itself around him. In a minute, he was out.

Jackie got another room a few doors down. He pulled out a New York Times. He was lying on the bed, a few pillows piled up behind him. He had his boots on.

He started to read a piece about Saddam Hussein. He read about Saddam's wives, his money, the people who jumped when he gave orders. He'd been a vicious tough guy all his life. The story said he'd tortured neighborhood pets when he was young. Jackie raised an eyebrow.

He read about a speech Saddam had given to a bunch of his Republican Guard commanders – telling them what they'd do to the infidel Americans if they tried to cross his borders. Saddam, the story said, banged his fist on a desk as he shouted at his men.

Somebody had written down what he said:

"They will become as a river of blood when we mount our relentless attack. They will quake like twigs beneath a gale as we sweep over them in a torrent. They will shriek like mongrels cast into the fire. They will weep as women swept into the raging waterfall. Their bones will snap like dried leaves under the tracks of our armored vehicles. They will utter our names with their final breaths. Their pleas for mercy will be like so many kittens whimpering."

Jackie thought it was flowery, but a good speech. He tore it lengthwise, on the thread of the paper where it would tear nicely, folded it up and stuck it in his shirt pocket.

He threw the paper down and walked over to the corner of the room, leaned over and put his hands on the floor, shoulder width apart. Lifting gracefully into a handstand, he began lowering himself slowly toward the floor, and then back up again. After 25 repetitions, he stood, threw a pillow onto the floor and began to hop back and forth over on his right foot, jumping from corner to corner, clockwise. It was all he'd salvaged from learning the box step in junior high.

No brothers and sisters. Just his mom. Jackie's father had been out of the picture since the boy was eight.

He'd been an indifferent student, although he got good enough grades to stay on the baseball team. After school he ran around. Smoking cigarettes, drinking beer, breaking into the neighbors' houses to steal jewelry and money. It was better than flipping burgers.

Then he'd joined the Army, found out what he was good at.

After a few minutes, he changed legs, hands on his waist, standing straight, focused on the mirror across the room, watching himself. There was a knock. It was Herbert and Otis with some deli food.

They came in and sat on the bed. Herb started to eat, then thought better of it. He stopped and turned toward Jackie.

"When are we gonna talk?" said Herb. "What happens now?"

Jackie unwrapped a ham and cheese.

"I have a guy I'm gonna call tonight. He's the Cuban I told you about, our contact person."

"So what does he want from us?"

"I told you. He's a guy I did some work for. He sent word that he could break me out if I'd do a job for him. I came up with the idea to break out a bunch of guys to give us more of a chance."

Herb stuck a finger in the air. It looked like the butt end of a hammer.

"Well what does he want us for? I didn't care much, if it was gonna get me out. I said I'd go along and fuck if we didn't make it. Now I wanna know what the job is. More people gonna get killed?"

It was Otis' turn to talk: "Herbert, before too long, you're going to be on the strategic command team. You've just been a product of the pygmalion effect."

"I don't know what you're talkin' about, Otis. Use words I can understand."

"It's quite simple. What I'm saying is that, once again you impress me. You see through to the horizon. You cut to the chase."

"Cut the crap Otis."

Otis reached out and gave Herb's shoulder a squeeze.

"Ok. Ok. What I'm saying is you're pretty smart. You're not a bullshitter. You figured out pretty quick that Jackie is up to something big, or we wouldn't be here. Isn't that right, Jackie?"

"You guys have already heard enough to get you to come along. I have an assignment. I need you two to watch my back. When we're through with this, we get a bag full of money and we get transportation to Havana. Where you go from there is your own business.

"I still expect you to keep up your side of the bargain."

Herb raised his hand like a kid in school.

"What are you up to, Jackie, and what kinda spot is that gonna put us in?"

Otis laughed again and snapped his head in the big man's direction.

"Fair questions, Mr. Barnett. And it's high time."

"OK. I'm going to kill a man, right here in River City. Turns out it's more difficult than I expected. So I expect you guys to stick until I need you. Now give me some peace and quiet. I'm going to get some sleep."

19

"YOU EXPECT me to sit here, day after day, go to volunteer meetings, attend lunches, write notes to ladies? I don't even know where you keep him. I'm sure it's safe by now. The police aren't coming around anymore. No one will know and no one cares. I want to see my husband. Now."

It was late afternoon. Juan made it a practice to see Isabel every day. He did it to calm her down. Sometimes she gave him a note to carry to her husband. She'd behaved well, as expected. But she was beginning to show some rough edges. The daily cell phone call from Alfredo had been tolerable for a time. Now it was becoming a nuisance.

They were sitting in the sun room at the back of the house. It overlooked the immense backyard and the boathouse. The gardeners were packing up for the day, bringing in their tools. Along the water and at the edge of the property, Juan could see the men, standing in pairs. There was a man on the roof with a rifle that he kept out of sight and, down the hallway, the room with the closed circuit screens. No wonder she found it claustrophobic.

"You don't have to tell me, of course. Nor does he. But perhaps it will gratify you both if *I* begin searching for him, telling everyone I see that I cannot find my husband, but I know he's around here somewhere."

Now she was out of her chair, standing over him. He started to laugh, a reflex, a defense. But her expression stopped him. She saw the startled look on his face. She sat down. She put her elbow on the table, pointed at him.

"I have an idea. We can meet on the water. Surely you can get him to a boat somehow. I won't use one of our boats here at the house. I'll rent one someplace and we can meet offshore. And then no one can see us."

He wanted to appease her. He wanted to leave.

"That's not bad. Let me see what I can do."

He could see the storm returning. He held up a hand.

"I'm not patronizing you. I think you have a good idea. I wish I'd thought of that myself. But I can't make it happen unless he agrees. You know that. Let me talk with him. I promise you I will try to make this work, or, if not this, something."

Theirs was not a close relationship. They were cordial, but Juan was inside the circle and she was not.

Juan had been with Alfredo ever since a chance encounter years before.

It was a December morning and Alfredo was walking through a thin crowd on his way to a luncheon. He'd spotted the kid, leaning against the corner of a small shop like he owned the place. Alfredo watched as the boy walked over to a fruit counter and picked up a couple of oranges, ignoring the shopkeeper's shout.

The kid threw the oranges to two young boys across the street. The shopkeeper raised a hand, as if to strike him. The kid walked past him.

Later, at lunch, Alfredo was sitting by the window when he saw the kid sauntering down the street. He sent the waiter out to get him.

"What's your name?"

"Juan."

"I saw you take those oranges, Juan. Why didn't you pay for them?"

"He has plenty of oranges."

Alfredo pulled out his wallet and handed the boy a dollar.

"Go pay the man and bring me back the change."

"Why would I do that?"

"Because then I'll have something else for you to do."

He'd come back with the change. And the something else was a visit to the small row house where Juan lived with an uncle and six cousins. Alfredo had a long talk with the family. The following week, Juan began working after-school with Alfredo's landscaper. Later, there were tutors and many summer nights when Juan would sit cross-legged on the floor of Alfredo's sun porch, listening to the men talk about Castro.

It was Alfredo who had suggested Juan enlist with the Marines and afterward, Juan had come to live in Alfredo's house.

Isabel had asked Juan about Alfredo once, and had gotten no reply. And, once, she asked Alfredo about his other life. He had said only that he was involved in some things that he could not talk about, political things.

It is nothing, he had told her, nothing that would embarrass or hurt you. But it is something that no one can know about.

It was Cuba, she knew. And because it was Cuba, she knew he would not tell her more. For the first time in her life, she'd encountered a man she could not control. She did not ask again.

The sky was growing dark. Shadows rolled through etched glass, bounced off mahogany and rosewood, marble and glass. There were fresh cut flowers in the center of the room and in vases on the end tables beside the chairs.

On one wall, away from the sun, a large acrylic. Two musicians, a white-headed trumpet player in a baseball cap and another in an orange shirt and a straw hat, playing a classical guitar. On the back wall, its companion. Three men this time, one playing a clarinet, another with a standup bass and, in front of them, a grinning character in a yellow shirt thumping on a conga drum. They were contemporary pieces that fit well with the casual elegance of the room.

Isabel was still in her in tennis clothes, still wearing her shades. She was married to a man who provided for her in a way she never could have dreamed of, a much older man who still worked obsessively. Still, he was a vast improvement over Antonio, her first husband.

She passed her days with work and volunteering. The time crept by.

Juan stayed long enough to finish the salad and the crab and corn chowder she'd provided. Then he drove off. Where to, she did not know. At least she felt something would happen.

Isabel knew she had to be discreet. That evening, she called a friend who lived several miles away, a friend who had a house on the Miami River.

"Rachel," she said. "I want to use your boat, but I don't want you to tell Roberto.

"No, don't be absurd. It's nothing like that. I just want to get away from all of this hired help. They hover over me like turkey buzzards.

"Can I just come down there one day and take it out for a few hours? Of course. I'll have Juan with me. Alfredo says I can't go anywhere without Juan. But at least I can get a taste of freedom. Thank you darling. Let me call you back and we'll figure out a time."

• • •

SHARON HAD on a very blue dress and a thin silver necklace. And high heels. The earrings were small, but very distinctive, something her grandmother had left her. Diamonds in a tiny, ornate setting. The dress had no sleeves, showing off her muscled arms and shoulders and the softness of her neck. She thought the snails were salty, but it wasn't slowing her down.

"If it weren't bad form, I'd eat two at a time."

"Your form looks good to me. Excellent technique. Actually, I'm just waiting for you to finish so I can slop my bread around in there."

"You know, you might pretend like you don't know how to act in a nice restaurant, but I know it's a sham. And you know how to dress, I might add. That shirt looks so good – you know what? You ought to get a modeling job. Those guys make *tons* of money. And it's not exactly life-threatening work."

"I appreciate the sentiment Shar, but I just don't think the modeling thing is my shtick. The guys at the shop might cast a sideways glance."

"Whatevuh babe. The main thing is you look quite acceptable this evening. I just might let you take me home later."

"Well, if you're losing your appetite . . . "

"Nip it, buster. I'm getting the trout with risotto. The salad looks spectacular. I may even ask you to split one of those soufflés with me. I plan on being very busy for the next hour or so."

"How'd you know I was getting the trout?"

"Don't even try, babe. If I'd said I was getting the broiled saltines you would have bitched about me jumping on your game plan – or, what is it you Woodstock types like to say? – harshing your gig?"

They burst out laughing. That caught the waiter's attention. He refilled their glasses. She ordered the trout. He got the shrimp and lobster with mushrooms and scallions.

"I had planned to take you out for this meal last night. You remember last night? I do believe you were slightly shitfaced and soaking wet when you got home?"

"Yup, it was a memorable evening. Hugh and I ate at a quaint little place along the river. Got the peanuts. Nicely prepared in the shell."

"Just about what you deserve."

"Sorry I had to cancel our date."

"You've been going at it pretty hard."

"Is that why you wanted to go out?"

"Yeah."

"You're pretty good to me."

"Yeah."

"Not sure why."

"I like it when you check the air in my tires."

"So that's it?"

"Yeah."

"I'll have to keep doing that."

"And I like it when you hold the door for me. I'm glad somebody still does things like that. I like it when you tuck the sheet under my chin."

She was spinning her wine glass, very slowly. Tate reached across the table and took her hand. He held open his other hand and she took it.

"If I haven't mentioned it lately, I am incredibly aware..."

Tate's cell rang.

"Don't you even think about . . . "

It was too late. He'd already answered.

• • •

THEY WERE playing half court, a gentleman's game. It was nasty out and almost dark. The wind was blowing and it was starting to drizzle. Still, they played. Winner takes it out.

Jackie took the ball at midcourt, checked it back to his man, then held it chest high, two hands, looking for an open man. The big man posted up. Jackie lofted a floater to him, a bouquet, then slammed a shoulder into his man and cut past him up the lane. Big Man saw it coming. Touch pass back just as Jackie broke free, two long steps and the finger roll.

"Hey man. Wait til we're fucking ready before you start with that shit. That ain't how we clear the ball hereabouts."

Jackie didn't look, didn't give him the satisfaction of eye contact as he walked by, ball cradled under his arm. The guy never saw the elbow, never caught a glimpse of body language, just a juggernaut shot to his chin that lifted him up and back and you could see the jaw was broken. Didn't make much noise, save for the crack of his head against the asphalt.

"We're a man short here," Jackie said. "Is there anybody who knows how to play this game?"

He had decided a bit of exercise might be a good thing. Jackie liked roundball. He was good at it. He played rough, but this was street ball and none of the others were likely to balk. If Jackie took it up a notch from what they were used to, they'd adjust. A fundamental level of macho came with the territory.

Jackie hit some jumpers. He played pretty good D, cutting off a few passes, stealing a ball here and there. Mostly he was a terror on the boards. Jackie pulled down a couple dozen rebounds, four times as many as the rest. He boxed out real well and he was startlingly quick. Jackie was in far better shape than his pickup game companions and he could outleap even the taller guys.

"How often you guys play?"

"We're out here every day, man," the big guy said with a smile. "Ain't nobody here got jobs."

No questions were asked. Nobody asked for a name. He could identify himself if he wanted to. Mostly, in this world, guys figured out another guy's name after hearing what people called them, which, in the case of guys with nicknames, meant you could go all year playing with a guy, not knowing who he was.

Jackie jogged down the street, dodging the rain, out of sight. There were some glances back and forth. His new mates made no mention of the fact that the rules of engagement had changed. They hoped he wouldn't stay long.

20

MONDAY

THE DIRECTOR of crime scene investigations was a guy named Brent Story. He'd spent his day off working on the river warehouse thing because he knew how important it was, because Tate and Hugh had told him several times how important it was.

"We found dirt, insulation fibers, doubt if you care. We found a couple of things that were incredibly interesting… bits of wood, cardboard, traces of styrofoam and, scattered around on the floor, we found metal filings and a smear. Felt kind of slick on your glove. Turns out to be a synthetic teflon lubricant."

"So somebody had packing boxes or something like that down there and maybe it was crates of bicycles or… "

"I seriously doubt it, Hugh. We also found some traces of a compound – one of the guys had a hunch and it checks out. Called nitro-benzene."

"What's that?"

"It's a cleaner. So toxic it's been banned for years. Stuff gets on you, you start growing cancer like potatoes."

"So what are we looking at?"

"Can't say for sure. But, you know, you could find most all of that stuff right here in this building, if you were down in Russell's area."

"I'm still lost, man. Can you cut to the chase?"

Tate jumped in.

"I think I see where we're headed. Tell me Brent, what do you use the benzene for?"

"Bore cleaner. You clean rifles with it after you've fired them. So my thought is that you put together the teflon lubricant and the nitro-benzene and you've got guns. The wood, cardboard and styrofoam is pretty innocent. But, if you think in terms of the other stuff, it could be shipping crates for guns and ammo. I called Russell when you guys said you were headed down. He ought to be here in a minute."

Moments later, Russell Block joined them. He was the department's equipment specialist, an armorer. When he'd heard what they were up to, he concurred.

"It's not a lock, obviously, but it's damned suspicious. I agree with Brent. The lubricant could easily be connected with guns. The cleaner looks even more likely.

"Every time a primer explodes and a round fires, the barrel gets coated. Cakes right up. And the hotter the barrel gets, the harder the crap gets. Add the goop the Russians use to coat their cartridges and you've got shit in the pipe a plumber can't clean.

"You see it a lot with the 7.62 every gun nut, doper and freedom fighter fires in his AK. That's why you clean the bore. They call it "salts" because it attracts moisture and your gun builds rust. If these guys were storing guns in a basement along the river, they'd have to make sure to clean them after they tried 'em out. Otherwise they'd rust."

Tate slapped his hands together and began pumping his upraised palms toward the ceiling, slowly turning in a circle, swaying his butt back and forth.

"She's a brick... house. She's mighty, mighty, lettin' it all hang out."

They stood and watched for a second and, finally, Story put an arm around him.

"You really ought to have that looked at."

"How many times," Hugh said, "have we asked you not to sing?"

And then he turned to Story.

"How sure are you guys about this stuff? I mean, can that crap be used for something else?"

This time Tate answered.

"Hey man, we get paid to think bad shit about people."

As they walked upstairs, Tate pulled out his cell and called the chief.

"We need to talk."

Thirty minutes later, after a call to the judge, Tate had everything he wanted. He'd have wiretaps on every phone he could find that had anything to do with Gonzales. The chief had been reluctant, but not for long.

"Let me remind you of a couple of quotes from the notes from Day Two, the day after the shooting," Tate said, "when Juan the driver – the bodyguard – starts hitting the streets. What's he telling everybody? 'The Cuban community has nothing to fear. Castro will be taught a lesson.' "

"We could be wrong," Tate added.

And then he smiled.

• • •

"SAY OTIS, what you figure Jackie's up to?"

"I really wish I knew."

They were stuck in the room. Two double beds. A Mexican-colored, crappy furniture, fake laminated wood TV, cheap bulb from the ceiling kind of room. Otis was lacing up his Nikes and Herbert was looking through an X-Men comic book Otis had bought for him, his third pass through, and he was mouthing the words now as he read.

"So it don't bother you none, him not telling us?"

"I think if he brought us along to be of some help to him, he's going to have to tell us his plans, and I doubt he'll wait much longer. Then again, if he doesn't need our help, he probably has no reason to tell us anything."

"Whaddya mean? If he don't need us, why'd he bring us?"

Herb leaned into "need" and "bring."

"Smokescreen, possibly."

"Huh?"

"Herbert, you remember how Jackie got six other guys to break out with us? Well, he didn't tell them anything. They didn't know what was on the other side of the fence, or where to go. The only thing they knew was we would have a hole in the fence at a certain time. And they would be told when that was, as long as they agreed to do what Jackie said.

"I don't think Jackie much cared whether they got out. I think he just thought it might improve our chances of getting away if the guards had more people to look for."

"So... it's like all them guys kept the guards busy."

"On the money, my friend."

For Herbert, it was as if you had turned on a big light in a dark room.

"Them guys didn't know nothing about the car and the stash outside. And we already knew which way we was running. And they didn't know..."

"Right."

He shook his head. There were still dark corners in the room.

"So what about us? You think he figures having us around makes it harder for him to get caught? Cause that's the part I don't get. Seems like it'd be easier to hide on your own than with three guys, especially ... you know... me being along and all."

Otis got down on the floor and began to stretch. The right leg out straight, left knee bent, the bottom of his foot against the inside of the knee, reaching for his toes with both hands, slowly pulling his head and chest down flat to the floor.

"You afraid of Jackie?"

"Me? Nah. Jackie's rough stuff, no kiddin. But I ain't been scared much, not since I was ... nah, come to think of it, I can't remember being scared of nothin.

"So... back up a minute here. I get the part about all them other guys. They was just smoke like you say."

And then Herbert smiled.

"They was just more stuff for the dogs to smell ... get it?"

Herb made a big face, like a kid in a cereal commercial, like he always did when he made a joke. Otis didn't react. Herb made his eyes bigger still. He waited for what seemed to Otis like a minor eternity before going on with his questions.

"You know we coulda split up later, huh? How come we didn't split up later?"

"Real good question, Herb. So I think that means he does need our help with something."

"And you're sayin' if he does need our help, he's gonna tell us what it's for."

"Yeah."

"Ok, so you were in for murder, right? You killed somebody. That mean you don't care he kills somebody else?"

"You feeling some qualms?"

"Some what?"

"Qualms… means you're not comfortable with it. It makes you feel bad."

Herb gazed for a moment at the laces loosely snugging his size 14s.

"Paul, that don't bother me much. But he did kill him real fast. I was thinking mebbe he already decided to kill him, you know? It wasn't no temper thing. That woman, though, she just got killed cause she gave us a ride. I don't feel so good about her. She seemed like a nice lady and she sure got real scared when she saw us."

Otis walked across the room to the tv set, grabbed another slice of pizza off the cabinet and brought it to Herb.

"Whatever," he said, tossing a hand aside. "Pathetic victim… sad case… poor child."

Otis had switched legs now. He held each stretch a long time before moving to the next one.

"You're sayin it's sad, but you don't mean it."

"Look here, Herbert. You're a good guy. I'm not. You seem to want me to declare whether I believe there is some loss to mankind from the death of this woman. That's fallacy, my friend. As far as I can tell, she's a meaningless spot on the carpet.

Otis turned to face Herb squarely.

"Now if you want to get out of here, just say so. I'll cover your back. Leave right now if you like and I'll tell Jackie you went down to get something to eat and I'll discourage him from looking for you when he decides you're not coming back. If that's what you want, say so."

"I dunno. Maybe."

Herbert rubbed his hands on his pants, cocking his head from one side to the other, weighing his options.

"Maybe I'll stick around until I hear what Jackie wants. You know... see what he wants. But how's come you wanna do me a favor?"

"I like you Herbert. I wanted to get you out of prison and that's why I told Jackie to bring you along. I think at some point here I'll ask you once more if you want to leave and, after that, there probably won't be another chance."

"You say you wanted me to come along? Not Jackie?"

"No, my friend. Breaking you out was my idea."

Herb crossed his arms and stuck out his lips, fishlike. He shook his head.

"Well, I appreciate it. I'm gonna think on it. That woman, I remember her pretty good. She had a ring on."

"She had two rings."

"You know what I'm talking about. She coulda had little kids, that woman."

21

THEY GRABBED all the stuff and headed for Hugh's office. It was bigger than Tate's and they wanted to spread out. Tate was universally regarded as one of the best on the force, a gifted investigator, and he could have had something better. But he'd specifically asked for this address, a very small office in a very out of the way spot. He suspected it had once been an equipment closet. It was a bare room with some bookcases Tate had gotten on his own. He had no windows to see the out of doors, no distractions.

To keep that office, he needed to tone it down with the chief. Hell, to keep the damn job. He was too quick with an answer. Half the time, the chief didn't much care for what he had to say. The way he said it just made things worse. Took the chief a second to digest, another second to be pissed.

For all his fancy upbringing, Tate fell a little short in the area of corporate survival skills. Was he gonna be an idiot just so the chief could keep up?

It was close to quitting time. They'd been working hard through the afternoon as the weather turned bad all around them. The downpour had started hours earlier. Now it was practically dark outside.

As they came through the doorway, there was a huge crash and a brilliant shock of light. Tate dropped a handful of notebooks.

"Holy shit."

Not bothering to pick them up, he turned on the weather channel. Everything was a sea of green and yellow.

"Look at this thing."

The station was running a crawl across the bottom of the screen. Small craft advisories, torrential rain and flooding, school closings, wind gusts to 50 mph.

He edged toward the window. Traffic lights were swinging wildly, palm fronds bouncing like kites without a tail. Some of the streets were dark; others were still lit, but deserted. The sidewalks were under water.

"This is unbelievable," Tate exclaimed. "Where did all this shit come from?"

"Maybe if you looked around occasionally. This thing has been predicted for a couple of days."

"Man, you know I don't watch television. What are you doing? Are you putting boards on your windows and shit?"

"Nah. It's never as bad as they say it will be."

"Bullshit," Tate answered. "This is gonna be holy hell. If a storm like this came up in Atlanta, the whole city would shut down and people would head for their basements."

"Nah. This is just a big old tropical storm. Come on. Forget about that. Let's look this last shit over."

They had finally gotten the lab reports back on the dead guy in the hotel. He'd been drugged, a heavy dose of sedatives, more than enough to kill him. The autopsy showed that he'd been banged on the head and the forensic types thought the fatal injection had come after he was unconscious. Something about pooling in the tissues.

There was no carbon residue. It didn't look like the kid had fired a gun lately.

He sure as hell hadn't been in Gonzales' place.

It wasn't complicated. Basically, the guy had been out cold, on his back, when the drugs were introduced. Somebody hit him over the head, then shot him up. A nasty murder. Those pills by the bedside were a sham.

HHe was nobody. He'd just been in the wrong place.

"You know what?" said Hugh, "this is sadistic shit, whacking this guy."

The hotel clerk had remembered him. He'd come in with an older guy – swarthy, stocky built. He'd never seen the other guy leave.

"You got any radar on this?"

"Nope," Tate said. "Somebody tried to kill Gonzales and they thought it just cool as shit to whack this guy to see if we'd bite. We still do not have clue one about who or why. Only thing I can figure is they thought it would make it less likely we'd keep looking for them if we had this kid in hand."

"That's what I was just thinking."

Another shot of lightning burst outside the window. They both stood at the glass for a moment, staring out at a suddenly empty city. The sky was close in and black, heavy with the storm. The walls of the buildings had turned gray, as if they were absorbing all the wet. The wind scraped past with a faint shredding sound and, underneath it, a low rumbling.

The lights flickered. They came back to the table and began to look over what they knew.

Gonzales was a Freedom Flight kid, raised by distant relatives already established in Miami. Brilliant academically, he was highly sought after coming out of college. A few years with one of the big investment houses and then Chicago, where he rose quickly to the corner office, making his first millions anticipating the high-tech run-up and the growth in low-cost regional airlines.

"I've got two old magazine profiles where they talk about how this guy could easily have been CEO of one of the big nationals in his 40's and he chucks it to come back down here."

"Well, he's obviously kicking ass on his own and maybe he's just an entrepreneur," Tate said. "Or maybe there's some other reason he wanted to be in Miami."

"Yup, and maybe that's why somebody wanted to shoot him.

"OK, so we're sure nobody was after Simons?"

"I've done everything we talked about. There's nothing there. The guy had a key and he was at Gonzales' house almost every Wednesday night, 'cause he coached a little kids' baseball team and left the office about lunchtime on Wednesdays.

"Lots of times, he got there ahead of Gonzales and just started in on stuff. He'd come in through the kitchen and he'd been doing it for so long the rest of the household pretty much ignored him. His finances are completely boring, except for the fact that he was loaded."

There were two security men on duty outside the house the night of the shooting. Isabel was at a meeting downtown. The security guys worked as a team and their stories matched up. If one of them shot Simons, they were in on it together.

The jury-rigged alarm certainly made it appear as if someone had come in from the outside, but that could have been an effort to throw them off the scent.

"I don't think it's the security guys and I don't think it's the wife," said Tate. "But let's go through it anyhow."

Isabel was third generation. Her parents, both professionals. Father a lawyer. Mother a hospital administrator, well known in town. She'd lived the good life, only child, exclusive schools, a joiner. Lots of community projects, even when she was young.

"When I was out smoking butts behind the school, this girl was helping the city fathers raise money to renovate historical buildings," said Hugh. "Spent a couple of summers working for a congressman. Went to parties with the big pants people."

"Yup. She's either a very serious woman, or ambitious as shit."

Played competitive tennis in college. A degree in design, couple of years working for a firm that told rich people how to furnish their homes, stints on a laundry list of volunteer boards.

"This woman is too good to be true. And now she's married into a very fat checkbook," Hugh said. "I don't see where she's got anything to be unhappy about, unless she wanted it all. And I don't know why she'd want to shoot anybody. Besides, Simons looks like the ultimate family guy. If they were carrying on, why does he get shot sitting at a desk doing paperwork?"

"Yeah. We do what we gotta do. But I'll bet you 100 bucks Simons was a mistake. And if it was somebody on the inside, that mistake wouldn't have been made."

He finished his coffee, tossed his pen aside.

"And what about those escaped cons?"

"Yeah. What about them."

Hugh went down the hall for more coffee. When he came back, Tate was standing at the window, watching small stuff fly by.

"Probably not that great an idea to stand that close to the glass."

Tate and Hugh worked awhile longer, pausing every so often to look out. The rain stopped for awhile, but the wind was still ripping it up. At the end of the block, a section of plywood had broken loose from a billboard. It was a dentist's sign offering a perfect smile. Now the lady in the picture was missing an eye and part of her top lip. Soon her adoring spotlights were gone too.

They decided to call it a day. Tate headed downstairs, carefully pushing the door open. He stuck his head out, took a few small steps, then crossed the street, hunched over, and headed toward a small park a half block away. It was a struggle to keep his back to the wind and he turned every once in awhile just to make sure nothing was coming at him.

Trash and branches flying through the air. He saw a fluttering – a bird, but it wasn't flying anymore. It was just being blown across the sky, trying to hold its own and losing.

• • •

THE MECHANIC had been thinking long and hard. He knew one place where he could find a carburetor. Trouble was, it was under another hood. At first, he thought about asking one of Ortiz' men to come with him. And then he decided that might just complicate things, afford the colonel more leverage over him. He wanted to give Ortiz what he wanted and be done with him.

And so he cleaned his hands with degreaser and pedaled his old bicycle home. He went into the kitchen and washed his hands once again, very carefully this time, and found a clean piece of paper.

He wrote a message to Ortiz:

There is a possibility I will be able to locate the information the Colonel asked about. It will take a week. No longer than two weeks.

He signed it, put it in an envelope and delivered it to police headquarters. He thought the note was discreet and just slightly clever.

He began to grow a beard.

• • •

NOTHING WAS biting and nobody was paying for the gas and there still was a helluva chop from yesterday's storm. Conover loved to be on the water when the weather got bad. Today, his heart wasn't in it.

"Fuck it," he said. And then, because he was alone, he placed a hand over his chest, rose to his feet and bowed slightly.

"My apologies, madam. A most unpardonable utterance. Please be so kind as to have me properly chastised."

Then, because he was already standing, he went to the cooler and grabbed another Bud. He cranked up the Queen and headed in. The Cap'n felt the need for a nap. He hadn't had a drink for days and now he was drunk and tired and bored.

As he approached the pier, a couple of tourists walked over. The guy had on plaid shorts and black socks under his brand-spanking new tennis shoes. The dollars were practically tumbling out of his pockets.

"We saw you coming in. Wondering what your schedule looks like. We're here for a couple of days and we'd like to get in some fishing if the weather clears. Heard you were pretty good."

"I'm damn good," he said. "Damn good. But I'm just on my way out of town. Might not be back for a few days."

He reached into a waterproof satchel wedged behind the wheel and pulled out a business card.

"Sorry. If you're still around later, try this number and, if I'm home, be glad to take you out. And we'll catch some big ones."

And with that, he tied her off and stumbled down the walkway toward the marina, wondering why he'd turned down the job.

22

TUESDAY

SHARON HAD been asleep for a couple of hours. She stirred, rolled over and then woke up when she reached across the bed and found it empty. She put on a robe and started for the kitchen, then went back to the closet for her Yogi Bear slippers to keep her feet from freezing on the tile floor they'd put down just the week before.

Tate, surprisingly, liked home remodeling projects just as much as she did. It was one of the things they had in common. They both liked working in the yard. Earlier in the season, they'd put in a sprinkler system and Sharon had stuck a couple of banana trees behind the ficas and jacaranda on the side of the house.

They liked nice dinners, days at the beach. Tate even hung with her when she cruised the occasional antique shop.

Rain still coming down. Tate was sitting at the kitchen table, papers spread across it, making notes on a yellow legal pad. Big Bill Broonzy playing quietly in the background.

"You got this thing figured out yet, baby?"

"Nah. Sorry, did I wake you up?"

"By not being there."

"Sorry. Couldn't sleep."

She came alongside, hovering, until he pushed back from the table. Then she sat on him and squeezed his neck. Ordinarily he was quite pleased when she sat on him.

"I can remember when you liked police work."

"Still do."

"Tell you what. You keep telling me bits and pieces about this case and now it feels like a jigsaw puzzle. Why don't you tell me how it looks?"

He pulled her tight and kissed her neck, holding his face against her. He slid his hands down to her waist and gently began to lift her up. She moved slowly, waiting.

He pulled a chair over.

"We have two crimes, probably three. Two related incidents. That's what I've been charting out here, thinking I might see things differently if I created more of a linear look at it.

"Let's start with the stolen boat. Looks like it was the guys who busted out of FSP.

"Let's assume those guys are the ones who tried to whack Gonzales. It wasn't a robbery. It was an assassination. Gonzales is big in the Cuban American stuff, so who's really interested in seeing him go away?

Tate had made a pot of coffee. She got up and poured herself a cup.

"Stealing a boat and trying to kill Gonzales. That's two crimes, correct?"

Tate nodded.

"Where's the third?"

"Well, I'm thinking that would be the crime Gonzales intends to commit. His people are like some kind of army. It's some kind of cult."

She didn't say anything.

"You've got that warehouse hiding place I told you about. There was something in there. That's going to be a key. So what was he hiding? Guns?

"Time out. Stop there for a minute. You said there were two related incidents."

"OK. First, there's that dead kid. I don't think I even told you about that. A young guy found in a hotel room with a suicide note about Gonzales."

"I read all about that. He wrote a note saying he was sorry, yes?"

"Yeah. Well, he's nothing. He's a diversion of some kind and he was killed by whoever tried to get Gonzales."

"Why?"

"Don't know."

"You've still got one more incident?"

"The shooting. The captain who owns that fishing boat is an ex-cop. He comes up here looking for whoever took it. Ends up at the hotel where the three cons were taken by a cab driver. He confronts them and they start shooting. Now they've disappeared."

"All right. Now you're trying to see how this all fits together. Back to Gonzales. You think he's a crook?"

"No. I don't think he has any criminal makeup."

He started to reach for the yellow pad. She interrupted.

"Ok. I'm going to run this back at you. You said he intended to commit a crime, that he was hiding something in a secret room and that it was probably guns. Do you have any...

"Castro," he interrupted. "It's the only thing that makes sense. He's a devout anti-Castro guy and he's huge in the Cuban community. He's got military people around him. He looks like he's got guns and Cubans are trying to kill him."

"Let me get this straight. You think Gonzales plans another Bay of Pigs?"

She was almost ready to laugh. Not quite.

"Maybe. It's possible. What if it's Fidel, or Raul? What if they're tired of waiting?"

This time she did laugh. Actually, it was more like a snort.

"Suppose you're right. It sounds crazy, but suppose you're right. What can you do? What should you do?"

"Find out. Stop him. Save his life. Arrest him. Save Castro. Arrest his hit team. Keep from being laughed out of the state."

"Who have you told about this?"

"Why?"

"Because I want to know how much trouble you're in."

• • •

SPORTS TALK in the background. Grady wasn't listening – background noise. He'd been given a spare office to use at the Miami-Dade Police headquarters on Northwest 25th St. He was re-reading files, looking again for something he might have overlooked, trying to reassemble the details, push them to the front of his brain.

Jackson Boyd Barnett had almost no visitors during his two-year stay at The End Zone, as some of the cons liked to call it.

His mother was still alive. She visited twice a year, on January 1st and July the 1st. One of the CO's had made a notation in the file. "Inmate refuses to spend more than a few minutes with his mother."

Jackie was named after his mom. Boyd was her maiden name. She married out of high school, a drifter who'd alternately kicked the hell out of her and the boy. She'd finally taken Jackie and fled.

What a heartache it must have been for her, Grady thought. Your kid turns up to be a complete shit and, when the world caves in on him, he still won't give you the time of day.

Safe bet Jackie wasn't running to mama, but one of Grady's people had been in touch. Mrs. Barnett was even more upset that he'd escaped. She hoped there wouldn't be more trouble.

Jackie had pleaded guilty to avoid a longer term, but she probably had attended his sentencing, where she would have heard some unpleasant details about her little boy's blunders. Of course she'd grown up with him. It must have been a thrill to discover your little angel pulling ruthless bits of savagery on the neighborhood youngsters.

There was one other visitor. Alicia McGovern. She had signed in, shown a Florida' drivers license. It was routine. Since the break, they had chased it down. Phony license. Though the photograph must have matched, the street address was phony. It turned out to be for the Wachovia tower, a skyscraper in downtown Miami. The officer who checked her in had remembered, because it was Jackie. Real good looker, he said. Memorable perfume. Wore a tight sweater.

Grady opened a manila envelope in the back of the case file, the supplemental investigative report. It was a one-page follow-up by a detective in Jacksonville who'd handled the hotel murders. There had been no progress in the case, the detective wrote. Then a package had been delivered. In it, Jackson Boyd Barnett's military service record, his photograph and a sticky note. "He's here," it said, listing an address.

And that's where the cops had found him.

23

ALFREDO WALKED several blocks, then hailed a cab. It was easy for him to move around, as long as he stayed away from places where people might recognize him. After all, he was the only one who wasn't being followed. He found a small marina on the Miami River and made arrangements to rent a 16-foot inboard. Juan let Isabel know. She rang up to borrow her friend Rachel's midsize Chris Craft.

"Help yourself, darling. It's full of gas and our gardener knows to let you in. Come anytime and, if I'm not here, just have yourself a ball. Keep it as long as you like. We hardly ever use the thing, anyhow."

Several hours later, a van delivering flowers pulled up to the Gonzales' gate. Nothing unusual – flowers were delivered every week. The driver parked underneath the porte-cochere alongside the house and carried several boxes inside. As he turned to leave, Juan and Isabel walked quickly from the house and climbed into the back. There were several more deliveries before they arrived at Rachel's.

Hugh's old Chevy was parked down the street. He grabbed the Nextel.

"Five bucks says this is it. It's that same van from the florist."

The phone taps were paying off. Tate cast off his stern line and eased the throttle forward. It was a very nice cigarette, something the department had confiscated in a drug bust, and it looked completely at home among the mansions on the river. He had on an old baseball cap and a faded Hawaiian shirt with purple flowers. He would try to stay out in front, a good distance away. The other boat would follow

Juan and Isabel. Hugh and Tate had thought it best not to advise Mr. Einberg of their plan.

"OK. The van's up against the house. And there they are. Two humans climbing out the back. I think we're good here."

"Cool. Get aboard, dude, and we'll see you in a minute."

Hugh only had a block to drive. He parked the car in front of a palatial Mediterranean and jogged down to the water. Detective Mike Newkirk already had the boat, one of the river patrol fleet, unmarked, cranked up and waiting.

"Where's the donuts babe? And who lives here, anyhow?"

"Thought you were bringing the energy food, man. Nobody. This place's been for sale for a year."

They were just backing away from the dock when Juan and Isabel pointed the Chris Craft north. On their right, the high-rise condominiums of Miami Beach and, on the left, Little Haiti. They cruised for awhile at about 20 knots. Hugh and Mike stayed a half mile back. There was a light chop and a breeze.

Isabel wore a light sun dress and hadn't expected the chill. She searched below and found a locker with slickers, hats and sweatshirts. She grabbed two of the sweatshirts and offered one to Juan.

"Thanks, Isabel. Do you like the water? You don't seem to get out much."

"I do. I'd prefer to sail. It seems more peaceful, but Alfredo isn't much for relaxing."

"You feel left out some of the time."

It was an acknowledgement, and a question.

"I knew I was marrying a workaholic. He was very honest with me and made sure we talked everything through ahead of time. He wanted to make sure I knew what I was getting into and he needed to feel confident that I would be happy. It's one thing to date someone – you may only see them part of the time, but you rarely see them in their down moments. But Alfredo liked the fact that I was very active, very independent. He thought that was one of the things that made us compatible."

"So that's been ... Ok?"

"One of the best things, for me, has been his involvement with some of my charitable work. At first, he reached for his checkbook. But I said it wasn't the money that mattered, at least not to me. I thought his personal involvement would make a bigger difference in the long run. And it has mattered. It's fun to see him working with people. And he's been very complimentary. It gives us something else to talk about."

She was a beautiful woman. He admired her coolness and he'd been impressed to see her sincerity. He had seen many women take a run at his employer. Isabel was the smartest and the most genuine. She hadn't chased Alfredo. She had simply been receptive and, over time, he saw that his boss had fallen in love.

"That wasn't what I asked. I won't pursue something that's none of my business. I just wanted to know if you'd been lonely."

"Yes."

They motored on for awhile without talking, past Barry University and on toward the Oleta River State Recreation Area. They came to a causeway, ducked underneath A1A and headed outside. Bal Harbour. The waves were bigger here and they both were glad they'd gotten a boat large enough to ride them comfortably.

A half mile offshore, they killed the motor and threw out an anchor.

Hugh and Mike had turned slightly south when they followed them out of the bay. Tate had already stopped and had thrown some lines out.

A small launch was headed up the beach. Hugh spotted it and called Tate.

"Here's something. There's a guy behind the wheel – older, shades, straw hat – could be Gonzales. He's alone."

The launch struck out from shore and the driver poured on the gas. The cops stood by, watching as it cut its engines just past the Chris Craft. It drifted alongside and the two men tied some bumpers between the hulls and lashed the boats together.

"You wanna go see?" Hugh was getting impatient.

"We don't need to. Hang tight."

They sat for a 20 minutes. Hugh had to split his lunch with Mike, who hadn't thought to bring any. The guy in the straw hat climbed back aboard. Juan and Isabel cast off the lines and turned south.

"They're going back on the ocean side," Hugh said.

Straw hat turned toward the beach. He was going to pass close by Tate's boat. Tate went to the wheel, killed the fuel switch and started cranking the starter. The boat was 50 yards away. Tate turned, caught sight of the man at the wheel and began waving his arms. The guy in the hat waved back and started in his direction. In a moment he was alongside. It wasn't Alfredo.

Hugh and Mike were staying a good ways back. Juan and Isabel were still poking along. Suddenly they began to pull away.

"What do we do now, man?"

"Stay with 'em," said Hugh. "We got no choice."

He squawked Tate.

"They're going to light speed, dude. We're on 'em, but we're made for sure."

Tate had made a pretense of continuing to tinker with his engine. The guy in the straw hat had thrown him a line and now he was towing him ashore. Tate flipped the fuel switch and the cigarette roared to life. The old guy looked back, saw Tate grinning and waved. Tate tossed him his line and threw the wheel over.

They were way out in front. He rammed the throttle forward. The cigarette growled like a P-51, lifted out of the water and, in seconds, he was flying. Tate reached into his cooler and popped a Budweiser. He tweaked the wheel from side to side. If there'd been a moon, he would have howled..

Hugh tried calling again and he thought Tate had answered, but he couldn't make himself heard. They were gaining on the Chris Craft, which was suddenly nosing close to shore.

"What'd he say, man?"

"He's running balls to the wall. I couldn't really tell. It sounded like he said: "Call some fucking people.' I dunno. But you know what? I'm gonna call some fucking people."

They were in the middle of the hotel strip. Hugh radioed for some patrol units to parallel their track. They were gaining quickly on the slowing Chris Craft and Mike eased back on the throttle.

"Here comes Tater. Fuck. I hope he don't hit us."

The cigarette was practically out of the water it was moving so fast. Hugh didn't take his eyes off the Chris Craft, though. Juan had taken it very close to shore, too close. Then Isabel was in the water. A surfer was paddling to meet her.

"Mother fucker these guys are sharp."

"Look out! Holy Shit!"

Tate was on them. The roar of the engines was ear-splitting. The cigarette was descending over their stern like a tall building crashing to earth. Hugh dropped the binoculars.

"Grab hold!"

Tate passed just feet from them, killed the engine, snapped the wheel hard over. He heaved a line at Mike Newkirk and leaped over the side. The much heavier cigarette settled in the water, but the patrol boat rocked and spun like a toy in the sudden wake.

Mike was knocked to the deck, staggered to his feet like a drunk, then fell hard.

"I think we're sinking, man."

Tate was swimming hard, but Isabel was riding ashore on the front of a surfboard. She was half a football field in front, running across the beach when Tate came out of the water.

Whoever had helped her ashore made no effort to get in his way. She bounded up the stairs toward the pool as he sprinted to catch up. How could she be that fast? He cleared the corner just in time to see the taxi burning rubber out of the parking lot.

"Tate Drawdy!"

He was inside before the patrol car got stopped.

"Get on that cab!"

But it wasn't one cab. There were three. He just prayed it was one of them.

They pursued for a mile. Then one cab swerved right. The other two accelerated past it. The front car turned into the center lane and headed in the other direction. There was no one in the back seat.

They'd been joined in the chase by an unmarked car. Tate was on the radio.

"Turn around and follow the guy coming back at you, but not too close. Just see where they go."

After a minute, Tate changed his mind.

"Swing back around. It's the guy who changed direction. Let's see if we can find them."

The patrolman sputtered: "There wasn't anybody else in that car."

Tate slammed him hard with his elbow.

"How do you know?"

• • •

THEY WERE in a little park in South Beach. Gonzales was wearing a straw hat and shades. Isabel sat pressed against him, holding his hand, her head on his shoulder. The cops kept their distance. They'd put several more cars around the park on side streets. Gonzales might have spotters. Then again, he might think he was home free.

Tate was across the street, sitting in an unmarked car. He made sure no more cops drove near the park.

"Gimme a smoke, man. I just did a fucking triathalon."

"You want to pick up the wife, too? Doubt if she's going to stay with him."

"Let's see how it goes down. I want to approach him before he gets into a car."

An hour passed. The back door opened and Hugh climbed in.

"Whoa, scared me, man."

"Guess you guys will forgive us for not being here sooner, but we were trying not to get drowned and then we were trying not to leave any boats lying at the bottom."

"Yeah. Sorry."

"Yeah."

He handed Hugh a smoke.

"Tell you what, let's see if we can't get that boat again sometime, just to party. But it will get out of your hands before you can turn around. That thing, you know you could go a whole lot faster, but you'd lose it and you'd be doing gymnastics out there and it would be all over.

"Wait a minute. I see somebody getting up."

Alfredo and Isabel were walking slowly toward the street, their arms wrapped around each other. Tate held up a hand and radioed the others to sit tight. Isabel walked right past the car, not seeing them as she mopped her eyes. She climbed into a cab, leaving Gonzales on the sidewalk.

Now Alfredo was heading back across to the other side of the park. Tate motioned to Hugh and the two of them jogged up alongside.

"Mr. Gonzales? I'm Tate Drawdy. This is Hugh Brice-Whittaker. We're with Metro-Dade and we've been looking forward to seeing you."

Gonzales nodded and shook their hands.

"Tate. Hugh."

There was no hint of disappointment, no hint that anything out of the ordinary had occurred. Tate hesitated. He had at least expected an acknowledgement of their persistence.

Gonzales reached out and grabbed him around the elbow. He looked at the wet clothes and smiled.

"I know a nice place just a block down. You look like you could use a drink.

"And you," he winked at Hugh, "look about the same."

Gonzales paused in front of a tailor's shop. There were hand-printed signs in the window. On display, several evening dresses with matching handbags.

"That man," he said, "begins his day at 4:30. He works until 9 or 10, every night. He works on the weekends and everything he does is by hand. People from the neighborhood bring him their mending. Wealthy women bring him gowns worth tens of thousands of dollars to alter. That's where he lives, upstairs, with his four daughters. All of his children are in the best schools. Each one of them has a full academic scholarship.

"He always stands up and walks to the door to greet his customers, although that is painful for him after the abuse he suffered in the prisons."

They walked on, together.

"I think I could use a nice bowl of soup. And you two? I wonder if you might have missed lunch."

• • •

"I THOUGHT it might be best to stay out of sight for awhile. I was nervous, of course, and I also considered that my wife might be better off if I wasn't seen around the house or the office for a time. I don't have any idea why someone would try to break in, but I could not discount the possibility, at least, that somebody was after me. And that meant that I needed to be away for her best interest."

Hugh was starting to think about how much trouble they might be getting into. And Tate was pushing pretty hard.

Where had Gonzales been? What was the warehouse used for? The hidden room downstairs?

As for Gonzales, he could not have been more calm. Here Tate was, treating him like a suspect and Gonzales was behaving like a gracious host, encouraging them to sample things, drink some tea.

He'd never really found time to develop any use for that warehouse. He'd bought it some years ago to help out a friend in need of some cash. As for a hidden room underneath, he seemed quite amused at the thought.

"Are you sure? I don't think we were told anything about a room under the first floor. I believe I saw those purchase documents myself and I don't remember anything about a room. What an adventurous life you two lead.

"Of course this has made your job even more difficult. And I don't blame you a bit for pushing your way into that old building. For all you knew, I could have been inside and injured or something. I'm grateful to you for taking such pains."

He took a cigar from a case in his shirt pocket, snipped the end with a fancy cutter and lit it.

"I want you to let me know anything that I can do that will be helpful."

And so they had a nice lunch. Tate passed on the food. But he'd gotten some drinks, doubles. He was beginning to slur his words. He was beginning to repeat himself. Why had Gonzales stayed away so long? What was the purpose of that hidden room?

Gonzales looked at his watch and remembered it was time to go.

They walked outside. Across the street, Hugh could see two men standing under a tree. One of them was Juan. The other man, he did not recognize. They made no attempt to approach.

Gonzales cheerfully shook their hands and flagged a cab for home, as if he were by himself. He said he hoped they would stop by soon, even tomorrow, to catch him up on their investigation.

Tate and Hugh stood there outside the café. It was a pretty afternoon, hot, and the birds were singing. There were some nice flowers in boxes on the sidewalk. A young girl sat on a bench playing a clarinet. It sounded like Malaguena.

"Not being able to find that fucking guy may be the worst thing that's ever happened to me," said Tate.

"And finding him is worse than that."

Hugh started to take his arm. Tate yanked it away.

• • •

LITTLE SUSIE, he liked to call her, like the song. Bill Conover had tried mightily to lower his voice around his wife, to walk softly. But then time passed and their conversations grew shorter. He thought he might be trying too hard. Then it had been a long time since he'd had a cold pizza for breakfast or a warm beer for supper and he hadn't shot the shit with a bunch of assholes at the pier and he thought he might be losing a step.

He was pretty sure she had a couple of disappointments as well – no white tablecloths, no Stan Getz aura to their Saturday morning errands.

What she'd like, he thought, is for me not to live with her, but still watch her back. I could carry the heavy stuff from time to time.

He could see that the eccentricities that had been so much an initial part of his charm had eroded into discouraging reminders.

What she thought now, with the passage of time, he did not know – another pretty catch spewing a hook.

Conover suspected he was becoming one of those rugged guys who looked pretty good across a crowded room to some spongy old broad having a few drinks on her salty, dark-skinned sabbatical, sprouting heavy armor around the neck, wrist and puffy fingers.

Like a lot of men, given the choice of cleaning up their act to meander back out into the fray, Conover instead hunkered back into a comfort zone of work and blue-collar self indulgence. I'll watch what I wanna watch, he thought, and leave the dead soldiers where they lie. There was a certain integrity there.

Susie's picture still sat on the dresser. She hadn't been back to see it. They weren't one of those divorced couples who still went on dates or visited each other's bedrooms. She checked on him once in awhile. He'd say something to make her laugh.

He threw some clothes and his shaving kit into a nylon bag and headed out for another run at being a clever investigator.

24

WEDNESDAY

MOST OF the time they laughed and told stories and grabbed lunch. Today was supposed to be like that, but there had been lots of phone calls lately and Donna could see Sharon was having a rough time. Tate had been moody, even angry. And Sharon, usually quick to distance herself from complication, had been sucked right in.

"You mind if I cut right to the chase?" Donna asked her kid sister.

She was the same height, same weight, same color hair. They looked like sisters. Except that Donna, if you saw her walking down the street, looked like a member of the school board. Sharon had a more purposeful stride, the way you'd walk if you owned an F-16 and kept it parked in your back yard.

Donna was a paralegal in a big firm downtown. Sharon had taken over their dad's insurance office. Donna was happy to let her have it, although Sharon gave her a nice cut.

"I'm not sure I'm going to like this."

"You won't. I've been playing by your rules. I've accepted your refusal to answer some things. But it's time you figured this out for yourself.

"I think you have been very reluctant to talk about Tate as a long-term partner. And things have been incredibly good. Now he's having a rough time and he's giving you a very rough time and, if I had to guess, I'd say you're more serious about him now, not less. That ought to tell you something."

Sharon gave her sister a dirty look.

"Sure, why not? But I don't know why. These days, I spend more time at my house, while he's at his house, than I have at any point since we began to get serious. And I have had a few nights when I was so offended by him that I wanted to puke. And, yeah, I am pretty much seriously thinking we have a future."

She opened her mouth wide and stuck a finger down her throat. Donna mimicked her.

"Wiseass."

"Better than being a smartypants."

Sharon grabbed her sister's hand.

"He's great with Ricky. He's great with me. I thought at first that this whole episode was going to be something temporary. Now, I think it might not be. This could really change his life. But I think he'll be the same person, even if he ends up flipping burgers."

"Flipping burgers? You think he's going to lose his job?"

"He might. He's planning to be the hero, of course. But I think he will see things his way, regardless. And he could lose his career, not just his job. He has this very wild theory about a case, which I don't think I can talk about. He could be right about it, and still get screwed. He could be wrong, in which case, he will probably want to move to Alaska and change his name."

"Our name?"

"Yeah. Maybe it'll be my name too."

"See if you can't talk him into surviving whatever it is. I don't know that I can make it for lunch in Alaska."

• • •

THE THREE of them almost never were seen in public together. Herbert, of course, could do little to change his imposing appearance, so he stayed in the room. Jackie had just gotten rougher – the beard, the tan and an unkempt look. Otis was much the same, although he made noises about taking on some sort of makeover.

Mostly, it was Jackie or Otis, separately, when they needed food. The shopping list for this evening, – a midsize used motorcycle for surveillance for the next couple of days. They'd already bought a nondescript sedan for the job, paying cash.

Jackie had wanted Otis outside watching when he was stuck inside a sales office.

"Money is not a concern," he told him. "Let's just get something invisible."

There was little love lost between them and so there was little in the way of small talk. Each recognized the other as the most intelligent of the men inside the razor wire. And Herbert, perhaps the strongest, though he did little in the way of exercise to maintain his brawn.

The sun had been down an hour. They were stopped at a light. It had turned green, but they were waiting for a young black man to finish his snail-like walk toward the curb.

"Always a pleasure to encounter someone whose last remaining shred of dignity requires moving as slowly as possible in front of anyone with any wherewithal."

Barnett flicked a butt out the window.

"Like people, don't you Otis?"

"Name me one friend you've ever had."

They came alongside a mom and pop grocery. Jackie saw a parking place out front and backed in.

"Let's stock up."

They went inside. There were hot dogs spinning slowly in a plexiglass oven, salsa playing from a small radio behind the counter.

Otis was sizing up the magazine display. Jackie had just grabbed a 12-pack when the little cowbell tinkled.

He set the beer down on the floor and pushed it aside with his foot, squaring his shoulders as he walked deliberately toward the door. The two uniforms looked at him.

"See some ID?"

Jackie flashed a grin and moved toward them, hands hanging loosely at his sides. The cops were still standing next to each other, their ponderous mistake. The one on the right, Johnson, his name tag read, puffy with the kevlar vest his wife demanded he wear. Patel, a small dark-skinned man graying a bit along the sides, unprotected. They were letting Jackie in too close.

Otis reached for a Motor Trend and opened it to the specs page for a new Maserati.

"Did you want a drivers license?"

A convincing southern drawl had appeared, the smile still there, the head tilted just slightly to the side, an unthreatening posture, but now one foot was in front of the other, the body angled a few degrees off center, not something the street cops would fix on.

He was the right height and, with a shave…

Patel slid his right hand slowly toward his waist, his palm coming to rest on the butt of his 9 mm, his index finger stretching for the safety.

"A drivers license would be fine, sir. Do you have something you can show me?"

Jackie, all innocence and boyish charm.

"Geez, I'm not sure I do, officer. I wonder if that young'un of mine's been playing in my wallet again."

"Not sure how you know, sir, not having looked…"

"Hey, Mr. Manager, you got any more of these car magazines."

Otis, suddenly in Patel's ear, crowded up against him. Patel started. He hadn't seen the other guy and now it felt wrong. He jerked the 9 mm free, stretching his left hand out, wanting Jackie to step back, wanting space, another second.

Like a barmaid casually wiping a countertop clean, Jackie's right hand sweeping against the policeman's wrist, palm pressing downward, forcing the gun away, down across his body, Jackie's middle finger pushing the trigger. Patel looking straight into Jackie's eyes, no longer seeing the grin.

And Johnson, understanding it all in just that moment. He took the bullet in the top of the thigh – no protection there – and went down quickly. Patel, struggling, trying to hold on, trying to win back control of his gun. Even as the shot fired, Jackie's hips rotating, his left foot up high, angled, smashing down against the inside of Patel's knee. There was a crack as the bone broke, Patel reaching to break his fall, screaming.

One, two. The barrel against each of their temples and Jackie was headed for the door, following Otis outside. Jackie started the car, made a quick right, forcing his way into traffic. He lit a smoke with his free hand.

"You're good, Jackie. Real good. And I loved the Tom Sawyer thing. You spend any time on the stage?"

Jackie chuckled. He chuckled some more. He put on his blinker and moved carefully into the left-hand lane, waving a thanks to the driver behind. Then he laughed out loud, a cascading, sing-song, childlike laughter, shaking his head, dabbing at his eyes. He smacked his hands together, flicked on the radio and cranked it up.

"I fucking love Miami."

They headed back to the hotel, rounded up Herbert and moved out, heading immediately for another dump Jackie had rented the day before. Otis ditched the car and got back to the room in time to see Jackie with his basketball. He told them he was headed for the city courts.

"I'm gonna shoot a few."

They could hear him laughing as he skipped down the stairs.

Otis went into the bathroom. It was awhile before he came out and he didn't look much the same. He had used a platinum blond dye for his hair, almost devoid of color now. He had shaved off the beard he'd grown after the break. Though his hair was longer, he trimmed the sideburns up high, above the tops of his ears. He was wearing a sleeveless T-shirt.

It was a startling look that had provoked Herbert to tell him he "looked like a flamin' fruitcake."

"Thank you my friend. That's the look I'm going for."

25

THE PLACE was crawling with cops. One of the metro detectives had taken charge of the scene, officers pushing back the crowd, stretching yellow tape across the parking lot.

Tate and Hugh made their way to the door... lots of cops standing around... and then they got inside, where they found a couple of techs working. The shop owner was telling his story for the 10th time.

Tate got where he could see. One of the officers was on his side, a nasty wound in the leg, the side of his head disfigured. The other was on his back, one leg twisted awkwardly underneath him. His head, like his partner's.

Tate crouched in front of them, pulling on a pair of gloves.

"Clear the room."

For a moment, they hesitated.

"Clear the mother-fucking room."

Hugh started with his back to the front door. He stood there for several minutes, slowly turning his head. He took a couple of steps into the room, moving his head an inch at a time. They were there for some time, Tate staring at the bodies, Hugh seeing the room.

• • •

THE NOTE had come to Lex Dean marked "Personal and Confidential." An inmate wanted to talk. He set a lot of conditions, all of which Lex agreed to immediately. The man's credentials were impeccable.

And so began the deal-making between the federal government and Otis Chandler. The break would not be interfered with. Lex liked the idea of having Jackie out. It would mean they could squeeze him, in order to find out some things. In return, some promises were made to Otis, who could not have cared less what happened to Barnett or Rutledge.

Herbert, however, was to suffer no consequences. He wouldn't be breaking out if it weren't for me, Otis had said. And he's here on my behalf.

They weren't really sure why Herbert was part of the deal. Perhaps he was a muscular convenience, some protection for Otis, a buffer between Otis and Jackie or, as Lex termed it, a "bit of neon" to make them easier to find if that became necessary.

And now, late in the day on a Monday afternoon, Otis had gotten in touch with Dean again, for the first time since the break. He was covering his bases.

"How in the hell do you think the cops won't find you now? If you're anywhere within 20 square miles of that cop shooting, you'll be found. All they need is for someone to have seen Dodds."

"Perhaps," Otis said. "That's why I was inclined to call. On the other hand, Herbert hasn't been seen outside for our last few moves. It might be a matter of whether anyone has seen me or Jackie.

"In any case, I thought you might have been missing me."

Otis said he'd be in touch. He headed back for the hotel.

• • •

BUDDY LEE Osmund and Grady were sharing a room. Fred had gone back to Starke to be there when Adam Pinckney, an assistant in the state attorney general's office, began to turn up the heat on Johnny Cordele, the tower guard. They had little doubt Cordele had been on the take. The escape was too easy. Pinckney would play the role of the bad cop.

Buddy Lee had gotten them a hotel room north of Miami. The trail seemed to be heading there. They had spent most of the day with a captain for the Metro-Dade patrol division. The street cops were all carrying photographs of Herbert, Jackie and Otis.

Grady and Buddy Lee were reviewing local incident reports to search for anything that could have involved the cons, trying to deal with the reporters.

The TV stations and papers all over the state were beating the hell out of them. It was all taking too long and people kept dying.

They'd gone on a couple of calls in the early afternoon. A manager at a fleabag motel who said two guys had left without paying their bill and a salesman at a used car lot who'd gotten spooked by a guy with a crewcut who wanted to take a test drive. They had shown them the photos and come up empty.

Buddy Lee and Grady were watching a game when the phone rang.

Grady answered. It was Tommy Becker.

"Yeah. Ok. How do you know this?"

"Uh-huh. And what is it you expect us to do with this information?"

"Ok. I think we'd better meet."

"Think this through, Tommy. You're doing the smart thing, making this call. But it sounds like you know more than you're telling me. What happens if this thing blows up? By then it might be too late."

"Yeah, Ok. You give it some thought."

Grady hung up.

"I think I'm ready for that beer now."

They got a booth in a bar they'd heard about, four or five blocks down, a neighborhood joint. Sinatra was playing. Buddy Lee ordered a wineburger... "the best burger in town, simmered in chianti."

Grady got one too. And a draft.

"Becker says he has reason to believe the cons are still here in Miami and they're getting close to making a move. He says he can't tell us how he knows this, but he wanted to talk confidentially, which means he doesn't think Lex Dean is going to come clean."

"Wonder if those guys are into something."

"Looks like it. They could have an informant, some associate who's in contact with Jackie or Otis. For all we know, they could be talking directly with one of the cons. Wouldn't be Herbert, obviously. He's along for the ride. Somebody's dirty."

"So is Becker doing the right thing here, or is he hedging his bet?"

Sinatra was done. A sweet alto started in. *That old black magic… has me in its spell.*

The place felt good. For lights, somebody had put little bulbs inside antique trumpets and trombones and saxophones and hung them on the walls, which were covered in bamboo.

A little bell, then somebody shouted: "Mikey…. Burgers up."

Mikey was a fetching character, about 5'6" and equally wide, a couple days growth, anchors and chains tattooed over both forearms and a gut broad enough to hold a TV draped like a lava flow over a massive belt buckle. He had a face like a frying pan and some kind of world record nose.

"You fellas want somethin' else, you holler."

He had a big chaw in one cheek and his knuckles looked like they'd been broken repeatedly over somebody's skull. To get that voice, he'd swallowed hot coals as a child.

"If this thing tastes as good as it looks," Buddy Lee said, "I may propose."

"Haw, haw, haw," Mikey said, and lumbered off towards another table.

"He looks like he's been rode hard and put up wet."

Buddy Lee leaned over the table.

"I never saw that much bone and gristle in the middle of a face before."

"Who gives a shit," said Grady. "This is the best burger I ever ate."

A couple of exquisite bites later, Mikey brought over two more drafts.

"Hey, we didn't order these," said Grady.

"On the house," Mikey said. "We ain't got no desserts here, just beer."

Buddy Lee snorted.

"Geez, I hope we don't catch those guys before I get in here for another burger. I think Mikey likes me.

"And, come to think of it, I was hoping maybe we might catch a Dolphins game while we're here. You know, after we're done. I talked to a couple of uniforms about it. We might could get some tickets.

"And isn't that part of the reason we're here?"

Grady chuckled and started to wipe off the juice running down his chin, then decided not to bother.

"A game would be pretty nice. As for being here, I think we're where we ought to be, but I'm not sure we're doing that much good. Seems like we're just waiting for somebody to see them so we can be there when it goes down."

"Tell me about Becker. I heard you say something about saving his skin?"

Grady finished the burger and mopped up his plate with his last fry.

"Damn, that was good. Now I know why Mikey's got that big belly."

He pushed the plate aside, pulled a small notebook out of his pocket and began to scribble.

"Making some notes. There's not much more. It was obvious from his tone that Becker wanted me to know he was freelancing. Dean doesn't know about it. All he said was they don't know why the cons are here, but it's for some kind of job and his source says it's going down pretty soon.

"He's starting to think. That remark I made about saving his skin was something to get him thinking some more. This is all pretty convincing evidence we can't trust the feds and, if we end up holding the cards, Becker may be stuck on the wrong side. I wanted him to know we're keeping score."

"Sounds like he's hearing footsteps."

"Yeah. Let's just hope they're loud enough to make him talk."

"Yeah... might help get the newspapers off our backs."

"Just doing their job. It's been a week."

"Why'd you wanna let that guy take pictures of Fred taking target practice?"

"Cause Fred groups his shots like nobody you've ever seen. And they'll get a nice picture of him smiling. The public wants to know we're just as scary as the cons, but you can invite us home for dinner."

Mikey was headed in their direction. He stopped midway and pointed at them.

"Nuthern?"

Buddy Lee waved him over.

"Nope. That was great, though. Hey, that Black Magic tune… you remember who wrote that?"

"Johnny Mercer. Everybody knows that," said Mikey. "You guys were trying to stump me. Haw, haw, haw."

He sauntered off, rocking from side to side, working to take the pressure of his knees.

Grady pointed at him.

"When the world ends," he said. "I want Mikey on my side."

• • •

BILL CONOVER walked into Tate's office wearing a grin, a pair of jeans, some high-toppers and an old cotton shirt dressed up with pelicans and palm trees. Tate's place was stacked high with folders everywhere. There were pictures thumbtacked to the walls and diagrams taped to the pictures.

"Think any of this shit will fool anybody?"

Tate stood to slap-grab a handshake and gave a shrug.

"It's a competition, man. He with the most clutter wins. And I am fearless when it comes to accumulation. Besides, you see all these drawers? Bone empty. My stuff is just for show."

"Well you ain't got a place to sit, so how about I buy you and your buddies a beer."

Tate gave the Cap'n a squint. Then again, there was nothing the slightest bit suspicious about Conover.

"I think that might be a good idea. Might give you a chance to explain what the fuck you're doing here."

He called Hugh. And Booker. And Sharon. She gave him an earful.

"Don't give me that shit you're going out drinking. Other guys lie so they can go drink. You go out drinking just so you can keep working."

It was completely true. But she said it with a smile. And it was his night – their new arrangement. There were nights when he was actually supposed to go out and run around with the boys. Be good for him, she said. She'd brought it up one evening after work when they were sitting outside. Tate thought Sharon was thinking long-term, but he wasn't sure what that meant. So he played it cool. Yeah, I can hang with the boys once in awhile, he told her.

They went to the Warm. The real name of the place was Warm Beer, Lousy Food, but everybody just called it the Warm.

It was a little brick building next to a dry cleaners and a travel agency. It had a cheesy dago fountain out front and, just inside the front door, a refrigerator case full of plush desserts. The four of them grabbed a booth under a big TV screen showing sports highlights. At the bar, a half dozen electronic poker stations, busy with guys who couldn't stand not to be doing something for more than a minute and a half.

Conover had lots of questions and they didn't have too many answers.

"You guys are just full of cop snot," he grumbled, and ordered another round.

"Sure," said Hugh. "Call us cops, right to our fucking faces."

Booker hit it on the head. "He's got a big case of the nags, looks like. He wants to play detective."

"That true, Cap?" asked Tate.

"Yeah, 'fraid so. It's not like bad dreams or anything, and I'm over being pissed off about it. They didn't do the boat any harm. But it's like it interfered with my life and now it's unfinished business."

"Finishing that business is a real good way to get hurt, or get somebody else hurt, or fuck up police business, or break a bunch of laws, which is another real good way to get hurt, so I think maybe we'll get the next round and later on you can just count on us letting you know if something breaks," said Hugh.

Conover nodded.

"Yeah, OK. Fine. So anyhow, after those three motherfuckers showed up here, anything weird happen? Anything bad, where you mighta said, 'Hey, I wonder if it's those guys that stole Conover's boat?' Cause you know, they really wanted to be here."

Tate paused, lifted his glass.

"Nah."

Conover told fish stories for an hour and gave them each one of his cards.

"Come on down. You can come together or separate. No big deal. I'll take you out. Be a good break from the city for you. The Silver Queen's a sweet boat and she'll make you think you're in some old Humphrey Bogart movie or something."

That sounded good to everybody. They shook on it and called it a night.

Conover pushed one more time for some information, got nowhere and told them he was heading south.

26

THE MECHANIC had one very nice outfit. It was a guayabera in the shade of a ripe banana and a pair of sandy colored linen pants. They had a faded quarter panel, not too noticeable, from being folded on the top shelf of his closet. Because there was just the one outfit, the mechanic rarely chose to wear it.

Likewise, there was a decent pair of shoes. Tonight, he came home early, washed up, put on his good clothes and tied a piece of string around his right pant leg to keep it from soiling against the chain of his bicycle. He pulled a wide hat over his eyes and rode across town. In the basket of his bicycle, a long-sleeved apron and some tools wrapped in a towel.

Until now, he had never been to the home, but he knew where the man lived, the man who had been one of his best customers. The man who always paid for his work. The man who never sent armed thugs to chase off his clientele. The man whose vintage American sedan sported the right kind of carburetor.

As he had the night before, the mechanic waited under some trees down the street. There was a wind. The weather was turning bad, but it felt like it would hold off for a couple of hours.

He heard them laughing as they left the house and watched as the man held the door for his wife. They had on evening clothes. Dinner, dancing, perhaps.

Tonight would be his chance.

The mechanic followed at a distance. There was a little traffic and their pace was slow. Here, as in much of the city, there were no streetlights. Just the crumbling reminders of the departed aristocracy.

There was no sign. The restaurant was illegal. The owners took the risk, not enough income to pay the tax. It was a nice restaurant.

They parked just down the block. He had already discounted the idea of waiting for a chance to work where no one would chance to see him. He might wait weeks. There were too many problems. Too easy to get caught. No, he would work openly, with a flashlight propped on top of the battery. It wouldn't take long.

He had nothing to hide, and, if he did not get the Colonel off his back, nothing to lose.

He stopped across the street, watched them enter the restaurant. He waited five minutes, pulled on his apron, pedaled over to the car, popped the hood, pulled off the air filter and soon was hard at work.

A passerby stopped to watch, make conversation. The mechanic grunted. When he had the carburetor free, he wrapped it along with his tools and stuck it in his bag. He gently closed the hood and pedaled away quickly. Ducking in an alley, he took off the apron and put it in the bag.

He pedaled the rest of the way home. When he got there, he washed his hands and hung his sweaty evening wear over the closet door. He would wait awhile, then take the carburetor to Ortiz and install it on the spot. Best not to do the work in his own shop.

• • •

OTIS CHANDLER brought back a used Honda and rested it on the stand in a back corner of the parking lot. It was quiet and quick. Otis would be the go-to guy now, the guy who did all the shopping.

"Your own momma won't know you. Least, she won't wanna know you," Herbert had said, after he got a little more used to seeing Otis looking that way.

It had been a bit disconcerting. That first night, while Otis read – he had been walking past a yard sale and spotted a stack of books, bringing back a bag full and just now he was into a four-book series on the Civil War – Herb sat watching a western. He loved them. He liked to lie there, concealed behind a couple of pillows, and make a pistol out of his thumb and forefinger. With a quick release of air through clenched teeth, he would shoot the bad guys dozens of times while they drank shots at the bar or plug them full of holes while they rode across the prairie. He would shout a warning if a good guy was about to walk into a trap.

Herb had dropped off about 9:30. Otis read awhile, then turned out the light. He rolled off the bed and headed for the bathroom, closing the door while he pissed.

He flushed the toilet, opened the door and was reaching to click off the light when he heard a muffled scream.

"Shit!"

It was Herbert.

"Leave it on. Jesus Christ leave it on."

"It's me, Herbert."

"I know who you are, dammit to hell. That don't mean I don't want the light on."

By the next day, Herbert was pretty used to his new roommate. Otis had brought back some breakfast sandwiches and Jackie was with them. All of the sudden, Herbert got up and began to cross the room, moving slowly just on his toes, crouching, hands lobstered out in front of him, like a hippo sneaking up to scare a butterfly.

"Who'm I imitatin? Who'm I imitatin?"

Jackie began to choke on a mouthful.

"What the fuck are you doing?"

Herbert flapped his arms and hopped up and down.

"It's me, Otis. Sweetie Otis."

This time they had to laugh. Otherwise, who knows how long Herbert would have stood there, mouth great big, eyes bulging.

When they were done eating, Jackie had a few things to say. He didn't want anybody leaving the room unless he said so. He was going to use the Honda to follow the banker, Gonzales, the man he was going to kill, to get a sense of his routine. When the time came, Otis was to drive. Herbert would be in the passenger seat. Neither one of them was to get out of the car. They would not be needed for this part. They both would carry guns, though, in case there was a change in plan. Gonzales would have a driver and perhaps another bodyguard along.

Herbert wanted to know if Jackie was going to kill all of those people. Not all of them, Jackie said. Otis could tell Jackie was starting to get impatient. Shooting the cops had started the clock running and now Jackie was thinking about the next phase, something he was disinclined to talk about.

"I've already got it all worked out. Let's just focus on what's ahead of us."

The TV was still on. As before, when Jackie was done talking, the conversation seemed to be over. Otis appeared to be deep in thought, but then he gestured toward the television.

"Here's my idea," Otis said. "The funeral network – 24-hour hours a day, seven days a week – cable TV for those who have passed on.

"Tasteful coverage from the service, the grieving family members, long recountings of the life of the deceased, hand-held video from the cemetery, intrusive closeups of the distressed, pipe organs, children crying, flickering candles, somber voice-over.

"Can't sleep? Just flick on a funeral. Must-watch TV. Make us all rich."

Jackie snorted at him.

"You're some kind of fucking nutball, man. When I was in the service, we used to tell guys like you to shut the fuck up. Or else we helped 'em shut up."

Otis leaned back. He pulled his lips into a tight grin under that hawkish nose and held his hands out in front of him, waving his fingers.

"Boogedy, boogedy, boogedy."

Jackie stuffed the wrapper from his biscuit into a bag and tossed it into the can next to the dresser. He had on an old jeans jacket with the sleeves cut off and he had pasted on a couple of temporary Harley tattoos on his shoulders. Pair of jeans. He had a full-sized helmet and some gloves. For a belt, a length of rope and a big black wallet that was clasped to a short steel chain wound through a belt loop. It had all been on Otis' shopping list.

He stood, pointed a finger.

"You guys sit tight."

He closed the door behind him.

27

THURSDAY

THE NEXT day, an hour at the public library was all Conover needed to decide the timing had been just right for his bad guys to be the same bad guys who had gone after a rich Cuban named Gonzales. He didn't get close enough to ring the buzzer in front of the Gonzales home before somebody intercepted him.

"Tell Mrs. Gonzales, if you would please, that I own the boat that was stolen by the men who tried to kill her husband."

The guards were ready to send him packing, but Isabel spoke over the intercom, asking who it was. No one had come to the gate for a long time.

"Send him up to the house."

He walked in, past the wrought iron and the exquisite landscaping. A paid person met him at the door. Conover looked at the walls, the chandeliers, the molding and the marble. He had on his newest jeans and a nice pair of topsiders and he felt hugely out of place.

Isabel sent away the security man and offered him a drink and fed him several of the smallest corners he'd ever seen off what must have been sandwiches.

Here was someone who wanted to talk with her, which was rare. As for Isabel, she knew virtually nothing. But she made it clear that her husband's people thought the connection between the prison break and the shooting was obvious. Conover thought that was interesting.

Juan came in. Conover repeated the story about the cons and the theft of the boat.

"So, if you don't mind my asking, why are you here?"

"I wanted to find out why those men stole my boat and why they were willing to kill me to avoid being accused of it. Now I know."

"Kill you? I thought I read in the newspaper that the boat was stolen at night when no one was on board. And then it was beached somewhere south of the city."

"Sounds like there's a good bit you haven't heard."

Conover folded his napkin, laid it beside his plate and stood.

"I sure wish I could be of some help to you. It's been a pleasure Mrs. Gonzales. Thank you for your hospitality. Your home is absolutely beautiful."

She walked him to the door.

"Are you staying in town, Mr. Conover."

"I haven't decided, but perhaps we can talk again sometime."

"I'd like that very much, Mr. Conover." She walked over to a chair by the door and took a card out of her purse. "Here's my number. I'd be happy to see you anytime. If I'm not here, whoever answers the phone can reach me."

She made no effort to include Juan. It felt good to have her own piece of something.

Juan held open the door.

"I'll walk you out."

"Good bye Mrs. Gonzales."

"Good bye Mr. Conover. Please come back soon."

The two men headed toward the gate, surrounded by legendary oaks, statuesque palms and, everywhere, mounds of flowers. They were about the same height, though Juan had less of an investment in his waistline. Conover, enjoying the view on a muggy day when what you knew was all that mattered and arrogance was a good play when you knew next to nothing.

They walked slowly. Outside the sitting room window, suspended over a corkscrewing shadow, a couple of fat bumblebees slowly hovered around a swaying sunflower, softly flexing, foraging, dazzled by their reflection. He thought about taking a nap. He could just stretch out there, under a tree. He thought about Isabel, trying to memorize what she looked like, searing her image.

Juan started to press, but Conover interrupted him.

"You seem to have gotten less from the cops than maybe you thought you had. I'd hate to be in your shoes, not knowing what they know. But if you want to know what I know, you're going to have to play ball. You'll answer my questions, and mine come first."

"You seem to think your information is pretty valuable."

Conover let out a grandfatherly chuckle, realizing his presence was a disruption in what must ordinarily be a very tidy world, realizing he'd be up shit's creek if the wife hadn't spotted him at the gate.

"Let's talk about why they're willing to stay here until they finish the job."

"I don't think so, Mr. Conover. Is there somewhere I can reach you?"

Conover smiled and offered his hand, then walked on toward the gate.

Isabel watched through the window. Juan hadn't gotten anything. Conover was still hers.

• • •

HERB WASN'T eating. He just stared at the tv. He reread his comic books. Otis felt sure he knew what the problem was.

"Tell me, Herbert. Are you really looking forward to this?"

"To what?"

"You know, Jackie's little plan."

"Oh, you mean... shooting some people?"

"Exactly, my friend."

For Herb, it was very much like one of those horror flicks where what got you the most was not just what was happening on the screen, but your imagination running wild about things you could not see, things just below the radar.

He shook his head, tight-lipped, a toddler refusing asparagus.

"I'm not gonna do it. You guys go ahead. I'm not gonna kill nobody."

"I was thinking that might be the case."

Herb was sitting on the edge of the bed. Otis grabbed the chair and pulled it over in front of him. Jackie was in his own room. He stayed away most of the time.

"So how to you want to handle it? Do you want to leave?"

"I was thinking it might not be good for me to leave now, cause if I get caught someplace close around here, then the cops might know where to look for you. I was thinking I need to hang out until you guys get outta here."

"A noble sentiment, my friend. But that assumes Mr. Barnett is agreeable to your plan."

"You mean Jackie might wanna whack me? He can try. I ain't gonna kill nobody. I already decided."

Otis chuckled. "Good for you."

"And I'd just as soon you don't kill nobody neither. Met a cop from Miami, real nice guy. Hate to see us get in trouble with him."

"Might be time to begin thinking about our exit strategy. What if there was something I could do, somebody I could call."

"Like who? You got friends around here you ain't told us about? I never thought you had any friends around."

"It sounds like you're saying I'm not the kind of guy who has any friends."

"I don't mean no harm by it. Behind bars, you never know about nobody."

Herb was talking slowly now, as if he didn't want to hurt Otis' feelings.

"I dunno what you do on the outside. You might not of had friends. You're real smart. Seems like real smart people don't have as much truck with regular folks."

Otis chuckled and offered a little feint, like he was going to throw a punch. Herb's smile was a hair tentative. Otis just went on.

"Once again, you have a natural-born diplomacy. Actually the friend I would call is not what you'd call a personal friend. We don't like each other at all, I would guess. But I think it would be a good idea to talk with him anyway."

"What kinda friend we talking about here?"

And so Otis explained, patiently and carefully, that he knew someone in the government, that the only way to ensure Herbert's safety was a deal with the cops, that he already had a kind of deal with them, that he could intercede on Herbert's behalf.

Herb found it all quite startling, that Otis might have an understanding with the "guvmint."

What really boggled his mind was when Otis explained that he had a relationship with a federal agent.

With that, Herbert was genuinely impressed.

"Otis, I always thought you was extra smart. But you know what? This beats the cake."

It sounded like a good plan. And Herb said he was glad Otis wasn't going to kill anybody either.

"Oh I don't know about that," Otis smiled. "I might just kill Mr. Barnett, just for the hell of it."

At that, Herbert felt a huge weight lifted from his prodigious shoulders, so he talked Otis into going out for some subs.

"Lots of onions," he said.

"I don't know about that, my friend."

"Whaddya mean?"

"We've been sharing quarters for some small time now. And I've come to the realization that onions aren't necessarily the most forward-looking decision."

"Huh?"

"Windows. When you eat onions, we have to open the windows. And it's real hot outside."

And then Herbert figured it out. He nodded somberly and hung his head.

"Geez," he said.

"That's all right, my friend. How about some pepperoni?"

• • •

GRADY WAS back. He'd called a meeting. They ran a checklist.

Cops were stopping at hotels and short-term rentals, talking to streetside car dealers, clerks at takeout joints, sandwich shops, gas stations and liquor stores, hookers, gun shops, goodwill and second-hand clothing stores.

The area around the cop killings was wall to wall.

The Miami-Dade cops thought there was a good chance the cons might try to leave town, probably by car and probably at night. Grady said it was more likely they'd still be around.

"Makes no sense," one detective told Grady. "They're in too deep here. It's a matter of time. They were already on thin ice and now they've killed two cops. Ain't no way they're going to stick around."

"We think they might," Grady said.

The detective asked why.

"That's what we believe."

"Well, I promise you, if they're still here, it won't be for long. You can't hide three guys that long, not when we're looking this hard. There is no place we're not looking."

"I'd like to feel that way too. But these are not kids we're playing with."

They had decided to withhold the connection between the escape and the cop shootings from the public. Grady didn't want to see the thing splashed over the front pages. Better to treat it as if it were something random. The story, as the city officials were telling it, a robbery at a convenience store, interrupted by a couple of cops, shot dead by doper. There would be nothing about a second man, nothing about martial arts. Grady had talked with the store clerk himself.

They set up a schedule, broke the search area into grids. They were hitting every mom and pop hotel in the area. Cops were going in on different shifts to make sure they didn't miss anybody, talking with all the late-night staffers.

"While they're at it," Grady said. "Have a guy work the record shops. Show the mug shots. See if anybody bought any Louis Armstrong lately."

Buddy Lee stuck around after the cops left.

"We're doing the right things, you know," he said.

"Yeah? So why are you shaking your head?"

"Because this isn't like anything we've ever seen. We've chased cons before... not like this."

"Barnett."

"Yeah. I don't like how we don't know stuff."

"Me neither. Why don't you track down that Jacksonville cop?"

"Good idea. I'd really like to know who dropped a dime on Jackie."

• • •

ADAM PINCKNEY slid the photo across a steel table. He had Johnny Cordele, the tower guard, in the interrogation room next to the sheriff's office holding cell, a barren, lime-green vault with a sizeable two-way mirror on one wall. Adam thought it was a good spot. He'd had a long talk with Grady earlier that morning. Grady had put it bluntly, telling him to "break the kid now."

Short, curly headed, a perpetually youthful look, Adam Pinckney was the kind of undersized teenager who got bounced into the lockers half his life at school. Those who had known him since saw in him a razor sharp prosecutor, driven, who had enormous sympathy for the victims of crime and none whatsoever for the perpetrators.

He had what he needed.

"The woman's name is Pat Eldredge. That's her husband, Jeff. Their wedding. And this," sliding another shot across, a Polaroid from the crime scene, "is Benjamin Whitley, a mechanic from South Florida. And this," sliding across a single sheet of paper now, folded into thirds, "is something you'll want to read carefully."

It was an arrest warrant. Cordele was being charged with assisting in the escapes, 10 counts, dereliction of duty and a variety of lesser things. It was the three counts of first degree murder that caught Johnny's eye.

"What the fuck is this? Holy fucking shit, what the fuck is this?"

"You're an accessory, Johnny. And this is Florida. You helped those guys get out and they committed two murders of innocent people. They also killed Paul Rutledge. For your part, you get three capital counts. The very best you can hope for, the best, is life. And I'm going to be adding two more counts, by the way, for the two officers who were killed yesterday. But this little document..."

He tapped a leather binder.

"Is something I'll give the judge declaring my intent to seek a one-way ticket in your case, since you decided to let this scum out in public."

He pushed his chair back and walked to the door, opened it and called out to a deputy.

"Would you mind joining us for a moment please?"

As the deputy stepped inside the room, Adam turned back to see Cordele looking just this side of apoplectic. He spoke to the deputy.

"I want a witness."

He then read Johnny his rights, asked him if he understood them.

Johnny, speechless.

"Let me know if you want the court to appoint you a lawyer, unless of course you have resources of your own."

Then, turning to the deputy – "cuff him."

Johnny sunk back into his chair. It was time to get his attention. Pinckney smashed his fist violently onto the table, rattling Cordele and prompting just the beginning of a smirk out of the deputy. He turned to the officer and pointed to the door.

"Get out."

When the deputy was gone, Pinckney stood.

"There is no give here, Cordele. None. I'm going to put you the fuck away. Life without parole. And a shit like you... I promise you that you'll go right back to your own prison, where everybody knows. Your ass will be shredded the first week. Get a fucking lawyer. Do it quickly and then have him see me. I'm giving you 24 hours, one day, to come across with everything you know. After that, I promise on the souls of that skinny kid and that sweet woman and the children she'll never have, I won't give you the fucking time of day. No pleas, no bargains. I'm gonna fuck you up so bad you'll kill yourself in a year, you fucked up little slime.

"24 hours."

Pinckney kicked over his chair, turned to walk to the door, turned back. With his eyes riveted on Cordele's reddening face, he picked up the chair and threw it against the wall. It bounced back hard. The impact broke the mirror and sent shards crashing to the floor. Cordele wrapped his arms around his head and started to whimper.

Pinckney closed the door behind him and turned to the slack-jawed sheriff.

He smiled.

"Whaddya think? Fear of God time, or what?"

• • •

CORDELE HAD arrived home one night to find an envelope on the floor inside the front door. Someone had picked the lock, put the envelope down and left. In it, small bills, not new, more than three month's salary. And a note. This payment, it said, is for reading the note. An equal payment for meeting us tonight to discuss a business proposition. More later.

Cordele made the meeting. And the deal was quite simple. He was known for his inattentiveness in the tower. That was to continue. The money was simply for his collaboration. Someone was going to cut the wire when he wasn't looking.

There was nothing for him to do. He was just an insurance policy.

He turned over the money. They sent it to the lab.

The man's name... Smith, John Smith. He was Hispanic, had an accent, drove a rental. They had met at a rural driving range, virtually deserted with the exception of a couple of guys hitting some golf balls. They had talked in the parking lot. Smith had a cooler in the trunk and they both had a beer. Pabst Blue Ribbon. Smith had kept the empties.

The directions were simple and Smith was quite clear about the money. Cordele got another envelope to match what he'd gotten already. In 30 days, he was told, he would get $10,000 more. If he spent a dime of what he'd gotten before then, he wouldn't get paid the rest.

And Smith had threatened to make him a cripple if he showed up with so much as a new pair of shoes. Cordele had signed on happily.

The night before the break, the Wagoneer had been planted off the road at the far edge of the woods beyond the north fence. The only other nugget of information he could recall was that Smith had described his boss as someone "young and beautiful," eager to see her boyfriend again. His information was next to worthless.

Fred said he wondered if the boss woman was the same one who had visited Jackie.

"No doubt," Buddy Lee said. "Problem is... we don't know squat about her. She made a strong impression on the C.O. who checked her in. But he can't tell us a thing, other than the fact that she looked really good."

"So what if we had him work with a sketch artist?"

"We've already talked about that. He can't remember enough to get started."

"Yeah. But we don't have a whole lot else to go on. Maybe we ought to hypnotize the guy."

"Are you shitting me?"

"Not a bit. It works with some people."

And so they called the sketch artist and had him work with Johnny on Mr. Smith, and with the officer who had checked in Jackie's visitor.

He brought along a hypnotist who was with the bureau in Orlando.

The officer, Danny Gifford, was a little uncomfortable with it all.

"You're not going to tell any of the guys I did this are you?"

"Listen," Buddy Lee told him. "This doesn't mean you have psychiatric problems. We're just trying to get you to remember something."

"Yeah, well I don't want to wake up someplace acting like a chicken or nothing like that."

Dr. Garner put a hand on Buddy Lee's shoulder.

"Maybe you'd better let me do the explaining. Danny, I work for the FBI. We don't play games like that. I have a degree in psychiatry. I want to try to reach back to your long-term memory, things you saw and remember, but under the surface. That's all."

Danny groused about how it might be worth a shot, if they insisted.

"The thing is," Garner said, "if you saw her on the street, you'd probably recognize her. You just can't remember her features well enough right now to draw them. But you might, under the right circumstances. The reason I'm hopeful is that you told me she was here to see Jackie Barnett, who never really had any visitors. And so it might have been unusual enough that you took a pretty good look at this woman. You might have been trying to figure her out, figure out who she was or how she knew Barnett. All those things will make it easier to bring that memory back.

"That memory's there. You just haven't needed it for anything."

Danny said it sounded halfway reasonable to him. Before they got started, they went to a room just off the hallway where visitors check in.

"What difference does this make?" Danny asked him.

"I think many memories are triggered by sound, Danny. I'm hoping the noises here might help you connect with whatever sensory information you've stored away from that day. We can't recreate the woman, or how she sounded. But in a moment I'm going to ask you to relax and we'll put you in the chair out there and then you can speak to me as if I'm that female visitor."

When the time came, Garner had Danny shut his eyes and try to remember that day, what the woman looked like. Then they did a sketch. It wasn't much. A good looking woman. Nobody who saw it recognized her.

28

NELL OSMUND put on a pair of rubber gloves and shoved her hands down in the mucky mix of topsoil and manure, stirring it up nicely. Then she dug three good-sized holes in a sunny corner of the garden. She'd already moved some Indian Hawthorne out of the way. She made the holes for the roses too big, so she could surround the root balls with the good stuff. French Roast, she liked to call it, "cause it smells so good it'll wake you right up."

Florida took its toll on most attempts to cultivate roses. Nell's garden was resolute defiance, a blend of tough climbers, heavily mulched, that could stand the heat.

It didn't take long. Soon she had them wrapped through a rusty trellis and she was ready to get at the weeds.

Gardening was her passion. They'd never had children, never been able to. On her own, Nell had seen a doctor, suspecting. And when she had told Grady that she was the problem, he had told her it made no difference. He was happily married. It was that simple.

She went inside to call him. They hadn't talked in several days.

"I just wanted to see how you were," she said.

"Not good. Not good."

Two more people were dead because he hadn't been able to find the men who escaped from his house. Five dead, so far.

The convenience store clerk had said the two cops, Johnson and Patel, had been taken out in the blink of an eye, as if it were some sort of training exercise.

"It was like there was nothing they could do," the clerk had told them. "They stood there watching while this guy... me too, I mean, I never saw anybody move like that before, except maybe in the movies. Maybe one of them Chuck Norris films or something."

The store had a surveillance camera, but it wasn't turned on. They were, Grady told Nell, the luckiest cons he'd ever encountered. Luck had so much to do with it.

"You'll catch 'em, sweet. Hard work overcomes luck, always does."

Talking to her took his mind off the job and he didn't want that right now. She understood. She never called during the day, she wasn't the type to check in. But she had just felt something was wrong. Grady said he'd call her back.

Despite their changed appearance, the clerk's description had left little doubt. Right there with the baked beans and the beer and the lotto tickets and the skin mags, Jackie and Otis, downtown, just a few miles from the hotel where Grady Osmund was sleeping. It made his skin crawl.

There was no shortage of cops on the street. The word had gotten out quickly. Two good men had been killed on the job. Cops finished their shifts and kept right on working, some driving their own cars. Off-duty guys had come in, retirees. Buddy Lee was optimistic. There were too many uniforms out there not to be.

They were all asking the same thing, if anyone had seen three guys, one of them the size of a phone booth. It wouldn't be long before they found somebody who'd seen something.

• • •

TATE DRAWDY'S boss was off the deal.

"You know, when the guy was laying low, I was pretty interested in that aspect of it. Now I'm not so interested. He's back home. He's innocent as hell, unless you know something you haven't told me. If he's up to something, where's the proof? Tails, phone-taps... what for?"

Hugh figured it would be better if he talked.

"We were sort of expecting this. We don't have anything, just a lot of suspicions, but they are damn strong suspicions."

"Doesn't cut it, boys," the chief said. "I would have a hard time chasing any citizen around, based on what we've got, let alone chasing this guy. He's a superstar for chrissake. Frankly, you guys owe me one for letting you go this far. I never asked you to get specific and I certainly never asked you to put anything on paper. Two cops dead and you guys wanna chase a citizen.

"You guys need to focus on who killed that guy Simons."

Tate knew they didn't have anywhere near what they needed to keep the surveillance on Gonzales' people. It didn't stop him.

"Look. There's some nasty shit going on here and we need some time..."

"That's all for now, gentlemen."

"This is a huge deal. We have got to hang on here."

"I'm sorry Tate."

He was ready to take the fight up a notch. Hugh took his arm and led him outside.

Gonzales had politely declined any offers of help from the police. His own security was far more extensive than anything the city would have provided. He hadn't broken any laws. But Tate was convinced the only way to find out who killed Simons would be to know who wanted Gonzales dead.

Now they'd need to find another way. The wiretaps were over. The surveillance, the chief said, stops now.

• • •

ISABEL WAS sitting by the pool, drinking green tea, working on a letter soliciting donations for the Historical Society. She was on a committee collecting artwork for a new exhibit on the development of South Florida's fruit packing industry. Staying under the umbrella on a hot day, a nice skirt, a light blouse.

The security men were walking the perimeter just before a shift change. They kept a respectful distance.

"Good afternoon, Mrs. Gonzales," they said.

It's what they always said. She saw them watching her, stealing glances. Veiled by her shades, she glared back. They were always there, watching, always watching.

And, as always, she resisted the temptation to swim or to strut past them in a skimpy suit. She resisted the temptation to slap their perky little faces, to scream at them to get out of her sight or to turn her back and drop her skirt, peel off her panties and give them a little show.

She picked up the glass and turned it over, draining the tea into the pool.

It wasn't a lack of comfort, or money or respect. There was plenty of that. She loved being whispered about when she walked into a restaurant. She loved the deferential bowing and scraping. She loved the sound of her heels on marble, the perfect thump when she closed the door on her little Benz, the silks and the scents and the certainty of her empire.

It just was the way it took forever for the tiny diamond-encrusted hands to make their way around her monstrously expensive Cartier. She could putter in the yard if she liked. Or not. She could work, or not. Some days, she wondered if she could get fat.

It had been the same way with her first husband, Antonio. The closer, she called him, the deal maker. Antonio was a lawyer who had spent his early days connecting the dots for commercial developers. After a few years, he knew the drill and began his own real estate company, taking over decaying properties downtown, converting them to condos, lofts, shops and eateries.

They had lived well for almost four years and then Antonio, the man who thought he could keep a dozen balls in the air, got stretched too thin and lost his shirt. Thankfully, he'd had the good graces to get drunk and die behind the wheel.

He'd left her with a nest egg and she was already doing well with her boutique, an absurdly expensive interior decorating shop, although that, too, was swiftly becoming a bore.

Her customers, doctors' wives, cloying trust-fund upstarts and foppish retirees, eager to surround themselves with sophistication, eager to snatch up the fruit of the small back shop where a pack of old women created the extravagant pillows and other knickknacks she sold off as auspicious acquisitions from Kabul.

After a time, she tired of providing pedigrees for slovenly professional athletes and dim-witted dope dealers. The business of decorating mansions dissolved into a tedious muck of color and shadow, small talk and manicured nails.

Her life, a struggle against bonds and fences, her beauty a prison. With her strict Latin upbringing, she couldn't date without a chaperone, couldn't choose her friends, couldn't exceed careful boundaries.

It had been years since she had felt real excitement. She'd been 17 the last time, driving too fast, passing the police car, seeing it swing around. And in that instant she had reacted without thinking, stomping on the gas, dousing the lights, tightening her seat belt as she blasted through the neighborhood, leading him on a chest-pounding chase for blocks, the radio cranked up high, staying just far enough ahead. Window down, her arm draped over the door, and then cutting the wheel hard, feeling the big convertible slide back around, gunning it into a driveway behind some trees.

Watching him pass by, too dumb to see her.

Bingo.

There had not been enough opportunities to recreate that feeling. Capturing Alfredo was one. He was a fine catch and it had been an entertaining three years. But now, what was left?

Now he wanted to have someone drive her from place to place.

She had thrown up, at first. Remorse. But then she moved on. There would be new adventures.

• • •

TATE AND Ricky were firing a baseball out in the street. It was something they found time for a couple of times a week. Tate liked to tell

Ricky that the kids his age wouldn't put quite as much zip on the ball, so if Ricky got to where he could handle Tate's pace, he was a leg up.

Actually Tate was still smarting from Ricky's pace, which was cool.

"So I guess you can talk and throw at the same time," Ricky said.

"Yeah. Don't be so casual. Follow the ball all the way into the glove, every ball, not just the tough ones. What's up?"

"That's what I want to know. You and my mom are acting weird lately."

"Like what?"

"Like everybody's real polite. Are you guys still getting along?"

"I guess we better sit down."

It was kind of a jolt. Here, Tate prided himself on thinking he was doing the right thing. And now the youngster was bringing him up short.

They sat on the front step, Tate finding a place to lean, rest his back.

"Look. I want to be the right person for your mom and for you. I don't know why I never tried to express that to you before. I guess I didn't know what was appropriate to say. But I am not… I take this very seriously, this time with you."

His first instinct, of course, was to tell Ricky he had asked his mom to marry him, repeatedly. But he shut that thought down as quickly as it came. That would deflect the heat to Sharon, not the right thing to do. Better for Ricky to see him as conflicted.

"Your mom is being real careful with me right now and she's doing it to be nice. The fact is, I've been a real shit lately. I've been working on a case that bugs the hell out of me and I've been treating everybody around me like shit.

"I'm sure your mom wonders whether it's just this thing, or whether I'm some kind of head case who brings his work home all the time. Lots of cops have some kind of problem that way and lots of cops' spouses end up fighting this constant battle.

"So which are you, a part-time head case or a full-time head case?"

"Thanks a pant-load for nailing it like that. I would like to think this is a short-term hassle. But you know what? If I knew how to deal with it better, I wouldn't be such a shit, am I right?"

"I always thought there were lots of crimes that never got solved. So I guess there must be lots of cops who have to deal with that."

Tate nodded. The kid was smart. That much they already knew.

"What's the crime this time?"

"Ok. There's a wealthy stock broker named Gonzales. Somebody broke into his house and shot a man sitting at his desk, presumably because they thought he was Gonzales. Turns out it was his partner who was there working. Everything about the way it was done suggests it was a professional job, not some amateur robbery.

"What's bugging me is the unsolved murder of a citizen, obviously, but also the why of it."

"Gonzales doesn't know who would want to shoot him?"

"That's just it. I think he does know and he's not saying. There's a little bit more to it, but I don't think I should talk about that. I hope you don't think I'm just being cute about it. It's really just not ethical for me to divulge certain details."

"Does my mom know those details? Because I think it would be better if she did."

They threw for awhile longer and he was glad for the talk. He tried to come at Ricky as an adult and, generally, the kid came back the same way, though, of course, there were the times he needed to argue over everything, when anyone who didn't see it his way was a loser, or worse, Bogus.

And then Sharon pulled up and commandeered their help carrying some groceries. She had flowers and wine and a DVD.

"I was going to cook," she said. "And then I thought, you know what, I'll just pick up something really good."

And that she had done. Pistachio encrusted salmon with asparagus and a salad, with raspberries and slivers of almond, lightly coated with a peanut oil dressing.

Tate and Ricky were making all the right noises. And then Tate said, "I really don't deserve this."

She patted his arm.

"You're probably right. Then again, you may always be a cop."

Tate didn't stop eating.

"You guys are very tolerant," he said. "I know I haven't been real easy to live with. And the way things are going right now, I may be bad company for awhile here."

They cleared away the dishes. It wasn't too late, so Sharon told Ricky he could stay up. She'd gotten a horror flick about monsters in space that made a huge mess of their human prey before they gobbled them up.

"This is totally awesome," Ricky said.

• • •

GRADY ALMOST forget to tell him where to turn. He wasn't used to being in the passenger seat.

"This is it, the lane here."

The deputy eased the car through the trees. There were lots of branches that needed to be cut back. He hadn't noticed until now. It was cool, a few clouds, the sort of day it had been the first time they saw the place. You could see possum here, lots of them, and armadillos pretty regularly, tiptoeing down the lane like they hated getting their feet wet.

Grady looked up, amazed at how tall the trees were. They'd always been tall.

The deputy was taking it slow, assuming that was the proper thing. Grady hadn't bothered to try to make much conversation. He was tired. He felt a cold coming on, that thickness in his head, the sense of being a half-beat behind. It would be nice to stay home for a few days. He could read. It would be nice to sleep late. It would be nice to watch a cowboy movie in the middle of the day. It would be nice to finish something. He was partway through three or four books. He'd start one and set it down someplace and then need to read something and grab whatever looked appealing. He worried he wouldn't be able to remember the characters' names; he'd have to backtrack.

Out back, there were two dozen tree sections, 18 inches apiece, waiting for him to split them up. Weeds all in the yard. Nell kept them out of the garden. The yard was his turf. It looked like crap. And he'd been thinking about putting a basketball goal over the garage door. He could shoot a few before dinner once in awhile. He had put a mark over the garage door at 10 feet.

He had a list.

Nell heard the car door slam and she ran to the window. Grady had his hand on the roof of a sheriff's car, talking to the deputy. Then he patted him on the arm and the car pulled away. He slung his bag over his shoulder and started toward the house. Nell ran outside.

She didn't say anything, just ran over and hugged him. He wanted to kiss her but she wouldn't let go.

Finally, she looked up, tears in her eyes.

"I missed you."

"Yeah. Me too."

They went inside. She grabbed a beer from the refrigerator and opened it for him while he poured her a glass of wine. Then they went out back. He moved his chair closer, so she could lean her head onto his shoulder. After a minute, he put a hand under her cheek.

"You're going to get a stiff neck."

"I don't care."

She got out of her chair and came and sat in his lap. She kissed him. She kept kissing him. He leaned forward and then he was standing, carrying her inside. She wrapped her arms tight around his neck.

"You haven't picked me up for a long time."

"You won't let me. I have to sneak up on you."

"You can sneak up on me right now if you want."

He carried her into the bedroom.

"No. Don't you dare put me down on this bed. I don't want you hurting your back."

So he let her stand by herself.
"You Ok now?"
"Yes."
He shoved her onto the bed and climbed on top of her.
"Don't you want to close the curtains?"
"Not hardly. I want to see what I'm getting."

29

FRIDAY

JACKIE BARNETT was a Ranger when he'd met Manuel Ortiz. It was a long weekend in Cancun. Jackie's gaze had lingered for far too long on the woman at the bar and when he left he'd been followed by her companion and his friends.

They closed on him just as he passed the alley, a dark and lonely spot where an ill-bred tourist with a knife in his chest might not be noticed until daylight. They had Jackie backed into a corner and then, suddenly, a 2x4 from behind sent one of assailants well into next week and, between them, Ortiz and Jackie quickly dispatched the others.

They drank far into the night and found they had much in common. The next day, their discussions resumed and collaboration was born. The young American soldier and the Cuban officer, men on opposing sides who cared little for patriotism, but saw great promise in working for their mutual advantage.

Ortiz had an international clientele and Jackie was a man with special skills. After Jackie left the service, he began to work for some people in Washington. And, over time, the American would moonlight, collecting significant amounts of money as a freelancer taking high-risk assignments from an associate who worked with Ortiz, a senior man with the FBI in Florida.

And then he had gotten himself into a jam and it appeared he had lost his usefulness. Until now.

• • •

TATE THREW a folder onto the floor, slid back his chair and headed down the hall. He had been working other cases, spending his time the way he was supposed to. But he had managed to squeeze in some research. And now he was telling Hugh what he'd been reading about Gonzales' organization.

"Look here. Over the last 10 years, almost every guy in that crowd has been in the news saying something about Castro. Nasty shit. I gave Olga a list of names and a couple hundred bucks to sift through the Spanish-language papers for quotes."

"So what, man? Guys can say anything they want. That doesn't make them a hit squad."

"Yeah, I hear you. But here's my point. You can find some edgy stuff out of every single one of the guys on the board, except Gonzales. He has never said anything that you couldn't read at church."

"So he's more diplomatic? We already knew that. Maybe he doesn't have the fire in the belly. Maybe he's trying to lead them into the 21st Century. Maybe he doesn't give a shit about who's running Cuba."

"Nope. He's clean because he's smart. The guys on his team are fanatics, but he plays it cool because he's the ball carrier. It's as simple as that."

Tate had rambled on repeatedly about his theory. Hugh saw no reason to discount it entirely, but little reason to invest much time into tracking it down. Tate, he said, might spend years sniffing around the Cubans and not find a thing. And by then he'd be old and tired. Tate had to concede there was some truth to that. Still, he had a gut feeling, and there was the warehouse. And maybe the hit on Gonzales was a preemptive strike because something was developing.

But he was stumped. He held up his hands.

"Look, I know what you're saying. But can you think of anything we might do, within reason, to stay on the trail? Anything that makes sense?"

Hugh shook his head.

"Only thing I can even imagine is to grab one of his guys and sweat him. The surveillance thing is ridiculous at this point. We have some warehouse residue that would mean absolutely nothing even if we could tie it to Gonzales, and we can't, so it's all theory and fantasy and that leaves us the old-fashioned stuff. Find one of their guys who's in trouble and see what he knows."

And the chances of that happening were slim and none.

"OK, well I'm back to square one," Tate said. "All along I've been thinking we had to solve Gonzales to find who shot Simons. Maybe we'll have to flip it, find who shot Simons and get them to tell us about Gonzales."

Hugh just laughed and then he turned to look at Tate, surprised to see he was suddenly red-faced. There he was, off the deep end again, pissed off at a moment's notice.

"What the fuck are you doing? Look at yourself."

Tate walked over to the window.

"I'm sorry, man. I wouldn't have even talked about this shit with you if you weren't my friend. And I'm a complete asshole.

"But I am going to catch this fucker."

His anger subsided quickly. An hour later, he was back in Hugh's office.

This time, Hugh agreed to help, but only on the condition that this was to be an all-or-nothing venture. If it did not succeed, they'd pack it in.

• • •

THAT AFTERNOON, Tate and Hugh dropped in on Gonzales.

The passed through a security check and were directed to an elevator that skipped all the bottom floors – brass and glass overlooking a 24-story atrium. They exited onto a long hallway, very wide, with enormous sculptures that towered over them, mounted on stunning wooden bases.

There was a majestic carved buffalo, larger than life, an eagle roughly cut from a weathered trunk of something that looked like it came from the Pacific Northwest. At an intersection of two hallways, there was a huge foyer with, as its centerpiece, a bronzed whale 20 feet long.

"Holy shit," Hugh whispered. "This is better than any museum I've seen."

They had been met at the elevator by an elderly gentleman whose gait was painfully slow and they were glad of it. It gave them a chance to ogle.

"I didn't know you could buy carpet this good," Tate said. "I cannot imagine what this cost."

Their escort was accommodating.

"Feel free to take your time," he smiled. "It is really quite something, isn't it. Perhaps you'd like me to tell you a little something about what you're seeing."

There was a Remington, another western by Albert Bierstadt and another by Thomas Moran and an incredible sailing ship made of polished steel.

They passed by an office with a wreath on a closed door. Simons's office, the old man said.

"Gentlemen. Thank you for stopping up."

Gonzales had come out to meet them. He was exquisitely dressed. Hugh presumed that every stitch was hand done. Who wouldn't feel secure having this man handle their money?

They followed him into his office, which, surprisingly, was quite modest – superbly furnished, but not at all large. The elderly gentleman pulled back a sliding door in the wall and withdrew a plate of hot pastries with fruit. He poured them each a cup of Cuban coffee.

Gonzales took a seat at the head of the table and unbuttoned his jacket.

"I'm going to guess that you're here out of frustration, more than anything else."

And then he waited.

Tate answered.

"I'm afraid so, and we appreciate your understanding. You've already answered all of our questions and we've already told you what little we've been able to put together."

"At least it's good to meet with you when you aren't soaking wet."

Hugh snorted, started to respond, then changed his mind.

Tate set down his cup.

"I've just got a few questions. I'm wondering, again, about why someone would break into your house and try to kill you without, it appears, any real robbery motive. And, as we discussed before, there's the fact that they were able to circumvent your security staff and the system on the house, both of which are quite good."

Gonzales folded his hands on the table in front of him.

"It seems clear to me," Tate went on, "that this was a political assassination."

He had spoken slowly, letting the words sink in. Gonzales was able to interrupt without appearing too eager.

"How interesting. And why do you say that."

Tate took a short breath and gestured like a teacher at the blackboard.

"And I think we can feel confident that the men who were sent here to kill you had been instructed they could wait no longer, for fear that your activities were moving to fruition."

It was all he had, but his tone carried the suggestion that he knew more. Tate had interrogated men for years, men who had much to hide. He was skilled at the pretense.

Gonzales did not move, did not flinch. There was a slight narrowing above the eye. It was enough.

Tate heard a faint scratching of the carpet beneath Gonzales' chair. The door opened immediately, the elderly gentleman.

"Mr. Gonzales. Your appointment. I had them wait as long as I could."

Gonzales stood.

"My apologies. Mr. Drawdy. Mr. Whittaker. Please allow this gentleman to show you the way."

He had gathered himself quickly.

"I'm going to be fascinated to hear more about your incredible theory, detective."

He took Tate's hand, started to squeeze and then thought better of it, instead clasping both his hands around Tate's in a soft grandfatherly way. Any hint of recognition had disappeared.

The return trip down the long hallway was no quicker. This time they did not speak.

When they got off the elevator, Tate flicked open his cellphone.

"Is everything ready?"

• • •

JUAN JABBED the accelerator on the Mercedes, down the ramp. Hugh's man in the underground parking garage saw Gonzales step out and wave Juan out of the car. Gonzales got behind the wheel. Juan got in beside him.

The light at the corner was yellow. Gonzales shot through, punching the horn. The traffic wasn't heavy and he was making good time. Gonzales took a couple of side streets. They followed.

"This is too easy."

"Damn straight it is. I spurred him. But he's not rattled."

Gonzales went straight to the house. Not where they had expected him to go, but they hadn't really known what to expect. Tate's theory was simple. There had to be a meeting and Gonzales had to be there. Now the wheels would turn and they would pray for luck.

Inside, Gonzales and Juan were on the phones, assembling the group. Isabel came downstairs, surprised to find him home so early, surprised he had not greeted her when he came in, not surprised when she heard his tone of voice.

"Yes, I know. Come over now and we'll explain. Make your calls, please. Yes. Right now."

"Alfredo? What brings you home at this hour? I'm so sorry I didn't know you were coming. I've got a luncheon..."

He walked across the room quickly and took her hand.

"I'm the one who's sorry. Something's come up and I needed to get back here. I've asked a few people to join us for a meeting. We'll get some sandwiches. Please don't worry about us. Who are you seeing today?"

"The art league again, the budget."

He waved a hand.

"Now you know I told you we could take care of that."

"But that's just the point. I've told you that."

She gave his arm a hard squeeze. "The donations are a way to measure public support. And if we don't have that measurement, we have a hard time getting city money, and, especially, corporate support.

"So your money becomes something of a liability, my darling."

He had been attentive lately, particularly on their once-a-week date nights. Today was a reminder.

• • •

ALFREDO DIDN'T bother to sit.

"Our final timetable doesn't change. We stick with the plan, but, as we discussed, we release the team now and sever the connection here. I've got to get free of it or jeopardize the rest of you."

Manuel was angry. He'd been on the golf course. Now there was a meeting, an unscheduled meeting. Alfredo was telling him a couple of Miami cops were getting close. This could not be.

"It is not possible that someone knows what we intend. It is not possible. Who knows enough to tell the cops anything? No one. There is just us and we are all above suspicion. This is not possible."

He brought both fists down onto the table, splashing coffee from his cup.

Alfredo walked around the table and stood next to Manuel's chair. He crouched beside him, took him gently by the back of his head and pulled him close. He pressed his forehead against Manuel's shoulder.

"Do you know how well I sleep at night my old friend? I sleep wonderfully. I have slept… I have slept well for a long time now, ever since we decided to take action. Before that, my anger kept me awake. My anger and my fear."

There were tears in Manuel's eyes.

"Fear, Alfredo?"

"I was afraid I might die first, before I had done something, before I had realized what it was we must do.

"But now I do not worry. I sleep well. We have a plan, a strong plan, and we have anticipated many things. One of those things is autonomy. We have people in place who know what they must do. Juan will go to them now. He does not need for us to look over his shoulder. We have a way for them to contact us if they need to.

"What we will do now is tell them that time has arrived. No more review. No more last-minute walk-throughs. For some reason, we have two policemen looking at us, looking at me. And that cannot be an obstacle. We cannot permit that to stand in our way. We simply move things up a couple of days."

"No. We will find out. We will find whoever talked to these..."

Alfredo cupped his hand under his friend's face.

"Forty years, my brother. We have let nothing go, not the smallest detail. This, we will let go. Other men, younger men, are going to finish what we started. It will be done and we will be safe. And el caballo will be done. No more eight hour diatribes at the Karl Marx. No more cells. No more rats. No more stale bread. No more women's screams.

"I do not know what Drawdy knows, or how he knows it. I do not care."

"That is not good judgment, Alfredo."

This, from another at the table.

Alfredo hugged Manuel and stood.

"It is not a matter of judgment. It is a question of confidence. Nothing will go wrong. Our business is almost done. And a new business begins."

30

THE LIGHT changed. And still Juan waited. The cars were starting to fill the intersection, the turn lanes. Then he punched it and bulled his way in like he was at the start of a bumper cars ride at the circus, banging hard against a taxi crossing from the right, feeling the big Mercedes shudder as he was struck from behind, brushing alongside a dry cleaner's van, the clatter as his side-view mirror shattered. And then he was through, leaving behind the crowd and the shouts, the horns and the angry fists.

Half a block further, he darted into an alley, a dogleg to the right and he was on the entrance ramp for the turnpike, headed north.

He had lost the tail.

They'd had five cars on him and he'd shaken loose.

Tate drove with one hand, screaming into his Nextel.

"Anybody see him? Keep looking!"

Tate took a chance and got onto the turnpike. What kind of gamble was this? He couldn't go too fast. If Juan was up ahead, he might spot the Marquis. So he pushed on and prayed.

He keyed the radio again.

"Billy and I are on the turnpike north. Don't see anything yet. Traffic looks really fucked up ahead of us. Does anybody have him?"

One by one, they checked in. Nobody.

"Keep looking."

They drove for almost 15 minutes, scouring the traffic in front of them. But now, cars were stacking up, slowing to a crawl. A wreck ahead, something. They came to a stop. As far as they could see, nothing was moving.

Tate's chest was pounding. He yanked his hands from the wheel and began raking his scalp with his fingers.

"We're fucked," Billy said.

Billy leaned back, put his feet up on the dash, his face in his hands.

Tate stared for a second. Billy had on his Nikes, as usual.

"Get out. Get the fuck out."

"What are you talking about, man?"

"Run up the road. Just run. There's some shorts in my bag in the back. He doesn't know you. Jog your ass up the road and see if he's up there.

Billy, not understanding for a second. Then he quickly changed and started pounding the asphalt.

Some waved, some stuck their hands out the window to slap him five. Everybody understood. It was a way to keep from going crazy, jogging up the middle of the highway. It might have felt good, another day.

Kids making too much noise, moms and dads chewing them out, workmen in pickup trucks, a guy with a major comb-over in an old Caddy, couple of high school girls in a convertible.

"Hey baby."

Sweating now. Sun softening the asphalt, the sweet smell of exhaust. A couple of miles and an assortment of Mercedes later and still there was nothing. Then, up a slight rise, a quarter mile ahead, he could see the wreck. An 18-wheeler on its side, blocking three lanes. They were pulling it back upright, dragging it into the median. A cop walking out into the road, getting ready to wave people through.

Billy looked around. He was jogging up the center line. He'd have to stop. He'd have to get out of the way. Any second now. He sped up, running hard.

He was getting lightheaded. This wasn't going to work.

The cop raised a hand. Then it looked like somebody was shouting to him, the cop turning, walking back toward the wreck and Billy could see the cars in the front of the line, a van with a ladder tied to the roof. In front of it, the metallic blue Mercedes, banged up, Juan standing beside the car.

Billy slowed, staggered a few steps, then hopped his way to the side of the road and ran back, sprinting now.

Tate was on the Nextel, Billy hunched over beside the car, killing the grass.

"We've got him. Mother fucker's a couple miles up on us. Billy's half dying here, but he's my fucking hero."

They began to move. And then it was a matter of cheating his way up, edging closer. After a time, the traffic spread out some and they could see Juan up ahead. Back on the string.

Billy had caught his breath. He reached behind the seat and opened Tate's cooler. Tepid beers floating in tepid water.

"Want one?"

"Shit yeah."

And now it was getting dark. It was a South Florida sunset, orange, brushed in thick with purple, a trace of pink. Clouds moving slowly across the sky. Tate loved Florida. He loved the smells and the thick hot air. He loved sitting on a porch at night, the water. It was just beginning to cool off now, just a little breeze, and Juan was still making time.

He hit the talk button.

"Son of a bitch! Where are you guys?"

"Right behind you compadre. Wave if you want to."

Tate pulled his new Gator cap off his head and shook it out the window.

"Careful you don't lose that cute hat."

"Glad you can see me."

"We see you about as good as it gets, compadre. Danny sprayed some glow on your roof. So when it gets dark..."

Hugh and his pilot, Danny, were high overhead, 1,000 feet. Nobody on the road looked that high. Tate's volunteer army included a city chopper pilot with night-vision equipment. For this favor, Tate would owe something memorable.

"Can you see him up there?"

"Yeah, but we have to be sure, so you just make sure you stay too far back to be seen, but too close to lose him."

"Thanks, asshole."

All that needed to happen, the only thing that needed to happen, was for Juan to lose them. Then it would be over.

Up ahead, Juan was paying little attention now. If there'd been a tail, he'd lost it hours ago, he was sure. Soon he'd be at the camp. On the seat beside him, a duffel with a few changes of clothes, his passport. Everything else he needed was already in place.

There had been no promises, no effort to persuade him. He had volunteered long ago, when things first came together. You need someone, he told Alfredo, who will be predictable in all situations. Alfredo had balked, but only for a moment. Juan was like a son, but he was clearly the best equipped.

Juan had understood.

"You feel concerned about me, yet you know I can be valuable there. Don't worry. It is a good plan. And our focus has to be on the mission."

And Alfredo went along. He was too committed to see it any other way. He'd never been to Venezuela and would not ever go. Perhaps a sightseeing tour later, to see where it had happened.

Thank God it wasn't dark yet. And there were still other cars on the road.

Tate was on the radio again.

"He's maybe heading into the boonies. This could get nasty."

"Your job is to stay with him, and not to be seen."

"Like we don't know that," he snapped.

Juan had turned off on a two-lane. Tate was creeping along now, trying to leave enough distance between them. He came around a curve. The road ahead was empty.

He stomped on the gas. Around the next curve, nothing.

They'd lost him.

• • •

A WHOLE new ballgame.

Tommy Becker wanted a meeting this time. Becker was pretty uptight.

Lex was playing a long string and it looked as if it might break. Becker didn't like it. So he had decided it was time to work up his exit strategy.

Becker had a wife and kids. Lately, he'd been thinking it was time to find another line of work. In a nutshell, he was scared shitless. His boss might just be a psycho.

Skinny guy, glasses, a likeable preppy sort. Law degree, five years with the department, some solid work, most of it behind a desk. Actually, almost all of it behind a desk. Then he was assigned to work with Lex. People started being really nice to him. Sympathy, he guessed.

Tommy met them at the bar. He had on a striped business shirt, nice pants and loafers with little bows. The belt and sweater could have belonged to his dad.

They got a table. Buddy Lee asked about the scar across his forehead. Stick check, he said. Buddy Lee asked for a translation.

"Hockey. I grew up in Massachusetts and, when I was little, I could skate my tail off. Headed for the goal, beat my guy, and he whacked the shit out of me from behind. You know what? I was staring in the mirror, thinking I could see that stick coming at me again. That's when I decided to call you."

Grady waved for another round. Tommy Becker needed to work his way into this. Mikey sauntered over.

"You guys want some beers? Maybe a coupla wineburgers?"

Grady held up three fingers. Tommy lifted a hand.

"I'm not really hungry, guys..."

Both brothers immediately shut him up.

"Ignore this child," Buddy Lee told Mikey. "Go for it."

Grady asked about Tommy's kids, their ages, what they were up to, how Tommy had met his wife. Tommy obliged and got teary about it.

Grady patted him on the shoulder.

"You want to shed some light?"

Tommy drained his beer. He had expected this might be difficult, but he had the feeling it wasn't going to be.

"I know what they're up to now and it's pretty fucking scary. But let me start at the beginning, so you know the picture. Before the breakout, Otis Chandler reached out to the office and got through to Lex. He said he'd been offered a chance to go along on a break, a sure thing. Jackie Barnett was cruise director. Otis decided to hedge his bets. He'd tag along with Jackie, feed us some information at the right time, and we'd trade."

"For what?" Grady wanted to know.

"Freedom. Get out of jail card. Lex never hesitated. He said Otis was offering an inside story, information we might never have gotten any other way."

Lex had even visited the prison to deliver a note to a guy, another con, who'd passed it along to Otis.

Buddy Lee interrupted.

"Wait a minute. I haven't seen anything in the visitor files about a federal agent on site."

"Doesn't surprise me," said Becker.

They were into the third round now. Grady had gotten up to piss and stopped by to chat with Mikey. He told him to hold the burgers for just a few more minutes. And keep the beer coming.

"So now Otis has been back in touch. He's got new info, blockbuster shit, and he wants to tweak the deal."

"What is it now," Grady asked. "A cash bonus?"

"Nothing, for himself. Now he wants a break for Herbert Dodds, a promise there will be no repercussions. He says Herbert is going to bail because he doesn't want any part of the killing that Jackie has in mind. Otis, actually, doesn't either, and he's counting on us breaking up the party. But he wants us to play nice with Herbert.

"Who ever thought of Otis as some kind of good Samaritan?"

They talked for awhile longer. Then there was a nasty grating sound. They looked up. It was Mikey, the goodwill ambassador, subtly acquiring their attention.

"Burgers?" he asked. "Mighty good."

They did their best to keep Tommy talking while they ate.

"Here's the deal. The breakout is half of the package. Otis says they're down here to kill Alfredo Gonzales, the guy who runs the big Cuban-American foundation, and Jackie's been hired to mastermind the hit. Otis isn't privy to the details. Jackie's holding a lot of the cards close to his chest."

Grady and Buddy Lee looked at each other, then both started talking at once. Grady pointed a finger.

"This really changes things. I've read about that shooting, the Gonzales thing. Never occurred to us, obviously, that the cases were linked. Now our objectives are going to have to change. Catching Jackie is critical. But we cannot allow this thing to come anywhere close."

Becker nodded.

"I know. That's why I'm here. Lex is willing to let Gonzales be the bait. He wants to grab Jackie as the hit does down. It scares the shit out of me.

"And here's the thing. I've told you everything I know. I don't know where this is going to happen, or how.

"But I think it might be the day after tomorrow."

As they were leaving, Grady called Dwight Morrall, the Metro-Dade chief of police. They had spoken when he'd first arrived in town and the chief had offered any help necessary.

Grady said he wanted to set up a meeting with the Metro-Dade team investigating the shooting at Alfredo Gonzales' home. The chief said he'd call everyone in. Grady said two hours would be soon enough.

• • •

ISABEL KEPT the picture on her vanity. It fit nicely there. A handsome man in a silver frame. Her mother's brother. Her protector, her mentor, her babysitter.

She was 13, a gorgeous coquette, and her parents were away. He'd slipped quietly into her room, gently closing the door, and then he was on top of her, covering her mouth with his clammy hands, telling her everything was going to be all right, suffocating her. An hour later, he came again.

She said nothing.

It was almost two weeks before he returned. This time, she was waiting for him. She got out of bed and locked the door behind him. She was already naked.

He smelled victory and came toward her. And then he saw what she held in her hand. He backed away in revulsion, pleading. She pursued him across the room, slapping his face, hard, again and again, and then he was on his knees, sobbing from the guilt and the shame.

And the fear.

She stood over him while he undressed. Now she had him.

Over time, there would be other games. But then her beloved uncle would swallow a handful of pills and drive off a bridge. She'd hoped Alfredo might one day take his place. But Alfredo was too strong.

31

THE SWEAT stretched Tate's underwear, filled his socks, poured down the back of his neck.

"Maybe we'll get lucky and find some snakes."

The guys in the chopper had decided that Juan must have left the road someplace close by. They were guessing… praying really. They'd seen the farmhouse from the air. And, from the air, it didn't look that far. So Tate and Billy stuck the car under some trees and started in. The good news was they'd found a dirt lane that looked like it led back to the place.

Hugh was on the ground a few miles away. They didn't want to keep the chopper up for fear of being seen. And now it was dark. Tate called him.

"We passed a 'No Trespassing' sign, so we might be headed in the right direction and Billy says we're probably going to get shot and I was thinking maybe you'd like to join us."

Hugh came back quickly.

"This is not turning out to be an entertaining afternoon."

"Look, I know this ain't too cool. But it's the only thing we've got. If we go home, we're done. All we have to do is see something, so we know if we're in the right place."

And so they kept on. The lane wasn't hard to follow, but it hadn't been used much, not for a good while. Tate switched off the audio on his radio.

They moved slowly in the knee-high undergrowth. At one time it would have been Indian land, full of cypress and wild orchids, massive oaks and magnolias and palms, hickory and sawgrass. Panthers.

And it would have been wet. But this land had been drained a couple of generations ago.

Billy tripped on something and fell hard. Tate would have laughed, but then he was on the ground too. They went on for 10 minutes and then they saw the lights. Through the trees, they could see a weather-beaten colonial with a circle in front surrounding a grassy yard.

Moving carefully, they crept closer. Several men stood near a brick grill. They were cooking. Inside the house, a radio was playing some kind of Latin hip-hop. Under the spotlights at the corner of the house, a banged up Mercedes.

"Holy shit. Are we lucky or what?" Billy said.

They reached the edge of the woods, about 60 yards from the house. It was a big old place, lots of live oaks and spanish moss, a southern mansion hidden in the deep woods. They stayed close to the trees, moving carefully in the dark. The mosquitos had long since found them.

Then Tate grabbed Billy's arm, tugging him down onto his knees. He pointed. On the wide veranda, underneath a couple of rocking chairs, a big dog was gnawing on a stick.

They were away from the house, but not far enough away. And it was dark, but not dark enough.

Tate took Billy by the shoulder and spoke into his ear.

"I want to see around the rest of the house, but I don't want to push our luck."

Billy shook his head.

"No fucking way. We sit here and see what we can see and then we get the fuck out."

He pointed angrily at the ground underneath their feet. Billy wasn't going anywhere. He was rattled. They both were.

Around the grill, a handful of men, laughing and drinking beer, every one of them young and fit, as if they had come upon a group of athletes on a weekend adventure.

The guys by the grill were shoveling up some steaks. They filled a couple of platters and headed for the house. Inside, they could see half a dozen men gathering around a table. There was a whistle and the dog went in. Someone turned off the outside lights.

Tate began to creep forward. Billy reached out for an ankle and missed.

"What the fuck do you think you're doing, man?"

"They're in for the night. I'm going to see if I can get closer."

"There is no way I'm going up to that house. You got some kind of death wish?"

"Don't want you to. You sit tight. In fact, move over in that direction, away from this drive. Give you some time if you have to get clear."

"What are you going to see, man? Squat. Let's get back and call in some reinforcements."

Tate smiled.

"You know what? You're right. You start back. I'll catch up to you. I'm just going to go listen a bit. And quit worrying. It's too hot to get killed."

And, with that, he took off, low-running toward the house. Billy watched him move from shadow to shadow and stop under the window.

"This is fucked."

• • •

CHRISTINE DESILVA had been a U.S. attorney for seven years, in charge of the Miami District for the last two. During that time, she had prosecuted dope dealers, money launderers, tax evaders, investment fraud artists, Cuban spies and an assortment of other low-lifes. She had a political future, but seemed not to care. I serve at the pleasure of my superiors, she had said on more than one occasion. Her job simply was to prosecute anyone who broke the law.

De Silva was 45, single, beginning to show some gray, but didn't do anything about it. She had an exercise bike in her office with a tray on top so she could pedal while she read briefs. Just now, she was sitting at her desk trying to use one of those tiny screwdrivers that tighten the hinge screws in a pair of glasses.

She spoke without raising her head.

"I've about got this fixed. I was at home getting ready to put my feet up when you gentlemen called. I am in the middle of a very good book. And if you have not explained to me why you insisted on this meeting by the time I finish getting this screw in here, I am throwing you out and going home to finish it. So let's get to it, shall we?"

Tommy Becker knew what he needed to say. He gave her a quick summary and then sat back to let her digest.

His story made her angry.

"So let's get this straight. Your boss is running an off-the-books operation with an escaped con so he can catch up to a hired killer named Barnett. We don't know why he isn't willing to let Superintendent Osmund here take Barnett down, so we would have to suspect his reasons for wanting Barnett involve something distasteful.

"I guess we need to assume that it's for something that wasn't available to him while Barnett was incarcerated. That's an interesting question. And it seems to bother him little that Barnett is here to assassinate an American citizen. Am I missing any critical pieces in this completely screwed up story?"

"No."

"You're absolutely sure about this?"

Becker nodded.

"My instinct," Grady interjected, "is that Tommy has done us a big favor. I think Lex has been off the reservation for a good while."

She cussed under her breath. Then she poked in Becker's direction with her tiny screwdriver. She cussed a little more. It did not look the slightest bit ridiculous.

"The first thing I'd like to do is bring Lex Dean in and yank his chain. But before I go too far off, let's talk about what you've got that's admissable.

Becker ticked off a very short list.

"Not much. He received a couple of phone calls that could be damaging. We can probably establish his visit to the prison. My testimony.

None of that is a slam dunk. He's smart. He might have provided for himself. Ultimately, you have Otis Chandler's story, with me backing him up."

She slammed a hand onto the desk.

"You're insane. Why don't you have something better than this? You've never talked to Chandler yourself?"

"I can wear a wire, try to get Lex talking."

"That would have been a really sexy idea a week ago, Mr. Becker. Now, Mr. Osmund, I'd like to hear from you."

Grady reached over and laid a hand on Becker's shoulder.

"It's simply this. We're out of time and we need your help. I want to confront Lex now and find out what he knows about the escapees. And then I want them arrested. In the meantime, we have to keep Gonzales out of harm's way.

"There are only two things that matter here. One – we bring the cons back. Two – we make sure nobody else gets killed. Christine, I understand your concerns, but how effectively Lex is prosecuted is not the issue."

DeSilva nodded.

"You know what? I think you're right."

She stood, came around the desk toward Becker. Even in bluejeans she could look tough.

"You know where Lex is right now?"

Becker nodded.

"OK. We can talk in the car."

It didn't take her long to round up a trio of agents. One of them drove. De Silva sat in front. Tommy Becker and Grady were in the back and there were two more agents in a second car.

She turned so she could look at them while they talked.

"So… is Lex in it for the money? Is he a zealot? Or is he one of those angry types who thinks life has passed them by? Too smart for society, but nobody's noticed?

"I'd go with your third option," Becker said. "I've always thought Lex was a bully. He treats people like shit and he plays fast and loose. What I've decided is he's a psychotic, and a bully."

"And an asshole," she added. "A complete royal asshole. Unfortunately, he's also the most dangerous kind of malcontent."

"And why is that?" Becker asked.

"Because he knows the system. He knows the secrets."

Lex was on the bed in his hotel room, watching ESPN when he heard the knock. He walked softly to the door and listened for a moment.

"Yes."

"Lex, it's Tommy."

Grady pushed through the doorway first. De Silva was a step behind him. Tommy stood there a moment, studying Lex. Grady had one hand on Lex's arm. With the other, he took Lex's gun from his waist and held it up. The agent took it from his hand.

Grady went over to the desk and pulled out a chair. He pointed. Lex sat down.

"Lex, I suspect you know Christine De Silva. She's going to have a lot to say to you, but I'm going to set you straight on some things first. I'm in the middle of a statewide criminal investigation and I think she'll accommodate me."

De Silva and Tommy were standing next to Grady. One of the agents squeezed past them and planted himself between Lex and the window. Another agent stood inside the door. One remained in the hall.

There was another chair next to the bed. Grady pulled it over and sat down. He extended a hand slowly, reached underneath Lex's legs, and pulled his chair up close. Lex had yet to speak. His eyes darted quickly from De Silva to Osmund, back and forth. He wasn't looking at Tommy at all.

They were face to face, legs touching.

"Let me remind you," Grady said, "that I'm operating with special authority. I can guarantee you that I'll be able to ruin your life.

"Don't think about spin, don't think about cutting a deal, don't even think about trying to save your ass. I'm going to get some information from you right now."

He waited. Lex met his stare and said nothing. He was leaning back now, arms crossed, sticking his jaw out. His intent was clear.

Grady slapped him full across the face, hard, rocking him back, jarring his teeth.

Lex threw up an arm, teetering in his chair, then righted himself. For a second, he was tempted to fight back, then he changed his mind. He would say nothing. Do nothing.

Lex was trying work up a smile when Grady slapped him again, harder this time. Lex began to turn white, his head ringing. He forced himself not to shield his face. He cleared his throat and struggled to turn his head back toward Grady.

Grady leaned in just another inch. He hesitated. For a moment, Lex thought he was going to say something. Then Grady slapped him again, a round, sweeping shot that knocked him out of the chair. Grady nodded to the agent by the window, who lifted Lex to his feet.

Lex was shaking now, tears running down his cheeks, chin wabbling. Suddenly, at this moment, all he wanted was to get to the bathroom, but he was beginning to understand the rules. He tried to square himself, catch his breath. The agent helped him back into the chair.

"Can I get a glass of water."

No one answered. Grady was leaning forward again. Lex began to speak, forcing his voice into a lower register.

"I don't know where they are. Otis is going to call me here, probably in a couple of hours. I can tell him we'll meet him someplace, or ..."

"You'll tell him it's over. You'll tell him we want his location and we'll pick them up. You can tell him we will evaluate his status, but we will be inclined to honor certain assurances. And then you'll hand the phone to me."

"OK. Sure. That's fine. That's what I'll tell him."

It was over. Lex was whimpering now. He began to stand up. He looked cautiously at Grady and sat back down.

"I want to stay here for this call. Christine, what do you think about getting some phone people in here to hook on a couple of extensions?"

"Let's do that."

She turned to the agent by the window.

"He is not to be out of your sight for any reason. Empty his pockets. Lex, I'm going to read you your rights and ask if you understand them."

32

TATE WAS in the shadow, perhaps 15 feet from the porch when the door flew open. A young guy, wiry as hell, with a crewcut, a ragged t-shirt and shorts. All he had to do was look up.

Tate, his mouth hanging open, frozen, watched him set a soft nylon bag by the door and go back inside.

Tate felt pretty sure he hadn't pissed himself, but he looked.

He had thought he would just creep close to the window and see what he could see. What a grindingly stupid idea that was.

A bag by the door – they were preparing to leave. And wasn't that why they were here, because something was going down? There was nothing to do but run, quickly, quietly, back to the trees.

The porch was wide. Light poured through flimsy curtains across the front of the house and he could hear them jabbering as they ate. He put his foot down onto the first step and he was back in Atlanta, that night after graduation, the night his high school buddies had dared him to climb to the top of the water tower. He'd started up sprightly enough, but, as Tate had discovered, the higher he went, the heavier his hands and feet became until, near the railing, he could hardly move without superhuman effort. Forty feet below, they stood watching, whispering out taunting reminders that he wasn't yet to the top.

And then, just short of it, another ladder, this one leaning out to the walkway around the tank itself. He could barely keep his feet on the rungs. He couldn't stop, couldn't go any further, just pulsing there like a toy whose batteries had all but expired.

He was on the second step now, nothing to prevent anyone from seeing him from inside through those lacy curtains, or by bringing another bag to the door.

He tried to hurry but his legs no longer served him. He could feel the breeze prickling the hair on his arms, the hoot of an owl high up in the trees behind him, a cupboard door slamming shut, laughter. Suddenly, he heard a shout and then the music blared once again. He had forgotten to breathe.

He was on the porch now, moving toward the front door. He jammed his hand into his pocket, but couldn't seem to get it past the knuckles. The simplest coordination had left him. He wanted to crouch, but he was afraid of toppling over, afraid of losing his grip on that last rung, that long rocking fall. Slowly, he bent down, almost kneeling, put his hands on the porch floor, feeling the grit and chipped paint under his fingers, and counted to three. Heart pounding, he crept forward again.

Just on the other side of the door, more shouting. Spirits were high inside.

"Manuel, another Budweiser."

The accent almost made him laugh.

He was at the bag now, tearing at the zipper. Long, gray barrels, shoulder straps, the smell of gun oil. Underneath, a long metal box. More clips. He fumbled again in his pocket and reached into the bag.

Now, sweat dripping off his chin onto the bag. He had to wipe it clean. His shirt was short-sleeved. Tugging at his waistband, something to wipe off the sweat, and he could hear the hard leather heels smacking on the stairs inside the door. Someone coming down the stairs. They were coming quickly. Just a few more steps.

He tugged at the zipper. One quick swipe of his shirttail and he leaped backward, then off to the side, not risking the stairs, heading down the porch away from the light, against the house as the door opened, trying to get away without making noise and then he knew he was out of time. He froze, stood upright, pressing himself against the house, beginning to taste his breakfast, the ocean pounding in his head.

The man stood in the open doorway, then stepped out onto the porch. He stood for a moment at the railing, staring up into the trees, searching for that owl. He spit into the front yard, going for distance, turned and walked back inside.

Tate forced his breathing to slow. He looked slowly to his right, his left, then vaulted the rail, staying in the shadows, moving slowly away from the house.

• • •

TATE'S BOSS thought Sharon was the kind of woman men robbed banks for, which was odd, considering his profession. Still, he had never seen her at home, in a t-shirt and cutoffs, showing that much leg.

It took him a minute to explain himself.

"Why don't you just come in, Robert? Tate isn't here at the moment. Perhaps there's something I can do for you?"

He wasn't sure why he'd driven out. He could have called. He thought perhaps it was better face to face. He hoped she didn't mind. There were just a few things.

Sharon looked deep into Einburg's eyes. She thought about leaping across the coffee table and scratching them out. She thought about offering him a hose in the front yard so he could rinse that crap out of his hair. She got up instead and went into the kitchen. She came back with two glasses of Chardonnay.

"So far," she said, "I have not got a clue what you're talking about."

She raised her eyebrows and cocked her head just slightly to the side.

"Oh," he said. "Sorry.

"I was just saying I probably didn't need to come all the way out here, but it seemed like the kind of thing where Tate and I might actually talk it through."

"What kind of thing?"

"Well, he's gone off with some of the staff. Folks tend to be very loyal to Tate and it was quite by accident that I found out. But he's gotten a bunch of men and cars and a helicopter and they're off somewhere and it's all off the books. You know, unofficial.

"So I'm wondering if it's more of that Cuban thing and I'm thinking he really shouldn't be doing this."

Sharon leaned back and crossed her legs. She couldn't manage continuous eye contact, even though she knew that was the only way to keep him on track. She thought very seriously about wrapping a blanket around herself, so Einburg's eyes would stay in his head for half a minute.

"So are you here to chew his butt or are you here to help?"

"Well he can't be doing this, you know. This is completely against everything, you know, the rules and all."

He went on about nonsense for awhile. She held up a hand.

"Robert, you and I don't know each other very well. But I wonder if I might be completely candid with you."

"Please."

"Tate has told me that the two of you have had a little friction from time to time. He worries about that."

She leaned forward. He was blinking like a madman. He licked his lips for the 12th time. She had him.

"He has a great deal of respect for you and he feels that sometimes his tendency to be... very casual... might be off-putting. He thinks better of it, but then he hasn't felt comfortable taking the initiative to speak to you, to tell you how much he would like to improve the relationship."

"I had no idea. To tell you the truth, I've always thought that Tate saw me as an obstruction. To tell you the truth, I think Tate sees me as very naïve."

"Well he is acutely aware that sometimes he comes across in a way that is not what he intends. He has told me several times, particularly lately, that he wishes he had an opportunity to seek out your advice."

In lesser hands, it would not have been successful. On this night, however, and after another glass of wine, Mr. Einburg found himself developing a new regard for Tate Drawdy. He wondered, in fact, if he might reach a point where he might drop by more often.

They talked about other things. She rubbed a spot on the inside of her thigh. He reminded himself to close his mouth. He thought he might find a way to ask if she had a photograph of herself she might spare, something at the beach, perhaps. And then she brought him back.

"What do you think about all this Gonzales business? I don't know much about it myself."

Einburg leaned back, cleared his throat. He held up his glass.

"Would I be imposing?"

She laughed and let it dissolve into a giggle.

"Are you kidding? Let's look around in the kitchen and see if there's anything to snack on."

And then he was laughing and telling stories and pretty soon Sharon was thinking it was a home run and wondering where the fuck Tate was.

• • •

GRADY GOT his brothers on the phone. He told Buddy Lee to find Gonzales and get him someplace safe.

They were outside Lex' hotel room on a porch overlooking the parking lot.

"That may have been the finest interrogation I've ever heard," De Silva said. "And quick. Damn that was quick. Shame I wasn't here to see it."

She asked Grady if he felt better about things.

"I'll think about feeling good when we have those guys in cuffs. Right now, I'm worried about spooking them… a shootout… I don't know what kind of hardware they're carrying. Barnett could be a lot of trouble. We've got to surprise them."

• • •

TATE AND the rest still were parked in a field off the two-lane.

Robert Einburg called. The chief wanted to see them.

"I guess we're in some shit," Tate said.

"Actually, no. I told him I'd let him know when you were back. But we need to convene as soon as possible, right away. I told him you were on a case, following a suspect."

"Why did you say that, Robert."

"We can talk about that later. Right now, we need to get you back here for that meeting. Grady Osmund will be there and Christine DeSilva, the U.S. attorney. They've got a line on the escaped cons."

Tate said he'd call Robert right back, then he told the others.

"We can't go. We have to stay here and see where they go," Hugh said.

"You go," said Tate. "Take Billy with you in the car. We'll stay here with the chopper. It's the only thing that makes any sense."

"No way. If they leave before we can get back, we're fucked."

"Nah. I put a beeper in one of their bags."

"You did what?"

"Tracking device, in one of their bags."

"Holy shit. How did you do that? And what if they don't take that bag?"

Tate was leaning against the car, just the beginnings of a smile on his face.

"They'll take this bag."

"How can you be so sure? What are you talking about?"

"It's got sniper rifles in it."

• • •

ALFREDO'S BIFOCALS had slid down toward the end of his nose. He tilted his head back. It was a habit he had acquired. Sometimes he found himself tilting his head when he wasn't wearing them. He was working on a speech for the Senate Foreign Relations Committee. Mozart's Requiem playing softly from the bookcase.

The small lamp next to him was burning and there was light from the yard shining through the towering mullioned windows that overlooked the water.

He was in the upstairs office, in a stout leather winged back chair, working in pen, with a legal pad, working quickly without notes.

His back was to her. She didn't make a sound as she came in.

"You've been working a lot, Alfredo."

"Yes," he said, not turning. "And you've been very patient with me."

She walked in front of him, took the pad from his hands and turned to set it down on the desk. Alfredo watched her as she walked back toward him. She took his glasses and put them on. Except for the glasses, she was naked. She sat in his lap, facing away from him and took his hands and put them between her legs. She tilted her head back on his shoulder.

"You're through working tonight, my love."

33

TATE TOOK the old fire stairs, which put him on the other side of the building. He ran through the hallways, rounded a corner and heard the voices coming from the chief's conference room.

He was the last one there. A couple of guys were already sitting down. Somebody had made coffee. It was late.

Chief Morrall was standing at the head of the table, his face close to Grady's, nodding.

Tate walked quickly over to him and put a hand on his shoulder.

"I've got to catch you up."

But the chief shook his head.

"Give us just a minute, Tate. Why don't you grab a seat?"

And then he was introducing Grady to the group. They sat down, everybody but Tate. He stood, leaning against a wall in the back of the room. Most everybody was in their street clothes. With the exception of Tate, none of them looked like they'd been playing in the sewer.

Grady took charge of the meeting, told everyone time was running out. He quickly ran through the break, the killings – Pat, an innocent passerby found dead in an interstate motel room, Paul Rutledge, executed in an orange grove, the kid in the body shop, the two cops. He had Tommy Becker explain what they knew about Lex. Grady said they felt they were in a position to pick up one of the cons.

Gonzales and Isabel were in a conference room upstairs. The cops had sent a car for them. It was, they had said, for their own safety. Gonzales was staying pretty cool.

Tate was beginning to pace. His lunatic theory didn't sound so far-fetched anymore. And now he was thinking Hugh had done him a good turn, persuading him to take the chopper back for the meeting.

Hugh and Danny were still in the field, waiting, and this was all taking way too long. Somebody asked a question. Becker was starting to cover the same ground again.

Tate leaned over the table and held out his hands.

"Folks, shit is getting ready to hit the fan and we're having a conference. This is not the time to be worrying about getting everybody up to speed. I've got ...."

Morrall, in no mood, angrily motioned for Tate to sit down.

"Tate, we'll get to you in just a minute."

Morrall was a good cop, but he hadn't made chief by being informal. He gestured toward Becker.

"Please go on..."

Tate took a step back, his arms crossed over his chest. He was staring at the clock on the other side of the room. He could see that Osmund wanted to get moving. He wouldn't let this drag on much longer. Tate was just staring at the clock, and then he felt DeSilva's eyes. He looked at her.

She tilted her head toward the head of the table. Her eyebrows were squeezed in tight, telling him to do something. Becker was repeating what they had learned about the plot to kill Gonzales. He was beginning to speculate about motive.

Tate slapped his hands together.

"Yes. Now you're seeing a connection between the escape and the attempt on Gonzales. All you lack is a reason and I've got one."

Nobody spoke for a moment, once Tate had explained his theory, once he'd told them about a bunch of Cuban-Americans in the woods with guns.

He hurried through it. The lies after Simons' death, Gonzales' disappearance, the warehouse and nitro-benzene, Gonzales' sophisticated efforts to stay under cover and the elaborate code of silence, the place in the woods and the team there, the sniper rifles and a bunch of rich old men, still angry, still stoking the fire. It made too much sense.

A question or two. Tate quickly dismissed them. For a moment, the room was quiet.

And then they all began chattering. Morrall reined them in, running down the rule book, the way things were going to have to be done, obtaining proof, building a case.

Tate was boiling over. He cut him short, furiously massaging the back of his hand, realizing there was more edge to his voice than was advisable.

"Look, this is not the time to be tidying things up. We need to quit worrying about who's breaking what damn law."

The chief was not about to back down.

"But we are going to worry about who's breaking the law. That's what we do."

"We need to be making sure nothing else happens," Tate argued.

"Sit down please."

"This thing feels like a two-headed snake to me. Here's what ...

Morrall slammed a fist down on the table.

"Tate, you can stop interrupting me anytime. This is not how we get things done around here."

Tate took a breath. DeSilva cleared her throat.

"I apologize for breaking in here..."

Tate cut her off. He spoke slowly, hands held out in front of him.

"No, I apologize. Really. Chief, you're right. And I'm wrong. But just let me say this..."

He took a breath.

"Here's the thing. Half of the time, we like to let people get right to the edge of a thing, so we can get all our questions answered before we arrest 'em, so we can tie it up nice and tight.

"If we let another 12 hours go by, we may not be able to stop this. We need to be talking about stopping things right where they are – making sure nothing happens. We've seen holy hell on this. We don't need any more."

Grady cut in.

"I'm inclined to agree, gentlemen.

The chief studied the faces around the table. He nodded.

"I guess I do too, if Tate will sit the fuck down for two minutes."

Morrall never cursed. Tate sat down.

Grady took a quick survey of the room for next steps. It looked like a whole lot of cops were going to be real busy. They would borrow men and transportation from Palm Beach, Henry, Glades and Martin counties to set up a wide perimeter. A smaller group would go in, led by Morrall's SWAT team. DeSilva would line up a couple of agent teams. They outlined communications, the chain of command.

Tate was behaving. He waited for an opening and cleared his throat. He had one more thought.

"Listen here. Why don't I just tell Gonzales we have tons of guys out there right now, all around his farmhouse. We want him to make a call, tell those guys to pack it in. Then we just have Hugh and Danny drive in."

"And what if he thinks you're full of it?" the chief asked. "If we don't round those guys up…"

Tate had gotten himself under control.

"Here's how I see it. This guy is the ultimate planner. I could tell you a couple of stories about things he's done. He always goes that extra step. But today, I spooked him. It was a bluff, but I told him I suspected the reason somebody tried to kill him was because they'd found out about his plot.

"Ten minutes later, they were on the road. I figure he's punching the button on this operation. But he's not a fanatic. He's not a gangster. He cares too much about people. This is all about tradition and principle for him. We tell him he's caught and he'll pull the plug. He'll stop before anyone gets hurt."

He could see acknowledgement and agreement in the faces around the table.

"Let's give it a try," Grady said. "It's either going to work in 30 seconds, or it's not going to happen. You go talk to him now. If it doesn't work, keep both of them away from a phone. We'll have to roll people pretty quickly.

Tate turned to Morrall.

"Is that acceptable to you, chief?"

The chief shrugged.

"The fact that you are completely covered with mud and sweat may make your story more believable."

Tate was at the door.

"I'm going to get him away from the wife for this. I still haven't figured out where she fits."

He took one last look around the room. DeSilva was shaking her head, smiling. The chief had a different expression. Tate closed the door.

• • •

AND IT went much the way he'd predicted.

He had come into the room, all business. He'd asked an officer to take Mrs. Gonzales to a room down the hall, make sure she was comfortable, see if she needed anything. Isabel looked pretty irritated.

Gonzales sat, waiting.

"I have a call I need to make," Tate told him. "Unless you'd prefer I don't"

"And what is that, detective?

Still strong, still crisp in square-toed lace-ups, pleated pants, an elegant belt, a delicate shirt, hands folded patiently in his lap.

"I've got three choppers full of men sitting in a field down on 846, about a mile from your farm. We're about to go in, take down your team."

He paused, studying the man's face. Gonzales wasn't looking at him.

"You didn't think we'd let them leave?"

"What is it you want from me?"

The voice was hollow, from deep in his throat, from a very long time ago. He looked up and Tate saw the anger and the bitterness and the resignation and the pride and he admired it.

"The U.S. Attorney is outside. If you like, they'll fly you out and you can speak to your men. You can end this quietly."

Gonzales stood. Tate wanted to reach out, put an arm around his shoulder, shake his hand. Instead, he stepped to the door and opened it. Gonzales walked through.

"Thank you, detective."

34

THE CHOPPER set down in the field beside the house. They hadn't had a lot of chit chat on the way. Gonzales, his hands folded in his lap, spent most of the trip looking out the window or at the floor. He sat in the back with Tommy Becker. Christine sat in the front.

Gonzales had called Juan on the cellphone as they were preparing to leave police headquarters.

"Juan," he said, "I am on my way out there in a chopper. We'll meet you at the house."

"Who's we? What's going on?"

"Nothing. Nothing's going on. I'll see you in a few minutes. Have the men stand down."

"Are you sure? Are you sure, Alfredo?"

He never called him Alfredo.

"It will be just a few minutes and then I can answer your questions."

There had been no code word, no signal to the men. Just a straightforward telephone call. Juan knew something was wrong. He called the men together, told them Gonzales was on the way, that something didn't sound right.

The team put the weapons and the rest of their equipment in a cubby under the stairs. It wouldn't take long to grab it. The men got dressed. A couple of them washed the dishes.

As the chopper landed, Hugh and Danny bounced their way in on the lane leading to the house. The chopper pilot stayed behind. Gonzales took the lead, walking quickly enough, with Christine and Tommy on either side of him. Hugh and Danny in the rear.

"It used to be an old sugar plantation," Gonzales said. "It's a beautiful piece of property. We've done a little work, but mostly we've left it alone. It's very comfortable, a nice place to get away from the city."

He turned to look at Christine.

"You'd like it here."

Gonzales walked more slowly as they came to the yard. A few feet short of the driveway, he stopped for a moment, looking up at the old house. And then he climbed the stairs to the porch.

The men were in the kitchen, all of them standing. Gonzales spoke quietly. The police wanted them to come downtown. He would take care of everything. He'd arrange legal representation. He'd have someone go to their homes, be with their families.

The men packed their things. There was a police van on the way. Tommy Becker and Christine were waiting outside on the porch.

Tommy turned to her.

"Do you believe this is over, and so quietly?"

She smiled.

"I think Detective Drawdy might be one of those guys who make the right conclusions despite inadequate information. Intuition, I think they call it.

"And he's got balls, too."

• • •

THE NEIGHBORS were told to leave their TVs on. The hotel manager called the handful of occupied rooms and, one by one, they evacuated the whole place. They took their time. It was a small hotel, 17 rooms in a U shape, with the parking on the inside, and half the units were empty. Next door, along one side, a gas station converted into a neighborhood garage. On the other, a print shop, and behind, a couple of rental units. The cops got the people out of those too.

They had cops on foot around the back and the sides, with backup units in cars behind them. Lots of cops, all out of sight of the rooms.

When they were ready to move in, they closed off the streets. Because Otis and Herb were three doors down from Jackie, the cops felt comfortable reaching out to them. The phone rang about 2 a.m. and Otis picked it up.

It was Lex, doing what he was told.

"This is going down now, Otis," he said. "If you and Herbert will put the lights on and step outside. We have some people outside the door waiting for you. Are you ready to come in?"

Otis grunted.

"This needs to happen in absolute silence. When you're ready, open the door and come out slowly with your hands up, both of you."

Otis said Ok. He walked over to Herb's bed and put his hand over his mouth and shook him awake.

He'd already put the light on.

Herb woke up quiet enough. Otis told him the cops were outside, that they were giving themselves up. They dressed quickly. Otis took time to piss.

"Might be our last chance for awhile," he said.

Herb said he didn't think he could. In a minute, they were outside, walking quickly toward the street. Herb saw Tate and waved. Tate waved back.

Around a diagram of the hotel, Sgt. John Block gathered his men. They knew what to do. They had spent a considerable amount of time over the years perfecting their small team movements, first responder tactical angles, high-risk warrant entry. Block's plan was simple. Jackie's motorcycle was parked in front of his room. One of the officers would drive a junker into the lot. He'd smack it into the bike and then play the drunken fool. When they got Jackie to the door, they'd take him down with a taser.

• • •

THE DOOR to Jackie's room, a dismal reminder that this was not the nice part of town. Heavy rough-cut plywood painted in streaks of artificial-turf green, with cockeyed hinges and metal weather-stripping that made an overworked scraping noise when it opened. It didn't do much against the heat or the noise of the street, but it offered a little privacy.

The men took up positions on either side of the door. Everything was ready. Down the block, an officer stepped toward the car. Then Block grabbed him.

"Nah. You sit tight. I'll handle this part."

Block climbed behind the wheel. He put the windows down and turned the radio up loud. A moment later, he was careening into the lot, where he slammed on the brakes and began to back into a parking space, lurching his way along. And then a jab with the gas pedal and Jackie's new motorcycle went down with a crash. Block got out of the car and began cussing loudly. And then he was at Jackie's window, banging and yelling.

"Hey. Anybody in here? Somebody leave this fucking motorcycle out here? Thing was right in my way."

Block pressed his face against the glass.

"Hey," he shouted. "Anybody..."

There was a burst of gunfire. Block flew backward into the parking lot and then the team was on the move. Breaking glass as the tear gas went through the window and began to fill the room. They'd set a short delay on the flash-bangs. After three seconds, glass and light exploded outward. Jackie's grassy green door went down with a splintering crash under a 60 pound battering ram. From inside, the roar began.

The first man leaping through the narrow doorway twisted as the impact of the bullets hitting his legs lifted him off the ground. And then his partner, his shoulder pressed against his buddy's back as they went in, collapsed in an agonizing heap on top of him, screaming as he fell.

The two men at the window, cut down in the same instant, and suddenly fire was licking the curtains, dancing toward the ceiling, and smoke was rushing out through the broken windows and the shredded doorway and still that hideous sound came pouring out of the room.

Swat commander Ross McDonough, poised behind a car 60 yards away, screaming into his mouthpiece.

"Get out of there! Get out of there now!"

Outside, men staring in disbelief, trying to make out the bodies of their comrades through the smoke as the fire grew and after a moment, the only thing they heard was the crackling of the wood, the popping it made as it spread to the adjoining rooms. Buddy Lee clutched at Tate's arm.

"What's he done? Filled the place with gasoline?"

For a time, not long, they stared, trying to understand.

Then McDonough was running forward, half-crouched, running as fast as he could across the parking lot.

Barnett couldn't still be breathing in there. And the men, his men, might still be alive.

He'd covered half the distance and then Tate and Buddy Lee and half a dozen of them were racing toward the room, sprinting toward the fire now searing its way through the walls, flames pushing up under the eaves, bursting through the roof. Blocks away, the firetrucks and the ambulances screaming.

Nearly blinded, McDonough slid feet first, ducking under the window frame, a semblance of caution as he reached the bodies crumpled there like dirty socks. And then the others were there, dragging the men back, pulling on their legs and their flak vests to get them away from the room and the fire.

In the doorway, choking black smoke poured out so thick they could hardly see the two bodies.

"Leave their masks on them, just get them out," McDonough shouted.

And then they had them in the ambulances and the hoses were being connected and the fire department was doing its best to act like it cared about a shit-eating sleazy motel.

Otis and Herbert were standing on the street. They had handcuffs on. The cops escorting them, just standing there.

"Man," Herb said. "That Jackie is a mean motherfucker."

"Was," said Otis, his shiny bracelets and his milky hair shimmering in the yellow of the streetlights.

"Huh?"

"Was. Jackie's a crispy critter now. Went out in a blaze of glory."

"I wished I'd of stayed in prison."

Herbert, feeling bad, feeling bad for the whole thing.

As for Otis, he figured it just meant more time cooped up in a box. Their little jaunt had been a mistake, a big one. Add that to the man he'd killed. And he'd sassed that judge. He'd reached his limit.

They stood for a moment, hypnotized by the racing fire, stunned by the sudden violence. Men shouting commands, bells, chunks of roof crashing in, muffled belching explosions as TV sets blew up and the shrimpy motel owner threatening and crying and pleading.

Business was going to be bad for awhile.

They watched while the firefighters did what they could. Soon, the hotel would be gone, but they could keep it from spreading. And then, McDonough's radio. It was one of the ambulance drivers. It was noisy but they could hear him.

"You ain't gonna believe this, chief. One of your cops just jumped up when we were about to put some oxygen on him. Jumped up and ran out the back. And, from the way he took off, it don't even look like he's hurt. He was covered with blood, but he's gone now."

McDonough couldn't believe it.

"What the fuck? Is he in a state of shock?"

"Not hardly," said Otis, shaking his head, a wry grin.

McDonough, developing an instant dislike for this arrogant son of a bitch escaped con.

"I'm guessing your man's dead and he's still in that hotel room."

"What are you talking about?"

"Looks like you guys just escorted Jackie Barnett out of here, free and clear."

McDonough, blood pounding, reached for his 9 mm. Otis saw it coming and stiff-armed Herbert, pushing him clear. Then McDonough got hold of himself. He took a breath. Putting a bullet in the forehead of a piece of shit scumbag wasn't going to bring his boys back, wasn't going to erase the pungent series of career-ending mistakes he'd made tonight.

• • •

JACKIE RAN a few blocks, shedding the mask, the vest and the shirt into the first dumpster he passed. He was thankful the cop didn't have the wrong size feet. He hadn't had time to put on the man's gun belt or even lace up the shoes. No one had noticed. They were too desperate to get him into the ambulance. What a clever little terrorist he was. Clever and lucky.

Now he truly was on the run. No place to stay, no money, no gun. A grimy t-shirt and a pair of blue cop pants covered in blood and soot and the smell of smoke. In five minutes, every car on the street would be a cop. He slowed to a walk. A man was just coming out of an all-night convenience store. When the man turned down the street, Jackie followed him.

The young veterinarian was headed home after a very long day, an emergency surgery on a puppy that had swallowed a sizeable and indigestible chunk of a child's toy, a plastic garden tool, of all things. Young Dr. Curtis had worked on him for hours. Now he was looking forward to a pizza, a beer and a few minutes of any old movie that might still be on television. Something to fall asleep with. Jackie was about to cut his dreams short when he saw him reach into his pocket. Car keys. What luck.

As the key went into the lock, the young man felt a hand reach around his neck, wrenching it sideways, past where it wanted to go. Jackie shoved him into the passenger seat, got in behind him and started the car.

"Hey!"

A couple of guys just leaving a bar across the street, running. They'd seen him. Jackie gunned the motor, one hand on the wheel, the other reaching for the dead man's wallet. Ten blocks down, he hung a right into a street filled with small bungalows. Everyone was asleep. He pulled to the side, turned off the motor, emptied the doctor's pockets. He found his address.

Jackie got out of the car and walked around to the other side. The street was still. Slowly, quietly, he opened the passenger door, eased his young passenger onto his shoulder and stepped lightly over a low picket fence. He laid him on the ground behind a pair of plastic garbage bins.

The headlights on the Volvo came on automatically when he started the car. He drove to Curtis' house.

There were no pictures in the wallet. Perhaps he was single.

• • •

TATE WAS asking Herb about the break, why he went along.

"Not sure now why I did that."

"Me neither. You need to stop once in awhile, think things through. You know… count to 10 or something.

Herb just hung his head. Tate gave his arm a squeeze.

"OK. You behave real good, real tight now until you get back, you hear me."

"Maybe you could come visit me sometime."

"I could do that."

The TV guys surrounded him as he walked across the parking lot, on him before he even noticed they were there, and then he had a microphone in his face and a guy was asking him what the hell had happened.

Tate, too tired to dodge. He told them two of the three escaped cons had been captured. The third con, Jackie Barnett, had rigged some sort of booby trap in a hotel room. And he'd been waiting for them with an arsenal. There were a number of casualties among the men who had attempted to take Barnett into custody.

Tate said the chief would want to say something later, and there would be additional information about the men. It was just too early for that. The officers were well trained. They had done what had been asked of them. They were brave professionals dedicated to protecting society. It was a huge loss for the city.

They could hear the rage in his voice.

"What about Barnett?" one of them asked.

Barnett, he told them, was a "despicable loser." And then he stopped. He looked straight at the camera.

"And I'll be taking care of Mr. Barnett personally."

The interview was over. They moved aside to let him pass. It would make great TV and it would be splashed across every local station all morning long.

35

JACKIE PARKED in the driveway and walked up the narrow brick path to the front door. There were stones edging the garden, metal chairs surrounding a redwood table on the porch, potted plants. The veterinarian was a neatnik. If he'd had a burglar alarm, there would have been one of those signs.

He used Curtis' keys. There was a shuffling, an old lab coming toward him. The dog was almost to him when he suddenly lifted his head, backed up a step and growled. Jackie knelt and extended a hand.

"Come on."

The dog lowered his nose toward the floor, limped forward. Jackie gave him the back of his hand to smell.

"It's all right."

The dog bared his teeth, coughed up a bark. Jackie smacked the dog's face, sent him sprawling across the room. The lab lay on his side, whimpering.

A quick tour. Clearly the man lived alone. He tossed some food in a grocery bag, a six-pack of Bud. Throwing off his clothes as he walked, he headed for the bedroom in the back of the house, dressed in the dead man's clothes and put more clothes in a small bag off a closet shelf. He went through drawers, headed down the hall to a tidy office and rummaged there. No weapons, nothing worth taking, he stepped through the kitchen door into the garage. Another car under a cover.

He peeled it back. A vintage rag-top Studebaker, cherry red. Jackie hustled back into the house, saw a set of keys on by the kitchen door.

He put the food and the small bag from the bedroom by the door and took a last walk into the dining room.

The old lab hadn't moved, just laying there, breathing with difficulty. Jackie got down on one knee and reached toward him. The dog snapped at him. Jackie recoiled, leaning in to finish him, then stopped.

He went into the kitchen. On the floor by the back door he saw a dish of water and an empty food bowl beside it. He tried a couple of cabinets, found a can of dog food and poured the whole thing into the bowl. Then he carried the food and the water into the dining room and laid them down.

"Ok buddy."

The Studebaker cranked up on the second try. Leaving the engine running, he walked to the garage door and looked out. Still dark, the street deserted. He hopped back into the car and hit the opener. There wasn't enough room to get past the Volvo. Jackie mowed down a bed of roses and headed out into the street.

An hour later, he was registered under the name Curtis in a north Miami hotel, a nice hotel where he could park on the lower level. He was tired and he smelled of smoke and gasoline.

• • •

NO LIGHTS. No siren. But they were moving.

Hugh had ridden back on the chopper. The guys at the bar had taken down the license plate as Jackie accelerated away.

Hugh parked half a block short of the veterinarian's address. He tossed his keys and anything else that might jangle onto the floorboard and turned off the interior light before they opened their doors.

He unholstered his gun and hopped a picket fence, scuttling through the yard, staying close to the houses, his breath coming in spurts as his feet hit the ground. It was near dawn, but the night air was cool and the tops of the palms were swaying just slightly in the breeze. He was sweating hard, but not from the exercise.

In the shadow of a big water oak, he saw the Volvo. He stopped and, for a moment, he just listened.

Then he crept closer and crouched behind a palm three strides from the driveway. Hugh pulled a small flashlight from his back pocket and looked across the street, trying to find Tate in the darkness. There he was, down on his stomach, crawling, waving to the guys on the other side to move up. Hugh pointed the flashlight into the ground and turned it on, then swept under the car. Across the yard, two flashes.

And so they moved, a few feet at a time, making sure they wouldn't be surprised.

Finally, they were at the windows and there was little to be seen, an old dog in the living room, a car cover laying in a pile in the garage. Satisfied, they burst through the front and rear doors and found nothing. A pile of clothes on the floor.

"He's been here and it couldn't have been too long."

Hugh was on the phone, checking for another registration. Dr. Curtis had owned a second car, a classic Studebaker. He called out a BOLO.

Tate wrapped a blanket around the dog and carried him out the door.

SATURDAY

JACKIE AWOKE to the sounds of the street, the sun climbing into his window. The housekeepers were pushing a vacuum in the room next door. He rolled over and reached for the remote. Tate Drawdy was on. He watched for a minute, then switched it off.

Jackie leaned his head to one side and held it there until his neck cracked. Then he called room service.

"Gimme the businessman's special and plenty of coffee."

They said it would be about 35 minutes. Jackie walked over to the window. He had a nice view of the city. With a graceful sweep, he dropped into a handstand and lowered his nose slowly to the floor. He'd worked up quite an appetite.

An hour later, he was on a bus, inching along. Traffic was heavy, but he was in no particular hurry. He'd already hit a couple of ATMs and he knew a place, a pawn shop where they kept a nice selection of hardware. He just hoped it hadn't changed hands or had other complications.

He got off the bus a couple of blocks away and walked. The shop was still there.

Jewelry in the window, a boombox and a wooden sloop rigged with blue thread, a set of pewter mugs with glass bottoms. Hanging from a two-sided hook, a pair of guitars. In the other corner, a vintage Schwinn Cruiser Deluxe. It had fat tires and heavy fenders and a fancy cover over the center bar with a button in the middle for a battery-powered horn.

Jackie pushed open the door and let it swing closed behind him. He recognized the old man behind the counter. His luck was still running strong. He browsed awhile until couple of teenagers looking at a knockoff Gibson gave up trying to haggle with the guy. When the store was empty, Jackie walked over.

"I'd like something from your private case."

"I'm not sure I know what you mean."

"We've done business before Mr. Smith. If you'll move that last book from the third shelf, you'll find a small brass key."

The old man smiled.

"I think I remember you now, sir."

"Perhaps. What can you show me."

"What are your needs?"

"One piece that gets it done."

"I have just what you need, a gem from Poland. An Onyks."

"That'll do."

"It's the NATO version.. folding stock."

Jackie threw Curtis' Visa card on the counter.

"Don't you want to know how much it is?"

"That won't be necessary."

"Then you probably know I don't take plastic."

"You took plastic from me one day five years ago. It was a day you were closed, but you opened specifically to make this sale. It was Labor Day and it was quite a large sum. You had no trouble with it."

"I remember. This card will work the same way, then? I just call a number and someone brings the cash and I give the card back?"

Jackie nodded, gave him a big smile.

Mr. Smith took down the book, got the key and headed into a back room. In a moment, he returned with a cardboard box almost two feet long. It was for a pricey coffee maker, the home entertainment choice.

"I stuck all I had in there, a bunch of 5.56."

"How long's it been in the box?"

"Years. This one's still gift wrapped."

The Onyks was a Polish copy of a Russian gun – smaller, gas-powered, just under seven pounds. It could fire 700 rounds a minute. It was just 21 inches long and looked more like a sci-fi handgun than a carbine. The pistol grip, dwarfed by the banana-shaped clip, looked too small to control the thing. The muzzle, modified to launch grenades.

Jackie took one of the old man's business cards. He wrote a number on the back. It was for the pay phone on the north end of the S-wing at Florida State Prison.

"Don't call today. Tomorrow."

"Not a problem. It was a pleasure doing business with you again."

Jackie picked up the box and headed for the door. Then he turned back.

"Maybe you'd better tell me what we're paying. My boss... you know."

Mr. Smith held up five fingers.

Jackie laughed and turned toward the door.

"You have a good day."

He walked a few blocks and found a pay phone. At first, the woman who answered didn't want to put him through. Then he said he knew something about the fire, he had some information. And so they switched him over to Tate's number.

Tate said hello. He hadn't had a whole lot of sleep. You could hear it in his voice.

"This is Jackie Barnett."

"How do I know that?"

"Gee. I don't know. You're a clever guy. Why don't you ask me some tricky question? Would that make you happy?"

"Ok. I think that's a good idea, Jackie. Why don't you tell me something particularly discernable about your buddy Paul?"

"Good choice. Mr. Rutledge is a fruit lover – oranges especially. But I'm guessing he finds them a mite difficult to swallow these days."

"I think you just might be the real deal. What can I do to help you? Would you like to get yourself arrested today?"

"Actually, Florida is starting to wear thin and you'd probably want me to stick around. I did want to touch base, though, say hey, let you know I wouldn't want to leave town without making sure we connect at some point."

"Nothing would please me more."

"Cool beans. You take care."

Jackie hung up the phone. He waggled his head from side to side, feeling the looseness in his shoulders. He looked up and down the street at the crowd, bustling shoppers, tourists, businessmen, meanderers. It was turning out to be a good day. He pulled his lips back in a hard grin, picked up his brand spanking new coffee maker and strutted down the street.

The chuckle began in his belly, building into a full-fledged Sidney Greenstreet that echoed between the storefronts.

• • •

LOTS OF cops were looking for the Studebaker. But there was nothing.

Tate and Hugh were getting to know the Osmund brothers. It had been particularly interesting to see Grady confront the question of what to do with Herbert.

He was telling the story now.

"So I asked him, why did he go along on the break, what was he up to?

"And he said he knew they were not the kind of people you'd bring home to meet mom. Actually, what he said was, he knew they were 'for real.' And I said, what does that mean? 'You know,' he says, 'rough characters.' But they were going to break out and it sounded like a good idea. Later on, when Barnett began killing people, he knew he had made a mistake.

"The weird thing is how Otis took care of him. I asked him why. He said he had no idea. He said I should ask Otis.

"So I did. And, you know what he said? It was the day he saw Herbert stand up for a guy, some little snot who was going to get his throat cut over a pack of smokes, and Otis said he knew he never would have done that, not for anybody. And he thought Herb might not be safe, not on his own, not after they left.

"Weird, huh. I've seen lots of guys who were complete scumbags who nonetheless had their own sort of code, their own ethics. And I've seen guys get turned around by small things that made them regret their past in a meaningful way. In this case, I doubt Otis regrets much of his past. We may never know. But I think he regrets getting Herbert into trouble."

Tommy Becker showed up, fat briefcase, wearing an old pair of jeans.

Buddy Lee had greeted him loudly, with a "Who the hell is this guy?"

Becker smiled.

"What? You didn't think I owned any?"

He'd been doing some homework. He turned to Grady.

"Let's sit down. I have that background on Barnett's last job, before he got nabbed. The guy he killed was a top exec for this big French communications outfit. I have somebody checking on why he was here. His company had gotten real fat during the tech run-up. Then the bubble burst. Lot of investors – lots of them were employees – got burned on the stock. The French government bailed them out. Maybe something like us and the airlines. I dunno."

Grady nodded.

"So it was a hit and there was a lot of money on the table. Question is, who was Jackie working for?"

"I don't have the slightest idea. But I bet I know who does."

36

ORTIZ WAS napping. And then the telephone rang. It was Barnett. He wanted to leave town, leave the country.

"How do you want to work this?"

"Work what, my good friend?"

"I need to get out of here. The cops grabbed both of my guys. I'm running. I'm going to need money and transportation...."

Ortiz sighed. The association with Barnett had always threatened certain liabilities. He unwrapped a cigar and rolled it under his nose.

"I'm not sure how I can help you with that, my friend. Our agreement was for a piece of business, support, resources, preparations. It appears that you have botched the job."

"You cannot be serious. We have an understanding, Ortiz."

"I would call it... an arrangement. I wouldn't go so far as to say it's an understanding. In any case, there is scarcely anything that I can offer you. Perhaps if you were to come here, we could talk about things, take a look at your situation..."

Jackie was beginning to lose his temper.

"Just get me out of here. Cut the crap."

Ortiz didn't reply. He just sat, drumming his manicured nails on the desktop. Jackie tried another tack.

"Look, we've got a lot of history, you and I. A lot of work. Surely you can get me in touch with your guys up here, get me on a boat."

Ortiz lit the cigar. He leaned back in his chair, put his feet up.

"That history was quite some time ago. A lot has changed. You've been in prison. Perhaps you haven't kept up to date. You're already in debt to me, my friend. And I suspect you aren't going to be able to fulfill your part of this bargain. Frankly, I suspect that you don't have much time."

"But you've got guys here and you've got a way you get them back when you need to. I can tag along."

"Actually, I have already expended a great deal more energy and resources on this problem than I should have. I can remember when you had resources of your own, my friend."

Jackie's head was pounding. Lately, he'd lost a few rounds. He was losing this one.

"Ok. Tell you what. I'll just wrap up this job, finish it up, and then get down to Matamoros, grab something headed your way."

Ortiz stubbed out the cigar.

"Yes, of course. That is a good plan. Give me your location, my friend. I'll have someone bring some cash to you. That is the least I can do for an old friend."

A bit too cozy. He'd allowed Ortiz to hear his desperation.

"Sounds good. Sounds real good. Tell you what. I'm sort of in-between locations right now. Call you a little later with an address. Thanks for the help."

He hung up the phone. Now the Cubans would be after him, too. He was a liability. He would remain so until he got back on his feet. Right now, he needed time. And space.

And payback.

• • •

THERE WAS some arthritis, some bone density loss, a finicky stomach. He was a little hard of hearing. Otherwise, he was in decent shape for a real old dog.

Sharon and Ricky had gone down to Curtis' office. The staff was there, clearing things out, calling the clients, cleaning the place up, sharing their grief. They all thought it would be fine for them to keep the dog. His name was Albert. Curtis had raised him from a puppy.

"If you want to have somebody look him over," one of the techs had said, "his former partner has an office a few miles from here."

So they'd gotten a checkup. The doc said Albert looked fine, but he might feel better if they increased the dosage of an anti-inflammatory that helped with the arthritis. Ricky was all gaga about Albert, so Sharon thought she better get some things clarified.

"How much time does this old boy have?" she asked.

"Hard to say. Maybe a year, not long. He's to the point that he needs a little exercise, but there isn't much point in dragging him out if he isn't feeling like it."

She put her arm around Ricky and pulled him close.

"I think sometimes," she said, "people hang onto a dog too long. They don't really know when is the right time and they're afraid of making the wrong decision."

The doctor smiled.

"That's absolutely right. It's a good idea, I think, to have a few barometers in mind. Then you can be clear on it and you won't worry. Would you like a few suggestions?"

He gave them a checklist. Can't eat, can't sleep, can't stand up, can't hold his urine. When any of those occur, it's time.

He turned to Ricky.

"You'll remember those? You're probably going to see more of old Albert than your mom will. I'm thinking maybe you ought to be the one responsible for knowing how he's doing."

"We'll take good care of him for as long as he's got left."

They thanked the doc and headed outside. Albert had gotten a cortisone shot to get him moving again. They lifted him into the car and started home.

Sharon turned off the radio.

"How do you think Albert likes getting in and out of the Jeep?"

"Probably not much. We can lift him, like we did today. But he might not always feel like it."

"Yeah. So is that going to make it harder, you think, going back and forth to Tate's?"

"It could. I've been kinda thinking about that. What do you suggest?"

"What do you suggest?"

"I don't know. Maybe we could spend more time at Tate's now?"

"Is that something you could live with?"

"Sure."

She took a breath, tried to keep it light.

"Tate's been wanting us to move in full-time, you know? He wants to get married."

"I figured that. I thought maybe you weren't sure about how I'd like it, or maybe you weren't sure about you."

"But you'd like it Ok?"

"Yeah. I think it would be good for us both."

She pulled to the side and put the Jeep in park. Then she grabbed Ricky and gave him a big hug.

"Thank you baby."

And then she straightened herself out and started back up the road. She brushed the tears out of her eyes.

"We're just doing this for Albert."

There was a car dawdling along in front of them. Sharon punched it and took them on a curve.

37

TATE DRAWDY'S Nike high-toppers squeaked ridiculously on the tile floor, echoing in the empty spaces. He'd missed a lot of sleep, but there was too much still undone. Almost running, he hustled down the long lime green and fluorescent hallway and took the stairs two at a time.

He unlocked his office and stood a moment in the doorway. It felt as if he hadn't been there in months. He stayed just long enough to review a list, grab a file, then took off for home. He wanted to change into something a bit more formal, a tie perhaps.

He had called Gonzales from the office, asking him if he could swing by and now he was jogging down the street to the car, oblivious to the helmeted guy on a midsize Suzuki, the guy in the old jeans jacket with the sleeves cut off, the guy who followed him home.

Tate went straight into the house, made a quick change. The biker was gone when he came back outside.

He climbed into his car, pushed in an old Mike Bloomfield CD and headed for Gonzales' place. He kept the windows up, the volume just halfway, listening to Bloomfield's sweet vibrato, the emotion, waiting for the flurry, the notes cascading like water over a gutter in a hard rain.

They opened the gate and he drove right up to the house.

"I don't believe you've met Grady Osmund. He's the superintendent at Florida State Prison. He's been in charge of the search for the escaped cons who came down here and killed all our guys."

"I know, of course, about that horrible shooting Friday night. I hope those men were not personal friends of yours."

Gonzales' concern was genuine. He was subdued, almost relaxed, it seemed. He had on a casual shirt and some slacks and was sitting in an Adirondack chair out back, by the pool. He'd gotten them both a beer from a rather stupendous little refrigerator inside the cabana next to the shallow end.

"Actually, I've been asked to come downtown in the morning, to meet with Mr. Osmund and Ms. DeSilva. I was expecting you would be there as well. I suspect they want to talk about the men at the farmhouse."

"Good. Yes, I'll be there. Why I came by. I was wondering if you wanted to talk about it, about what you expect to happen."

"Perhaps tomorrow. Can I get you another beer?"

He'd hoped Gonzales might want to open up, now that his scheme was a bust. But that clearly wasn't going to happen. Tate stayed a few more minutes. They talked about Florida, Gonzales waxing enthusiastically about the economy. He called it "abounding." Tate wondered how often he used the word.

The next morning, things did not go as he'd expected. Tate got a call at home at about 8. The meeting was postponed. He'd probably get a call in the afternoon.

And he did. The meeting, once again, was postponed. They might be called in later that evening. He called Grady. They decided to meet.

Tate suggested a pasta place around the corner from the Osmunds' hotel. Buddy Lee was there with Grady and Tate brought Hugh. Grady had on his jacket so he could hide the .45 under his arm. When the waitress came over, Tate felt a kick from under the table, from his trusted subordinate, no doubt.

Grady was on the cell with DeSilva. In 15 minutes, she was there.

Gray suit, white blouse, string of pearls. Nothing too threatening, but folks still gave her room. She came in under a full head of steam and was in the booth before Hugh had time to get out of her way. She set her purse under her feet and, catching the eye of the server, raised one hand and snapped her fingers.

"Double martini."

The men looked at each other, at their iced teas.

The waitress hesitated.

"Go ahead and bring the lady's drink, if you don't mind," said Grady. "And then we might want something else."

He turned to Christine.

"I get the sense we won't be meeting tonight."

"That's right."

She looked over her shoulder.

"I have sworn to say nothing. So you guys are gonna swear, am I right?

Everyone nodded.

"My boss is a very straight up guy in Washington, close enough to the action to know what's going on, far enough away not be a part of the deal-making, capiche?"

And then she laid it out, as much as there was. Gonzales' men had not been charged and it appeared they would not be. None of them had any kind of criminal background.

As for criminal intent, none of them had any of that, either, other than that one thing.

Gonzales had not asked for any help, any intervention. It simply had been offered, once he had agreed he would stop. There would be no further escapades.

The waitress arrived with a tray, one double martini and four beers. Tate, it seems, had connected with a little sign language while the others were intent on DeSilva's explanation.

DeSilva waited until the waitress was well out of earshot before she went on.

"Here's the thing. It's not just a matter of covering up for some guy who's buddies with a bunch of Washington big shots. They think – 'they' being the oval office – that popping Gonzales creates this massive uncontrollable shit storm.

"An inner circle player wants to kill Castro, so the whole world would think that meant the United States government was behind it.

Or else the White House fries him as some rogue con artist who fleeced everybody, and then there's a rift that lasts for generations between Washington and the Cuban community. And there are all sorts of problems with other countries that still think it was Washington and he was just cut adrift. Americans are pigs. It just goes on and on."

"Not a surprise," said Grady. "Underneath it all, we're talking about a guy who was doing something people aren't supposed to be able to pull off. It makes us look bad to have it happen under our noses."

"Not only that," said Hugh. "He was going to do something that really doesn't bother a whole lot of people."

Tate gestured with his beer while he wiped some foam off his mouth.

"Yeah. Well, there's still a pretty short list that knows about it. If everybody in the loop keeps quiet, it goes away. It's crazy. The greatest law enforcement minds in the free world and he's got a million-dollar hit team running around in complete secrecy.

"And it's not just that. It's who he is, the fact that people just flat adore the guy. I'm having a hard time staying clean on it myself. I keep thinking about finding some way to wrap this up without it ever becoming an embarrassment to him."

Grady shook his head.

"Sounds like you approve of letting this all slide. Well, that may make sense. But there are an awful lot of loose ends and an awful lot of people..."

He turned to Christine.

"I don't think you've told us all of it. This might be written off. But Lex won't."

"No shit."

She laughed, downed another swallow. She was raising her hand to snap another time when the waitress appeared. She was holding another double. DeSilva took it from her and kept talking.

"Tommy's on his way back from Washington now. I talked to him a couple of hours ago. He was at the airport. Said he couldn't talk. He said to tell you, Grady, it was all about the French thing. Said you'd know what he meant."

"Let's call him," said Grady. "If he's back, he could join us."

• • •

BY THE time Becker showed up, they had decided they'd better eat dinner.

"Before I tell you guys anything, I have to say I've been..."

They all spoke at once.

"... sworn to silence?"

"Bottom line is whether Lex was the guy or whether it went higher up. I sat in on a meeting with a presidential adviser named Lionel Twiggett. Did anybody ever hear of Lionel Twiggett?"

Tate, his usual self. "I think I went to the fourth grade with him. I think I used to kick his ass after school."

"Geez, this guy is a total bookworm. But everybody shuts up when he talks. Anyhow, the guy Jackie killed over here, he and his wife, actually, worked for this huge telecom. I'm not going to try to pronounce it. Lot of French people bought stock in it. That was a major cultural change. Turns out the French weren't that big into investing, not mom and pop anyhow, not like in this country.

DeSilva jumped in.

"At some point here, I suspect you're going to explain how this matters to us?"

"Yeah, I hope so. Twiggett talks a lot about how government ownership of the company was this colossal mistake, how it gave the competitors a big edge."

"So the government had to sell out."

"Right."

"What was the job," Tate asked, "of the guy who got killed?"

"He was their money guy. He was trying to talk them out of doing the deal with the government."

"So Tommy," said Hugh. "Can you boil this little economics lesson down for us?"

"Only with assumptions, I'm afraid.

"I was just there in case anything that came up triggered any more nuggets I might offer about Lex, anything he'd said. Twiggett has one theory, although the general view of the folks in this meeting, they all seem to think that somebody in France hired Barnett to quiet this guy, or somebody in France knew one of Barnett's bosses and paid him to get it done."

Buddy Lee had been waiting for a chance to get a word in.

"I think we might have a useful nugget... I reached out to the Jacksonville shop to find the detectives who handled that killing. For a while, they had nothing on it. Two bodies. Then one day a note shows up fingering Barnett. The detective told me he was pretty damn skeptical, except for the sticky note. It was a question... 'victims' fingers folded together?'

"Then he knew it was the real deal. They'd held that piece back. Hadn't told anyone."

Tate set down an empty mug, waved a hand for the waitress.

"But he doesn't know who sent it?"

"Nope. Only thing he knew... there was a postmark. From Tampa."

"You know," Becker said, "I'm beginning to think this case may just be a whole lot less complicated than we thought."

"Maybe," said Buddy Lee. "But what about the killing at Gonzales' place?"

"One thing to let Gonzales' little army walk," said Tate. "Strictly another thing to deal with the breakout – how those guys got out, who got them out."

"That may be a lot tougher," DeSilva said.

Grady waved over the waitress. He handed her a handful of 20s.

"Coffee for me. One more round here, please ma'am, and a check."

There were protests, which he deflected.

"You guys can drink more than me," he said.

"I didn't tell you this part," said Becker. "Twiggett says whoever's dirty, whoever sent Barnett to kill the French guy, was working with the Cubans. That was the relationship he cared about. He says he wants to clear the air, whatever that means."

"It means finding out whether we're dealing with the Cuban government or a freelancer," DeSilva said, "and for those of us in this world, it means reassuring ourselves about whether Lex was dirty all by himself, or whether there are other nasties we still have to uncover."

When the crowd broke up, Tate and Hugh had stayed on at the bar. They persuaded Grady to hang on, staying to talk about how things must have worked, how they might never know a lot of the details.

Finally, Grady, too, headed back to his hotel. And now it was late.

38

SUNDAY

THEY WERE heading home. It was close to 2 a.m. when Tate's cell-phone rang. He jumped a foot.

It was Sharon.

"I'm a little creeped out."

"What's the matter."

"Well, I got up to go to the bathroom and I saw this car drive up and stop across the street. And there's this guy just sitting there, staring at the house."

"Are your lights on?"

"No. He doesn't know I'm looking at him."

"What kind of car is it?"

"I dunno. Very ugly, old, long, low to the ground."

Tate, trying not to sound too disturbed.

"Could it be a Studebaker? Is it... is it weird in the front? Are the headlights round, sunk in?"

"Yeah, like from a bad space movie. It's red, bright red."

"Jesus!"

"What is it? You're freaking me out."

He grabbed Hugh's sleeve. "My house. Haul ass. No noise."

"What is it? Is this something bad?

"Is he still in the car? Can you tell? What does he look like?"

"Yeah, sitting there. I don't know. Some guy smoking a cigarette."

"Listen to me. Stay on the phone. Go to the hall closet and get my gun. You know where it is?"

"Your gun? Jesus, Tate..."

"Do it Sharon. Right now. Stay on the phone."

He wasn't quite yelling... almost.

"Ricky's here. What do I do with Ricky? Can't we just run out the back or something? Tate... what is this?"

Hugh had it hammered, running his blue lights. Middle of the night, not much traffic. He was on the radio, talking quietly, sending cars to Tate's, telling them no lights, no sirens, to stay back.

Tate flicked his butt out the window. They pulled their seat belts tight. Hugh powered through a turn, then cut the wheel back hard to the inside to counter the skid, flooring it to pull them through.

"Tate?"

He took a breath.

"Have you got the gun?"

"Yes and I'm in Ricky's room. Hang on."

She shook Ricky awake. He started to complain.

"Shush. Something going on. Get up and shut up."

Ricky saw the gun. He got up.

She had set the phone down on the bed to wake him. She picked it back up.

"Ok. We're up. Where should we go? Tate, is this bad?"

He debated a second, and then said yes.

"You need to stay very cool. We'll be there in five minutes. Go into the office. He can't get in those windows. He'll have to come down the hall. Get Ricky in the closet. You get behind the desk."

"Ok. All right."

Creeping down the hall, looking over their shoulders, Ricky not saying a word.

"We're in there. I shut the door behind me."

She opened the closet door and pushed Ricky inside, pulled a coat down to throw over him.

She pushed a hand on his shoulder.

"You sit tight. Do not come out. Do not make a sound, no matter what you hear. You understand me?"

Ricky started to grumble.

"I can help."

But she was at the window now, looking out again.

"Jesus God, Tate. He's not in the car!"

He slammed his fist on the dashboard, forced his voice down a notch.

"Get down behind the desk."

Ricky was leaning his head out of the closet. She gave him a look. He slinked back, closed the door slowly, turning the knob behind him.

The cruiser skidded badly through a turn. Hugh couldn't hold it and they slammed into a parked car, bouncing off, still moving, fish-tailing. Hugh took his foot off the gas for a split second, then stomped the pedal back to the floor.

Tate just staring straight ahead, one hand on the roof because of the bouncing.

"Tater... I'm behind the desk."

She was whispering, her voice quaking.

And now Tate was whispering too, speaking slowly, carefully.

"Both hands on the gun. Don't make any noise. If he calls out to you, don't answer. Don't move. If the door opens, start shooting. Do not hesitate for one second. You hear me? The door opens, you shoot. Now put the phone down and get ready."

The house was still, a faint light coming in from the street. The Johnson's dog barked, the shepherd they kept out back. Not a friendly bark. Her own Albert, sleeping the sleep of the deaf in the bedroom.

She'd just looked out the window, that was all. She didn't know why. Now there was hell to pay and she didn't know she could be this scared. She was counting as she breathed, tiny breaths so there wouldn't be a sound, letting her feet sink slowly to the floor, gradually shifting her weight, everything in slow motion.

She got down on one knee, held the phone over the desk. Then she gradually set it down, easing it, just a corner at first and then the rest of it, slowly laying it down, the mouthpiece toward her. The gun, so heavy she was afraid of dropping it. She was holding it now the way he'd shown her, the butt of it in her palm, her finger on the outside of the trigger guard, the other hand wrapped around her wrist and the palm of her hand, down on both knees next to the chair, toes in the carpet, her forearms pressing on top of the desk.

It's like I'm praying.

The phone was under her chin. She leaned down and tried to talk, but her tongue stuck in her throat.

"I love you baby."

But he couldn't have heard it. She'd lost her voice. She stared at the door, looking over the barrel of the gun, bouncing in her hands like a fish flopping on the deck, her breaths coming in short, choking gasps, eyes stinging from the sudden sweat and the fear and then the creak, that floorboard right outside the kitchen.

She was thinking about where he might go first, where he might look, whether she'd hear anything, whether he'd call out.

I'm hardly wearing a stitch.

Jackie didn't come in. He didn't open the door. There was just the long hard obscene rush of the clip he emptied into the room and then the sound of him chuckling as he jogged down the hallway, the car starting, accelerating down the street.

Ricky heard the roar, knew what it was. Scrunching his face, he fought back a cry. He hadn't moved a muscle. He heard the footsteps, heard the car leave.

Moaning, he pushed open the closet door. There, in the dim from the streetlight, he saw the broken glass, the overturned lamp, the shredded curtains, still fluttering, too frightened to come to rest, the splintered wood, the chair, her body crumpled under the window, the gun lying beside her.

He could hear Tate screaming through the phone.

"Shar! Sharon!"

Ricky picked up the phone. He hung up, then called 911.

• • •

ISABEL WAS getting a bit more excitement than she'd planned for.

They had broken into her house – gotten past all that super-slick security outside and right into her house – without even setting off the alarm. They had killed Robert Simons and gotten clean away.

And now the cops were closing in, how, she did not know.

The money from that little slush fund she'd been so careful to amass, the very secure cellphone calls from the park, that remarkable plan and the ideal executioner – a mercenary convict.

It was during the Brothers to the Rescue trial. The Herald had covered the proceedings in detail. She read about one of the affidavits detailing the evidence against the WASP spy leader. It had named his boss, a ruthless guy who'd given the order to shoot down the rescue planes.

And so Isabel had taken a little solo shopping trip to Washington, hunting for some new clothes, she'd told Alfredo. One afternoon, she dropped by the Cuban Interest Office. A young man there explained he knew of no one named Ortiz, that it would be impossible to put her in touch with anyone in Havana. The man, a mid-level assistant, was charming, but not the slightest bit helpful. Nevertheless, she agreed to meet him later for a drink and, eventually, there would be another meeting. And then the infatuated young man gave her what she wanted.

Over time, she had reached an agreement with Ortiz, who found the whole thing quite amusing. Killing Gonzales would be a lark. Getting paid for it was all too – he couldn't quite think of the right word. And then it had come to him. American. It was all too American.

And, for Isabel, all too clever. Chances were damn good they'd be killed. And, if not, they knew nothing. None of them had ever seen her, ever talked to her.

None but Barnett. When she'd heard about Barnett, she just had to see for herself. He sounded so absolutely death-defying, so deliciously creepy. She'd walked right into that prison and sat face to face with him. It felt wonderful.

But now, things weren't feeling so good. They'd screwed up. They'd shot the wrong guy, for heaven's sake, and a whole bunch of other people. That wasn't the idea.

And getting caught certainly was not…

You made your bed, her mama used to say. You'll sleep in it.

Well, Isabel had wanted more. A very well made bed, she had, and she'd wanted more.

If mama could see her now, lying there staring at the ceiling, lying on her remarkable custom-made mattress in its gleaming cherry frame. She'd gotten it from one of her designer catalogs, the kind with long poetic descriptions of the furniture, no phone numbers and no prices. Just the showy pictures and the address. She got the handmade sheets, the covers, the shams and the duvet and the matching throws. For her frilly bed things, she had spent more than most people spent on a new car.

Alfredo had thought it was fine. He admired her taste.

What Isabel really wanted was to take a trip. A really nice trip. A long trip. Miami was feeling a little close.

39

MONDAY

THE FRESHLY-SHAVEN mechanic was at the colonel's office bright and early, tools in a little trailer he had built to pull along behind his bicycle. An officer in front of the building told him he was at least an hour early, perhaps two.

So he sat. He smoked. He read Granma twice.

And then Ortiz arrived.

"What brings you here so early this morning?" he asked.

"I have something for the colonel's car, a new carburetor."

"This is excellent news. Not too difficult a task, I hope…"

"It was no trouble."

"That is truly excellent. Will you do the work here? I see you've brought your equipment."

"Yes. It shouldn't take long."

"I will be upstairs in my office."

And, with that, Ortiz gave the mechanic a rousing slap on the shoulder and hurried inside.

He had not been long at his desk before there was a gentle tap on the door. It was the mechanic, the carburetor in his hand.

The explanation was technical. Ortiz waved it off. The carburetor did not fit. It could be remachined, but it would not work well. The mechanic offered to take Ortiz downstairs, show him the problem.

"That is not necessary my good friend. What will you do now?"

"There is not much I am equipped to do, my colonel. I have taken your carburetor out so I could take down the part number, and put it back. I have the number here. It will take someone with a computer to send messages back and forth to suppliers in America. It could take time and it could be costly.

"I'm afraid I do not have a computer, or the knowledge. If the colonel can find the part and have it sent here… in the meantime, if the colonel wants to bring the car to my shop, I can spend …."

He stopped. The colonel had turned in his chair and now he was looking out the window, not speaking. The mechanic held his breath. The colonel would hear only the sound of humility at his back.

He stood there, motionless, for some time, holding the carburetor. He looked at the massive portrait of Fidel on the wall. Above Ortiz' head, between the windows, a black and white photograph of Fidel, with Che and the troops, marching into Havana, surrounded by a cheering crowd. Next to it, a small portrait of Raul. A recent addition.

And there was a smaller photo of a stone wall taken late in the day. He could see the stones were pocked and crumbling and covered with stains.

He quietly backed out of the room.

He was sitting in his shop, hoping for customers, when a car stopped out front.

A tall man in a good suit stepped out.

"I hope you can help me, my friend. A few nights ago, while my wife and I ate supper, someone stole a carburetor from me.

A look of amazement stole across the mechanic's face.

"This is incredible."

He was practically shouting, grabbing at his hands.

"Those kids!"

"What are you saying?"

"This morning, early, three kids came by on bicycles. They wanted to sell me a carburetor, and old 2 x 4. 'Where did you get this?' I asked them. And, you know, of course, they had very little to say.

"I looked them right in the face and asked them if it was stolen and, of course, they denied it. But I knew. I sent them on their way. I told them the police would be here."

"Where are they? How can we find them?"

"No need, my friend. Of course I did not let them take it with them. I have it here. This could very well be your carburetor. Where is the car now, and we'll go see."

And with that dramatic performance, the mechanic once again was in the good stead of a longtime customer. He even wrangled a high-priced tune-up.

There was a modicum of guilt, not much. What choice had he?

And now, life would return, perhaps, to a semblance of normalcy. He would wait to hear from the colonel.

• • •

TATE WAS brushing his teeth when the tears started falling, just brushing his teeth. Pretty soon, he gave up and slid to the floor. He threw the toothbrush across the room. And then he sobbed, loud enough to be heard across town, sobbing like he'd been saving up.

After a time, he stood and threw some water on his face, found his toothbrush, rinsed it off, stuck it back in the little white container Sharon had bought for him, no longer willing for him to leave it on the countertop like he'd always done. He walked into the bedroom and did some more crying, sitting at the end of the bed. He pulled up the end of his t-shirt and blew his nose.

He tried lying on his back for a few minutes, imagining old age.

It didn't work.

He got down onto the floor, reached for the remote, punched up a sports talk show, turned it off.

He went into the office. It was pretty well cleaned up. The department had sent over a crew. They were good at what they did and they had replaced his window and his curtains, had fixed the walls and had taken away the bloodied carpet and the riddled furniture. So what he had was a bare, clean room. There was some painting to do.

He felt it coming and had no desire to run. He just got down on his knees, right there on the hardwood floor and threw up like a busted toilet. He lay down on the floor and stayed there until the phone rang.

40

THE STORM was coming in hard and Tate was discovering there were different colors of darkness. The sea, the clouds, the horizon – all complicated shades of black. But the sky was the worst of it.

Even as the waves gut-punched the boat, retching them up, tossing them like sudden leaves before a cloudburst, the sky held a promise of more. At first, he'd told Conover to put the Schnapps aside, but Conover had laughed in such a humorless way that he'd realized the foolishness of it.

They'd lashed themselves down, the three of them, there by the wheel. Conover had seen to it, tightened the knots hard on Tate and then Hugh, and then he'd tied himself in, snug up against the wheel, the three of them caught in a web. He had spent some time before they left, explaining the emergency beacons on the vests, what to do if they were swamped, how to stay alive. And then he punched it toward the open sea.

They had their emergency provisions, extra gas, extra water, a passel of guns.

On the shore, Einburg watched them disappear, forcing himself to stand there with the thunder and the lightning crackling around him, praying softly aloud as the tiny boat faded from sight. He'd even given them awkward hugs as they boarded, clutching Tate's neck, pulling him close.

"This may well be the most fucked up thing you've ever done," he shouted over the din.

And to Hugh: "You don't have to do this."

And then they were gone.

Ortiz had called.

"I'm looking for Detective Drawdy."

"Who wants him?"

"Is this Drawdy?"

"It is."

"I will tell you where to find Mr. Barnett."

And then, when Tate didn't answer, he had told him.

"I'm giving you the man you're after. And, at some point, like your Marlon Brando, I may ask a favor and I will expect you to honor our agreement. That is our understanding."

They'd grappled a bit and Ortiz had given him his telephone number.

"Talk to your State Department people. They will tell you who I am. Beyond that, all you need to know is that Mr. Barnett and I have some history. And I am going to give him up. Beyond that, I will expect that you will not betray our confidence. I saw your little speech on television and I think that, based on my long experience with men of strong conviction, I know who I'm dealing with.

"You check me out. And then call me back. And I'll tell you where he is. But don't let too much time go by. Mr. Barnett is in something of a hurry."

The meeting place was not convenient and it was not a good time. It meant Conover would get his chance to play cop once again and the Cap'n had not hesitated, although the weather was bad, he said, bad enough to kill them.

Puke swirled around their feet. For a time, Hugh watched it, thinking it might act as a compass of sorts, but that simply made him vomit all the more. On shore, he had weighed the odds. He had confronted the very real possibility that they wouldn't make it back, that it was all lunacy.

Now, well at sea, the storm exploding around them, the waves crunching against the hull like falling rocks, he had decided they would escape death only by being incredibly small and ridiculously unimportant, about as much chance as if he'd tried to stop the pounding with a wave of his hand or a few well-placed bullets.

A hellish sky. As far as the eye could see and for miles above and miles below, for all he knew, there was water and yet there was a hot stinging in his nose. There were noises he could not understand, above the shriek of the storm and the squall of the Silver Queen.

He thought about that time, the bruising late-night flight when he'd encountered clench your butt and pray turbulence, and had discovered what it was like to feel truly helpless. The shaking had lasted awhile. The passengers, save for a few crying, had gone silent. He had pressed his hands against the ceiling and shut his eyes, straining to hear the chanting coming from underneath the engines.

Puke on his chin and on his clothes and in his hair and the tears were streaming down his face and, as he struggled to stand while the boat winced and reeled in the waves and the wind, he was not sure he could remember anything at all.

Jackie, out at sea, waiting for the ship he'd been told would meet him there. Ortiz had told him. Jackie would be there, despite the weather.

The Queen was working hard, pushing up the arc of a wave, then falling back hard to slide down the other side. Tate, looking back toward shore to convince himself they were making progress, seeing nothing but wind and water.

The pumps were working now. Waves higher than the bow, violently muscling them aside. The Silver Queen, tiny against them, her big turbos no match, whining like they would shake themselves loose when they came clear of the water. Another jagged shock of lightning and it began to feel as if they were floundering.

Conover, eyes blazing, reached for Tate, grabbed him by the back of his shirt and pulled him close until their heads were touching.

"Watch what I'm doing," he shouted. "Take 'em head-on. Cut your way through. Try to feel the rhythm."

And then Conover was pulling the rope loose, untying himself.

"What the fuck are you doing?"

Tate, not sure he heard him.

Staggered by the pitching deck, Conover made his way forward, into the cabin, bouncing hard against the door frame, grabbing hold, then disappearing below. Hugh was holding onto the wheel, too, trying to help, the rudder leaden one moment, aimless the next.

In a few moments, Conover was back on deck, down on one knee, dragging a large padlocked chest made of steel. Wrapped around his shoulder, a thick line. Tate was astounded the man could keep his balance. And then a wave smacked down like a thunderclap.

Tate turned to see Conover on his back, clutching his ribs and then another wave was washing him across the deck and he was against the gunnel, flailing for something to hang onto and the chest began to shift, slamming against a deck chair, breaking it into pieces. Tate wrenched the wheel hard, trying to keep her straight, trying to help.

Conover was fighting his way back, dragging himself along the deck. As they crested a swell, Tate looked back again. He was wrapping the chest, doubling the rope over and through a pair of rings across the back of it.

Another flash. Conover on his knees, pushing it to the stern, holding it there with his weight while he tied off the other end of the rope to two large cleats on the stern, wrapping it underneath, then a figure eight, the last half upside down.

He got down low and lifted one end of the chest, tipping it up against the stern and then, waiting for the wave, he sent it overboard with a shove. The rope spun out and there was a shudder and then a wicked jolt as it snapped tight.

And now there was a new noise, the line straining with the violence of the drag, pulling against them, a brutal moaning that shook the boat and sliced the air with a terrifying reverberation.

Conover crawled back to the wheel and tied himself tight once more.

"Pray she don't rip us in half," he shouted.

But the wheel was firmer now, the old chest somehow stabilizing the Queen, keeping her ass down. He thought he saw a light in the distance, but couldn't be sure.

The storm teasing them with moments of puny retreat, then roaring back with an immaculate anger and, against the thunder and the lightning, the gunshots sounded like a cheap toy, as if you'd recorded the sound on a pocket tape recorder and played it back in a far-off room. And then the plexi shield in front of the wheel shattered and Tate was shouting and tearing at the knots and the ropes were all that held Hugh upright as his knees buckled, his blood spraying in the wind.

Conover was clutching the wheel in one hand, sawing through the ropes with the hunting knife he'd strapped to his belt, the wind carrying away his shouted warning and then Tate was free.

There was no way to stand. Lying on his belly, snaking his way along the bow and, in the strobe of the lightning flashes, he saw Jackie's big boat bouncing on top of a wave 30 yards distant, a rock in the storm, Jackie standing straight, grinning, one hand on the rail, the other holding the gun aloft, a war chief with his spear.

Conover was bringing them in close. Tate slid forward six inches at a time, an elbow, a knee, praying for friction.

The Silver Queen shuddered hard and slipped into a trough between waves and then Tate was accelerating, face first, sliding, nothing to hold onto. He slammed against the railing, all that kept him aboard, and felt a sharp pain. He dropped his gun and grabbed hold, wrapping his legs around the post and then they were climbing again, mounting another wave.

Above him, an anchor floated down, smashed on the deck and then it caught the railing and Jackie turned on the winch and began hauling them in, a modern-day grappling hook. He was fighting the sea, pulling them closer. Tate saw muzzle flashes frolicking against the blackness but heard nothing.

A grinding crash as the boats slammed together and Tate spun free, struggling to stand, his broken arm hanging loose, and then, as the boat heeled into another wave, Jackie was over the rail and in front of him. He'd left his gun behind.

Tate lurched forward, driving helplessly against the slick deck. Jackie, crouching, waiting for the boat to slump, letting him get close.

Tate was watching his face and then he saw the leg arcing toward him and there was an explosion of pain and he was over the rail, a drifting speck among the waves.

Jackie cackled with joy. Quickly regaining his balance, he turned back to see Conover crouching just behind him, his face taut in the wind, one hand on the rail, the other aiming Hugh's .357, pulling the trigger, shooting him up close, shooting him again, shooting him after he fell, shooting him as he slid over the side.

Jackie, sinking under the surface to a place where his mama would never find him.

And Tate, he was searching. For what comes next.

The waves tumbled down on him like an avalanche. He struggled to the surface and let out a scream.

Let them know I'm here.

The water churned around him, plunging him deeper, rolling him down hills of granite, draining the strength from him. He kicked with all he had, exhausted already. I've got to keep yelling. How else will they find me?

But how could they find him? So quickly he was tiring. He wondered if he should fight on.

"Here!"

But Tate was nowhere near the surface when he shouted and the water poured into his mouth and down his throat and his stroke began to slow. He pushed and kicked and tried to clear his lungs and then he thought he'd just float for a time and the storm began to quiet and the dark stole in and then he heard a splintering and opened his eyes.

Expecting a city in the clouds, he saw gray and black and uncertain shapes, the sky a foggy bed of gravel, waves still crashing around him like chunks of a deteriorating ice floe and an arm reaching under his shoulder and around his neck and then Conover was pulling them back toward the Silver Queen, hand over hand on the rope he'd tied securely to the railing.

Bloody Hugh holding the wheel.

41

THE WAITRESS brought over the pot and freshened up their coffees. Conover and Einburg and Tate were sitting in a greasy spoon down the street from the hospital, where Hugh Brice-Whittaker was said to be in good condition with a hole in his shoulder.

Conover thought Einburg wasn't such a bad guy.

"What will you do now about all this?"

"Privately, we're all in very deep shit. Not you, of course, but we're supposed to know better. Publicly Barnett was killed while attempting to elude capture. The chief agrees it's better to say he was killed by Drawdy. There will be some grumbling about the whole notion of chasing the guy out to sea, instead of calling the appropriate authorities. Chief says we'll circle the wagons on it and Grady Osmund will back us up."

Conover said that was more than fine with him. He didn't need anybody thinking he was some kind of Lone Ranger or anything. Word had already gotten out about their strange venture, about coming back into port with a cop who'd been shot.

They had radioed for an ambulance on the way back and there was a small group waiting there, locals who'd heard about it. Susie was there, too. She'd seemed awfully put out about the whole thing, didn't say much, just cried a little and went home.

They had deflected any questions and headed straight for the hospital with Hugh. Einburg met them there. He'd stayed around waiting for them.

"Tate says things were pretty rough out there."

Tate kind of rolled his eyes. Conover just laughed, and then he held his ribs.

"I need to remember not to do that."

"Last night," Einburg said, "while we were in the waiting room, Tate said something about you throwing something overboard on a rope. Is that a regular thing you ordinarily do?"

Conover shook his head.

"I wouldn't worry too much about it."

"No, really. I don't know much about boats, you know, and I was just wondering."

Conover leaned in and lowered his voice.

"Here's the thing. Now that we're back, I'd just as soon we didn't make too big a deal about it. I don't want people to think I do a lot of hair-raising shit. This is what I do for a living and I don't want to scare off the population.

"Fact is, that storm came in a lot faster than the weather guys were saying."

"Glad it wasn't just my imagination," said Tate. "I'd had this sneaking suspicion things weren't going real well out there."

Conover patted his arm gently, on the cast, just above the elbow.

"With the sea running the way it was, I figured we had about a one in 100 chance of making it. And that thing..." pointing to Einburg "with throwing the chest overboard – we had about a one in 100 chance of surviving that. Either it would have pulled us under, or it would have ripped the stern off the boat, or the lines would have chafed 'til they snapped and come back and ripped our heads off."

Conover had lost his tool chest. Rather than try to get it back aboard, he'd just cut it loose, hadn't wanted to endure that drag any longer than he had to.

Einburg's jaw was beginning to creep towards the table. Tate, he just nodded.

"And then there was your pal Barnett, with his machine gun. We probably had about a one in 100 chance of living through that little encounter as well.

"So I'm not much of a math whiz, so let's just say things were not working in our favor."

"Holy shit."

Einburg's eyes were getting big.

"You guys are scaring the shit out of me."

Conover shrugged. Tate was staring out the window.

"Let's go back out," Conover said, "when the sun is shining."

Einburg said he'd like to come along, if that was all right, and the weather was extra nice.

• • •

"ALEXANDER DEAN?"

"Yes."

It was absurd. The man knew who he was. Then, Lex was not likely to complain about his treatment. He'd been told to report in the morning, to his own office. When he arrived, he saw the place had been sifted and they'd been quite thorough about it. The files were gone. His computer was gone. The pictures were gone, along with the furniture.

All that was left was the chair. He was in it. On a small folding table, a recorder. In the corner, on a tripod, a video recorder. It was pointed toward the center of the room.

"Do you know who I am?"

"Yes."

"Yes sir."

"Yes sir."

"That's better. Mr. Dean, it might be a good idea if you treated this as the worst day of your life."

"Yes sir."

"Unless of course I find out anything that contradicts whatever you tell me about your activities, anything at all. And I'm capable of back-tracking at some length, you understand. And if I find any sort of contradiction, then that will become the worst day of your life. I assume we have a complete understanding."

Lex didn't reply. From now on, he knew, he'd speak on cue.

He took out a notebook. He reached over and turned on the tape recorder. Lex figured the video recorder was already on.

"You may begin."

42

HUGH WAS driving, Tate up front, Grady in the back with Booker. Fred had gone home. He got seasick easily, so this was not an invite he cared to accept. Buddy Lee had gone with him.

Conover had called Booker, figuring he'd be the most persuasive with the others.

"Bring you and the rest of them sumbitches down here right now, while you got a little room to breathe. Tell 'em it'll be good for 'em."

And so Booker had collared Tate and Hugh.

"May's well go now, before some other shit breaks down," he said.

Tate and Hugh weren't the slightest bit interested in leaving town right now, not even for an hour. And then the chief came by.

He ordered them off the job. They were toasted, he said. They were both a huge pain in the ass. And were swiftly becoming a liability for the department. If they wanted to keep their jobs, they'd take some time off.

Grady was no easier. Buddy Lee went over his head and called Nell. And she called Grady.

"Don't you dare work another day until you've gone fishing with that nice captain," she said.

"I appreciate that, sweetheart, but I really don't think I can leave right now, in the middle of things."

"Bullshit. You haven't been fishing since I don't know when. Buddy Lee can take care of things. He gave me the captain's phone number. I called him 10 minutes ago, said you'd be there in the morning. He's arranged a place for you, so you can drive down tonight if you want, or first thing.

"You have a good time, baby. Love you."

Click.

And so they went, leaving before dawn so they would miss the traffic, passing the fancy beachside hotels, the underwater parks and the dive shops at Key Largo, the Theater of the Sea at Islamorada, over the Seven Mile Bridge, past lighthouses and t-shirt and shell shops, past stopovers with names like Smuggler's Cove and Paradise, past the little side road where Conover had met the cab driver at the convenience store, seeing the water much of the way. The sun was starting to pop.

They had decided it had the makings of a good day, one of those days when your car seemed to know just where it was heading, the tires caressing the pavement. Conover was ready for them and now they were heading out onto the dock with the Cap'n's big chest full of beer and water, soft drinks and sandwiches. Booker had a couple thermoses full of coffee. Tate and Hugh weren't carrying a damn thing. Grady had his briefcase.

"Hope I don't accidentally knock that thing overboard," Conover told him.

Grady gave his arm a squeeze.

"I've already heard you're way too smart for that."

Conover took the boat out easy for a few minutes. As the sun began to climb, he edged the throttle higher and, before long, they were roaring out to sea. The water exceptionally smooth, bundles of clouds tossed across the sky like paint splatters, all the way to the horizon, gulls trying to keep up.

Conover was at the wheel up top. He leaned out and cupped his hands to his mouth.

"Booker, you ever drive one of these babies?"

"No, but I'm ready to learn."

Booker hopped up from his chair and climbed the steps to the big chair, his plump old calves just popping from the pleasure of it. Conover moved aside and sat him down.

"Here's your compass. Here's your captain's hat.

"And here," reaching into his pocket, "is your big ass Cuban."

Conover made his way to each of them, stuffing a fat cigar in every mouth. He thought they might throw mullet out and try to land some grouper. Kings and mackerel had been running. It was late in the season, but they might try for a sail.

Grady was sitting with his back to the sun, taking just one piece of paper at a time from his briefcase for fear of seeing something blow away. He was starting at the front of the pile, looking again at everything he had before it was all filed away.

Conover standing over his shoulder, his first beer in his hand, telling the one about the piano player and the guy outside the bathroom.

"So the piano player says... 'Know it? I fuckin' wrote it!' "

And then it was Hugh's turn and even Grady tried his hand. But nobody could top the Cap'n. Besides, Grady still had his head half in his work. He stuck a page back in his briefcase, pulled out another. He was reading the interview with the Danny Gifford, the corrections officer who had checked in Jackie's visitor. Grady put it back and took out the next page. It was the artist's sketch of the woman.

Conover was standing over him.

"Here's a beer, my friend. Help you with your studies."

"Thanks. I'm about to give up for awhile."

Conover stepped to his side and looked down.

"She is the babe, isn't she? Not that great a likeness, but she still looks good."

"What?" Grady snatched Conover's arm. "You know this woman?"

"Sure do. Looks like Isabel to me – the fabulously beautiful and fabulously rich Isabel."

Grady turned sideways so he could hold the sketch out of the sun. He'd never seen Isabel, although he had heard she was quite the showpiece.

"Holy shit."

He said it real slow. He'd been a fool. Now Hugh and Tate were looking too. Tate took the page from him, shaking his head, the wheels beginning to turn.

"What is this, Grady?"

"That is an artist's rendering of a woman who visited Jackie Barnett at the prison. The C.O.'s description. We never had a good ID. Do you think it's her?"

Before he could answer, Conover turned and walked to the bottom of the ladder.

"Hey, Booker," he shouted. "Shut that fucking thing down."

Booker turned the key and the boat settled almost immediately. He climbed down and then they were all standing there, rocking in the swells, staring at Isabel.

• • •

HE WAS a mutt, a scavenger, lean and quick to look over his shoulder, a veteran of Havana's streets spoiling for his chance. At the corner, he had learned to pop up his head and signal with his tail when a car rolled to a stop. Sometimes, they tossed him something.

It was a blustery midday. The mechanic was watching him patrol the street from a shady place against the wall. He was sitting, resting his elbows on his knees, watching the dog and the cars and the people going by. Then he saw the car pull up to the curb in the next block. Two policemen got out and approached on foot. The mechanic started to flick his cigarette into the street, then thought better of it. He would smoke it awhile longer.

The men walked casually. They seemed in no hurry and there was nothing about their gait to suggest this was a mission involving confrontation or arrest. He took heart in that. Perhaps they aren't headed here, he thought. And then they made eye contact. He stood. His hands were clasped in front of him. There was grease under his nails.

"The Colonel sent us," the first one said. And then he introduced himself.

"He wonders if you have time to visit him this afternoon."

"Without a doubt," the mechanic answered. "I am always happy to serve. When would you like me to come?"

"Now."

He took a deep breath. They did precisely as they liked, these men. They took their authority from their commander and had their way with everyone.

"Yes. Of course. Let me just lock up."

At least they didn't watch him. They stood out front and waited. Nevertheless it was an embarrassment.

He took a moment to wash up and then fell in behind them, walking quickly. There was nothing I could do, he thought. Like the dog, he chose not to worry about things outside of his control.

They drove in silence. When they reached the building, they pulled up to the curb. He understood he was to get out. Once inside, he was not made to wait.

The colonel was in good spirits.

"It has been weeks since I have seen you," Ortiz said. "You have been well?"

"Very well. My thanks to the Colonel."

"I hope this is a pleasant mission for you. I have just this morning received a package and I am hoping you will open it for me. I am most excited to see the contents."

He gestured toward the table, a cardboard box sealed in heavy shipping tape. The mechanic could see the Colonel's name in large letters on the front. There was nothing else to indicate where it had come from, or what it was.

"But why would the Colonel think of me?"

The question was irrelevant. Ortiz gestured toward the box, handing him a glistening bayonet from a table behind his desk.

He cut quickly. Inside, a note.

For services rendered, it said.

And then, a smaller box, surrounded with crumpled newspaper. It was heavy. He hoped it would fit.

"Shall I open this box as well, my Colonel?"

"Yes. Yes. I want to see the look on your face. I want to know if it is right."

And it was. A beautiful 2x4 carburetor, in beautiful shape.

"If the Colonel will permit, I will install this immediately, and a full tune up, complete adjustments, everything...."

"Another time perhaps. For now, let's just..."

"Of course. Of course."

He was stammering now, a great sense of relief.

"I will return immediately to my shop for the tools. Unless ...."

The Colonel jumped to his feet, raising his hands toward the ceiling.

"You are right, my friend. I will have a car brought around for you."

He picked up the phone.

"A car, immediately."

The mechanic grabbed the box, stuffing all the papers back inside, and shuffled toward the door, still facing Ortiz.

"But how did you find it?"

The Colonel smiled, a flip of the hand.

"A man in Miami owed me a favor."

The mechanic broke into a foolish grin.

"Naturally. The Colonel has many friends."

"And this," Ortiz said, "was a rather large favor."

• • •

THERE WAS a gentle knock on the door. Come in, she said. She sat up, smoothing her silk dress, adjusting the scarf over her shoulder.

It was Alfredo and David Harrelson, their attorney.

She couldn't help but sigh. Isabel had resigned herself to jail – green walls, gritty floors, steel fixtures. Her food would be ladled from an immense gray pot and she would trade her custom-made bed for something with rusted springs that bolted to the wall. She'd have a roommate, someone she could share her thoughts with. Wouldn't that be nice?

And now Alfredo was telling her she was free to go. Take whatever she liked, whichever car she wanted. David would have the title transferred. And he had a check, a very generous check.

Our thought, David had said, was that you'd eventually want to relocate. You might simply want to get a place downtown for a little while. And he had asked her to sign a few documents. That way, he said, she would be free to remarry.

"Isabel," Alfredo said, "I'm not sure we will have thought of everything. Is there anything else you can think of?"

She forced herself to meet his gaze. He was polite to a fault and incredibly calm. Unbelievably calm. She found that it made her stomach churn, this soft landing her husband had arranged for her. They were letting her go. Still, her comfortable world felt as if it were beginning to spin out of control.

Of course, there was no point in asking how he knew, or what he knew. Alfredo would have learned a great deal very quickly. People were quite eager to do what Alfredo wanted them to do. Someone would have provided him with all the information he needed.

She didn't know what to say. She tapped a finger on the end of her nose.

Alfredo stood. He put his arm on David Harrelson's shoulder.

"Thank you Isabel. Thank you David."

And then he had left the room. She saw Juan standing outside the door when he opened it to leave.

The lawyer told her there was a car waiting to take her to a hotel until she could arrive at some decisions. She could come back anytime she wanted to gather her things. She might just call ahead, so they would know to expect her.

Isabel put some casual clothes in a bag, some evening wear, some nice jewels. She might want to go out later.

When she got downstairs, the front door was open. The car was there, the engine running. It would have been running the whole time.

TWO MONTHS LATER

HUGH NUDGED his old Chevy ahead a few inches. He was four or five cars back. Damn good thing he'd gotten it washed. He felt hugely out of place, but he had on his best suit and had polished his best shoes. He could see the chief in the car in front with a uniform behind the wheel. Einburg wasn't with him, which didn't seem right.

There was a tap on the window. It was a big mustachioed guy in a sport coat.

"Good evening, sir. May I ask your name, please? And could I see your invitation?"

And then he was waved through. Funny, he'd felt far more comfortable entering the mansion as an investigator with scuffed shoes and a gun on his hip than as a guest for dinner. A police officer waved him into a space. Gonzales was letting some of the city's finest moonlight tonight.

The chief was getting out of his car and moving quickly across the parking lot to shake hands with someone. It was the mayor.

There was a buzz just ahead. The face looked familiar. He got closer and recognized the network anchor. Hugh stuck his hands in his pockets and slowed up a bit, looking around to see if he knew anyone behind him.

And then he was inside. The place even more stunning at night, all lit up. Juan was standing near the door. The house was crawling with people and there was a bar in every room.

Hugh circulated. Christine DeSilva was drinking a diet soda in a corner with Tommy Becker.

"Hello, Hugh."

He recognized the voice without turning, that smooth affection.

"Mr. Gonzales."

"Call me Alfredo. Tell me about your shoulder."

Gonzales just might be wearing the nicest suit he'd ever seen. If it had been a pool, Hugh would have jumped in the deep end.

"It's much better, thank you. This arm's not much good right now, but the docs say it will heal fine."

"A huge relief for all of us. I am so glad you were able to come. And I see now we've both got on the same tie."

That fatherly smile.

"They're both red, but I suspect the similarity ends there and I thank you for this invitation. It's nice to come here unofficially."

"It's nice to have all that behind us."

Christine DeSilva came over and made some small talk. She thought the house was pretty cool and she was admiring the fancy handkerchief in the pocket of Gonzales' jacket, the corners folded into little peaks.

"I've been meaning to call you," Gonzales told her. "I was hoping you could help me locate that prisoner, the one who arranged for the police to find out how all this happened.

She lifted a finger to point.

"You're supposed to behave."

Gonzales laughed.

"I want to thank him. I'd like to give him a gift, perhaps some cash."

"Mr. Chandler is back in prison, safe and sound, which I'm sure you know."

"Yes, and I know he turned himself in to the authorities rather than participate in some things he found disturbing. I think that speaks well of him."

"Let's not paint too rosy a picture of our young convict. A man died in this house, your house, at the hand of those gentlemen. At the very least, Mr. Chandler was along for the ride. Apparently, my superiors find him believable enough to provide him something of a break on his term. I'm not sure I like it very much, but it's done. If you've got something you want to offer him, you can try Hugh here, or someone else. I'm not sure I want to be involved personally in any sweetheart deals."

"I understand completely and I would not ask you to compromise your ideals. Actually, I supported the idea of giving the man a certain amount of credit for his help, which I communicated to others. I think there's a fair amount of forgiveness that's taken place here. And I don't simply want to be the recipient."

"Mr. Gonzales, you seem to be a nice enough fellow and people have very good things to say about you. But my job is the law, which is supposed to be blind to things like affluence and political influence. I think you broke the law. I think the cons broke every law there is. Actually, I think Brice-Whittaker here broke a few laws and I'm not too sure I'm very clean either.

"So you'll forgive me if I tell you this whole affair has given me some sleepless nights."

Gonzales gave her a long look. It was soft around the edges.

"Of course," he said. "Would you excuse me for a moment?"

He walked away. She turned to Hugh.

"Now why do I feel like a complete shit?"

"It's something of a mixed bag, Christine. The man wanted to…"

He looked to each side.

"….commit a big-time crime and, then again, he's an idealist and he thought he was doing a good thing and he probably has had a sleepless night or two himself, given the circumstances."

"Yeah. What a little snot his wife must be."

"Ex-wife I'm guessing."

"I would hope so."

Talking with Tommy Becker under the shimmer of the chandelier, a quartet playing softly from the dining room, the atmosphere improving everyone's disposition, giving them all a borrowed grace, and then they were interrupted by a commotion by the front door.

The guest of honor was coming in.

There was Einburg, grinning, shaking hands, gesturing for people to move back. Then he stepped aside to hold open that magnificent heavy door. Soft light reflecting off etched glass. The room quieted as people turned to look. Tate came in first, his back to them all as he eased the wheelchair over the jamb. And then the crowd gently closed in around them, and around Sharon, a festive blanket thrown over her, pale, still frail, but smiling.

ACKNOWLEDGEMENTS

ON AUGUST 5, 1980, 10 men got under the wires at Florida State Prison. It was the largest escape in history from the toughest prison in the state. Most were caught almost immediately, but a handful, including a long-distance runner with a remarkable IQ, had a nice taste of freedom. They'd cut the wires close to a tower manned by a young guard who regularly interrupted his watchfulness to do pushups and sit-ups. His employment was terminated. Everything else in this book is pure fiction and any mistakes are mine. I relied on support and invaluable technical and literary advice from...

Lou Arcangeli, former deputy chief, Atlanta Police Department
Dr. David Baker
Henry Pierson Curtis
Lynne Bumpus-Hooper
John C. Huff, Jr.
Lynn Kittson
W.J. Laudeman, Society of Naval Architects and Marine Engineers
Lawrence J. Lebowitz
Jacob Preston
Nancy Thigpen

Made in the USA
Columbia, SC
26 February 2019